THE PROTECTOR

FOUR FORCES SECURITY BOOK 1

ALEXIS WINTER

I'VE BEEN TO HELL AND BACK DURING MY TIME IN THE SPECIAL FORCES.

But only one woman has brought me to my knees, and I was just hired to protect her.

Billionaire heiress Blaire Hanson.
A bottle blonde, walking pilates ad with perfect skin, a designer wardrobe and a fierce desire to prove herself.
Not to mention, my little sister's best friend.

She and I got off on the wrong foot the first time we met, and the day after...we both woke up on the wrong side of the bed—her bed.

But now that she's my client, those days are behind us. No matter how much my body aches to remember her.

I thought *babysitting* the princess was going to be the hardest part of this job, until her father is taken hostage leaving her to take control of the company and my security firm to negotiate with the kidnappers.

There's one problem—in order to gain control of the board and the finances, she has to be married.

With time running out and her father's life and legacy on the line I step up—to the altar.

But the moment I start to see hope in her eyes, I'm reminded that in this game, falling in love with your client can end in a deadly tragedy. Something I learned the hard way.

At the end of the day only one thing is going to keep her alive—reminding myself that she is just a job.
Not happily ever after.

She might have control over my body, but she'll never have my heart.

1

JIMMY

"Have a seat, Jameson."

I silently huff at the sound of Mr. Hanson's insistence on my full name instead of my nickname, Jimmy. Of course, I'm not going to fight Charles on that matter; nobody fights Charles Hanson on anything.

I do as he instructs and take a seat in one of the black leather chairs in front of his glass desk. Charles Hanson, owner of Hanson Enterprises, has called me in for some help. He's not just a whale in the financial world; he's the giant fucking kahuna. We've rubbed elbows at a few events, me being the one to organize the security for several of his friends in the business world. He's a big client for the security firm several of my Army brothers and I have started, and I'm anxious to get the ball rolling.

"How can I help you, Mr. Hanson?" I ask.

The old man smiles at me, leaning back in his chair. "Please. Call me Charles. I've called you in because I need your help."

"How so?"

Charles shifts in his chair to lean on the desk with his elbows. His hands clasp together tight enough to turn his knuckles white, and his mouth presses into a hard line.

"Someone is after me," he says in a low whisper.

My eyebrows narrow together. "Do you know who?"

He shakes his head. "No. Unfortunately."

I try to show consideration and sympathy for this situation even though it's not uncommon. Billionaire sought after for money or revenge... I see it all the time.

"Where do I come in at?" I press.

For a moment, I think I see some sadness in Charles' eyes. They shift from me to a picture on his desk. He stares at it a moment before picking it up in his hands and showing me the picture.

"You see this girl?" he asks, the sadness now in his voice.

I nod my head, looking at the face of the familiar blond woman staring back at me. I know who's in this picture. "Yes," I say.

It's a picture of his well-known daughter, Blaire. Blaire Hanson, total bitch and spoiled brat, has been on the cover of *Forbes* and *Vogue* several times for her achievements while working for her father... and she's been in my bed... once. But that's a story for another time.

Who knew months later, I'd end up taking on a job for her father.

"This is my pride and joy. My only reason to live. My *soul*. My daughter means more to me than all the money in the world."

"Is someone after your daughter, sir?"

Charles places the picture of Blaire back down on his desk with a sigh. He rubs his face with both hands before settling his eyes back on me. "I'm not sure," he says, "but I want her protected in case there is."

"What exactly is going on?" I lean forward, resting my elbows on my knees. While I appreciate Charles' love for his daughter, I need to know the breach here.

"Someone—not sure who—has been making threats lately toward the company. I've had my men on it day and night trying to track down the son of a bitch, but so far, no luck. I need you to watch over

Blaire. Keep her protected at all costs. Every second of every day. She's all I have left, Jameson. She's the only one left."

Now I shift in my chair. Is this man asking me what I think he's asking me? To babysit his god-awful daughter that I thought I got rid of months ago? Fuck me.

"Let me get this straight," I start. "You want *me* to be your daughter's bodyguard? Follow her everywhere she goes day and night?"

Charles nods his head. "That's exactly what I'm saying, Jameson."

I suppress the need to sigh. I'll definitely be needing a stiff drink when this meeting is over. When I first started this company, yeah, I'd jump at these opportunities but now—now I organize security for high-ranking political officials and billionaires, *not* their spoiled kids.

"She's my angel," he adds. "She's—"

The door to the office bursts open. My head jerks to see who's walking in and—

Fuck. Me.

Speak of the devil. In she walks—Blaire Hanson.

Her platinum-blond-topped head is tucked down as she looks at the stacks of papers in her hands and walks farther into the room, her heels clacking on the tile. The sleeveless cream dress she's wearing hugs every slight curve of her lean body. Her nails are perfectly manicured an icy white, just like her cold exterior.

"Daddy, I've gone over these reports dozens of times now. I don't see the—"

Her voice stops the second her eyes land on me. Her whole body freezes, and I watch as the memory of the one dreadful night we shared flashes through her mind. It almost makes me laugh to know what she's thinking this very second. I nonchalantly cover my mouth with my fingers to keep from laughing.

"You," she whispers, narrowing her eyes.

Charles appears to be oblivious to the situation by the way he cheerily says, "Blaire, darling, excellent timing! Meet Jameson Maxwell. He's going to be watching out for you for the next little bit."

I smile at Blaire as she shoots daggers at me, obviously not looking forward to her new reality. My, my, my, how funny is this.

"You've got to be kidding me," she says, turning her attention to her father. She crosses her arms over her chest and shifts her weight onto her left hip.

"Sweetheart, we've already discussed this."

"I can take care of myself," she protests, now looking back at me. "I don't need some wannabe undercover spy attached to my hip."

Oh, I've been attached to a lot more of you, sweetheart.

"Blaire, this decision is final whether you like it or not." Charles' voice is more stern and forceful.

Blaire gives her dad a look that could kill. The room is silent for a moment as the two of them have a stare down with me sitting in between them until Blaire interrupts it. "What about when I travel?"

"He'll be right with you."

"And when I go to the store?"

"He'll push your cart."

"What about when I'm at home cooking or sleeping?"

"He'll wash the dishes and tuck you in."

Charles folds his arms across his chest as if he's sizing up Blaire. His mouth is pressed into a hard line, and the two hold each other's gaze for a few more silent seconds. Something tells me this man has seen a lifetime of her behaving this way. I love seeing this woman being put in her place.

Without another word, Blaire's heels clack loudly on the floor as she walks to Charles' desk and slaps the papers in front of him.

"Read 'em yourself," she says, storming out of the room.

The door slams with a loud *thump*, and it's all I can do to keep from laughing.

Aw, the princess doesn't get what she wants. How unfortunate.

Charles gives me an apologetic look. "She just needs some time to get used to it. She'll come around."

I give him a large genuine smile. Something tells me I might actually enjoy this job.

"I've got all the time in the world."

2

BLAIRE

I immediately hit the gym the second I'm done with work. I need something to release my anger and the boxing bag is *screaming* my name.

By the time I'm done with my workout, I'm drenched in sweat. The hour I spent punching the life out of that hanging bag should have left me exhausted, but instead I feel refreshed. The whole time, I pictured the bag to be Jimmy, his face the center of it. With every punch I threw, I pretended like I was aiming for that pathetic, sleazy smile of his. I even threw in a kick to his imaginary groin.

How could my father treat me like this? Like I'm some child who needs babysitting or chaperoning? I've heard the whispers from my father about the threats he's been receiving; I know he's in some sort of trouble. But still, attaching some man to me at all hours of the day? And it's somehow *Jimmy Maxwell?* How fucked up can this world be?

I chug some water as I push open the door to the gym. The cool autumn New York air greets my skin with a refreshing breeze as a contrast to my hot, sweaty body. As I start to walk to my apartment, my mind drifts off to dinner options. I have stuff at home for a grilled chicken salad, or I could stop by the Chinese place just down the—

My phone begins to ring, breaking up my dinner thoughts. I pause on the sidewalk as I fish it out of my bag.

"Hello?" I say into the receiver.

"Hey, girl!" my best friend Juliette squeals. "Where are you? Harper and I are at Murphy's, if you want to join us for drinks. She's having another one of her mope sessions, and I need you here to get me through it and cheer her up."

The sound of Harper's name makes my stomach churn. She's the last person I want to see right now, given that her older brother is now going to be by my side twenty-four seven starting who knows when and I can't tell her why I hate him.

"I can't, Jules. I just left the gym, and I'm sweating like a pig."

"So? Get your ass over here now. You can shower when you get home. Just for an hour? Please?"

I pause once more on the sidewalk to ponder over my options. I was really looking forward to Chinese once I thought of it, but I haven't seen my girls in over two weeks. I can push aside my anger at my best friend's brother for an hour or so.

"Okay, fine. *One* hour," I say when my mind is made up.

Juliette squeals again. "I'll have a cosmo waiting on you when you get here."

I hang up the phone and start walking back in the direction I came from. When I get to Murphy's, sure enough, there's a cosmo waiting for me at our table.

Juliette stands to greet me with a hug as I approach the table. To avoid rubbing my sweat on her, I lean into her for one of those awkward butt-out hugs.

"Sorry. I don't think you want my sweat on you," I say, sliding into my seat.

Juliette swats the air at my comment. "Please. I already have Harper's tears on me. What's a little bit of sweat going to hurt?"

"Where *is* Harper?" I ask, noting her lack of presence at the table.

Juliette rolls her eyes. "In the bathroom fixing her makeup."

"What happened this time?"

"Some guy she met off Bumble. I keep telling her Plenty of Fish is where the real ones are at."

"So, another bad date?"

Juliette shakes her head. "Another *stood up* date."

The problem with our friend Harper is her lack of social cues when it comes to dating. Harper Sinclaire Maxwell, voted Most Beautiful for our senior superlative, has never had a clue on how to date successfully. She's too naive and too... *much.* Always smothering the guys right away, talking marriage and babies and white picket fences. She makes herself too vulnerable, believing the cut and paste lies they tell every woman to get her into bed. I know part of her problem is she's too trusting but she needs to guard her heart and stop trusting every penis that tells her she's amazing. We've tried to tell her this gently before, but it didn't work. It just resulted in tears like it always does.

But out of the four of us—Juliette, me, Harper, and Aspen—she has the purest heart.

"So, how's your love life going? It's been a while since we've talked about it," I ask her.

Juliette shrugs her shoulders. "Same old, same old. Josh is great. Can't complain. Anything new with you?"

I give her the *I had a shit day and it's because of a boy* look.

Juliette's mouth drops. "Spill."

I take a long sip of my cosmo, savoring the slight burn as it travels down my throat. My, oh, my, I can't wait to see how she takes this news.

"You remember that night I went out with that guy Jimmy?"

Juliette narrows her eyes as she tries to recollect. Seconds later, she loudly gasps and her eyes widen. "Harper's *brother?*"

"Yes. That one." My voice is flat.

"Oh my God, is he hot?" She smiles.

"Yeah, well, I'm stuck with him now."

"You're what?"

"It's a long story. Basically, he's my protection now."

"I'm so fucking confused," she says. "You need to spell this out for me."

I feel hunger and annoyance beginning to build in me. I briefly wish I would have just gone home after the gym and fueled up on lo mein and egg rolls instead of rehashing today's unfortunate events.

I take a deep breath and reposition in my seat as I start to explain my situation, double-checking Harper isn't returning to the table. "My dad has apparently gotten himself in deep shit and, for some reason, thinks that I need a bodyguard at *all hours of the day*. So, who's the lucky man? Jimmy fucking Maxwell."

I chug the rest of my cosmo and set it down hard on the table. I glance around again. Where is Harper?

"Oh my God," Juliette says in a low voice. "Does your dad know about you two? Does Harper?"

I shrug my shoulders. "No, and I don't know. I don't think so or she probably would have said something to me. After the way things ended between him and I the first time we met, I'm sure Harper would be blowing my phone up if she knew he was hired to babysit me. It's all purely coincidental, which is the crazy part about it."

"But... what if it's not? What if this is fate?"

I roll my eyes. Typical Juliette being her hopeless romantic self. She knows I don't believe in that fate, love at first sight, romance bullshit. None of it's real. Even Jimmy proved that to me.

"I doubt that's what it is," I mumble.

"So, like, when you say he's your *bodyguard* at all hours of the day... does that mean..."

I nod my head. "Yeah. He *literally* has to be with me everywhere I go every second of every day."

A faint trace of a smile tries to spread itself on Juliette's lips. I shoot her daggers and she calms down. "This is crazy," she says. "Where is he now?"

"Who fucking cares. I need another cosmo," I say, looking at my empty glass.

I feel the need to drink now that I've refreshed myself on what's about to happen to me.

The conversation dies when a recovering Harper makes her way back to the table, sniffling and all. I look to Juliette to give a *keep this on the down-low for now* look.

"Hey, Blaire," Harper says with a weary tone.

I fight the urge to roll my eyes at her woe-is-me face.

"Hey, Harps. Juliette told me what happened. I'm really sorry. It's his loss, you know?"

Harper sniffles again and wipes under her smeared off eyeliner. Her lips begin to quiver as if she's going to break again, and I inwardly kick myself for opening back up the floodgates.

"I just don't understand why guys aren't into me. Like, what am I doing wrong?" she says through tears, putting her face in her hands.

We've heard these questions time and time again, and by now, all Juliette and I do is *shh* her and gently stroke Harp's back. It's not that we don't care about her getting her heart broken; it's that every guy she meets was going to be *the one*.

"It's going to be okay. You'll find your Prince Charming," I tell her, looking across the table to Juliette.

A waitress at the bar approaches our table and sets a new full cosmo in front of me. I look at it questioningly and then back to the waitress. "I didn't order this," I tell her.

She turns to look back at me. "The gentleman over there did. He said to tell you to watch your limit this time." With that, she turns to walk away.

I look at the cosmo and then glance around the rest of the bar to figure out who sent over this drink. My eyes scan the stools at the bar until they stop at the very end. My stomach sinks. I feel my blood beginning to boil, and I narrow my eyes at the smirk belonging to Jimmy Maxwell.

Great. This is all just fucking great.

"Holy shit," I hear Juliette say once her eyes find Jimmy.

Jimmy waves a hand at me with a boyish grin that tells me he's doing this out of spite.

Keeping my eyes locked with his, I pick up the cosmo and chug the whole thing, setting it back down with more force than necessary. Thankfully, Harper is too busy consoling herself to notice.

"I guess it's starting now," Juliette whispers.

I ignore her as I keep my eyes on Jimmy. I guess now is when it really does start.

I feel the urge to get away from him. I turn back to my friends and tell them goodbye before grabbing my wallet and heading out of the bar. It's now nighttime in New York City, and goosebumps form on my skin. I knew I should have brought a jacket. My teeth begin to chatter as I walk briskly through the wind to my apartment and away from Jimmy fucking Maxwell.

How did he know I was at Murphy's?

It's not a question I ponder over long as the thought to distance myself as far away from him as possible floods my mind. If Jimmy was going to be next to me twenty-four seven now, I was going to have to find a way to get in some alone time. It's what I do best. I enjoy my personal space, and it's what I love about living on my own. I've never been one to crave the company of a companion. I'm completely fine on my own. I *can* take care of myself, which is something I really wish my father would have realized before hiring me some hitman or whatever it is Jimmy does.

I continue to speed walk down the streets of New York City toward my apartment before Jimmy can catch up to me. *If* he followed me. My eyes want to look back to see if he's right there, following me to my apartment, but my mind keeps telling me to not look. Just keep going.

So, it's what I do.

I make the fifteen-minute walk in seven minutes, lightly jogging the last three to shorten the time and warm myself up. When I'm in my building and riding the elevator to my floor, I peek my head out of the elevator door to see if he's in the hall waiting on me. Relief washes over me when my hall is empty.

I open my door and quickly step into my apartment, closing the door and locking it like Michael Myers is chasing me. I double-check the dead bolt and slide the lock in the hole for extra protection from Jimmy and whoever is out there trying to get me in my father's mind. My apartment was dark from when I left earlier, so I turn on the lights and step into the kitchen. My stomach rumbles, and I'm instantly reminded just how hungry I am.

I could cook something, but I don't feel like washing the dishes... I'll just order takeout and make them deliver it.

I pull open the drawer that contains the take-out menu to the Chinese restaurant and scan the items. Once I've decided on the chicken lo mein and egg rolls, I start to dial their number when, out of nowhere, I hear a deep voice from across the room.

"I'll take the beef and broccoli with a side of steamed carrots, please."

I scream and jump in place at the suddenness of the voice. My heart begins to quicken and nearly beat out of my chest, and my knees buckle at the fear. *Who the fuck is that?*

As if he's in a movie, Jimmy Maxwell steps out of the darkness of my living room and into the light of the kitchen.

"What the hell, Jimmy? You scared the living shit out of me!"

He chuckles and takes a seat at my counter.

"Sorry, love. It was either now or let you turn on the light to see me. Either way, you were going to be startled."

"How the fuck did you get in here?" I yell, trying to calm down.

My knees feel like Jell-O, and my breathing is still ragged.

"The key." He holds up a brass key that looks like a safety pin in his massive hands. "Your father had one made for me." He smiles.

"My *father* shouldn't have a key to my apartment to begin with."

"How he made the key is none of my concern. I have the right copy, and that's all that matters."

I close my eyes and take a deep breath, partly to calm down my breathing, but also to try and not lose my shit at the man whom I hate more than my annual gynecological exam.

"I'm going to say this as nicely as I can, and I'm only going to say it once," I say in the best calm and collected manner I can muster right now. "Get out of my apartment and stay at least a thousand yards away from me."

Jimmy pretends to think this over. He taps his chin with his finger and looks up at the ceiling before shrugging his shoulders. "Can't do that, princess. I'm under strict orders."

"Ugh!" I fist my hair and begin to pace back and forth in the kitchen. "Why does my father treat me like such a child!"

"Maybe because you act like one?" Jimmy says sarcastically.

I turn on my heel to face him and point a finger in his face. "You don't know a *thing* about me, so don't pretend like you do."

Jimmy lightly grabs my finger and pushes it out of his face. "Hate to break it to you, kitten, but I know you better than you think. And you can't tell me what to do. I hate this just as much, if not more than you do. I've got better things to do than follow your spoiled ass all day."

"Then don't do it." I'm so angry, I overlook his insult.

He shakes his head once. "Can't. I've got a job to do."

"Why don't you lie and pretend to do your job? I won't tell if you don't."

Jimmy chuckles and leans back in the stool, crossing his arms over his broad chest. My eyes skim over his body in his white T-shirt. His muscles completely fill out the sleeves, making it look like they're about to bust through the seams. I remember his body and how attracted to it I was the first time I met him and, honestly, still am. Jimmy is built like a romance novel guy—cut abs, bulging muscles, rock-hard body, and a pretty face. But all of that means nothing with the shit personality that he has.

I had to learn that the hard way.

"See something you like, princess?"

His words draw me back to reality, and I'm forced to look at the smirk he's giving me. He caught me looking at him in the way I didn't want him to see.

"Or better yet, see something you *want* again?"

I narrow my eyes and bite my lip, trying to suppress the anger. How in the world am I going to survive this? I don't even know how long I have to put up with him.

"How long will this be going on?" I ask, hoping he knows so I can have a date on the calendar to look forward to.

"Until your father gives me the all clear."

I whimper and place my face in my hands. I hate thinking that Jimmy holds some kind of power over me with information that I don't know. It's like he enjoys seeing me miserable. It's almost like it fuels him.

I sigh and try to mentally come to terms with my present situation. There's no way around this. Jimmy will be with me every second of every damn day until he is told not to be. My life now includes Jimmy, whether I like it or not. The only way to get through this is to not play into his games and to act like he isn't there.

But with a face and body like his... that's going to be hard to do.

"Why don't we set up some boundaries?" I suggest, looking up at him.

"What kind of boundaries?"

"I get that you have a job to do, I really do, but you *are* invading my life and personal space now, so out of respect for me, there are a few terms we need to go over."

Jimmy quietly holds my gaze for a few seconds. "Shoot."

"First off, you have to text me when you are at the apartment before me, okay? I don't like coming home and being scared like I was today."

He chuckles and smiles. "What's next?"

"You *have* to give me my space. I cannot be smothered by you, understood?"

"Define 'smothered.'"

"I don't want you to be closer than fifty feet away from me at all times. I don't want to feel you breathing down my neck. I need to breathe and be alone every now and then."

"Fine. I'll do my best. Just know I have to obey your father's orders. Whatever he asks of me, I have to do."

I nod my head. I know he's right. He does have a job to do, and I know he doesn't want to be here with me, just like I don't want to be here with him. But at the end of the day, I am still a person who needs to be free and have their own space. I'm thirty-one. I'm an adult who doesn't need a bodyguard, whether there's a hitman after my father or not.

"One last thing," I say. "*We* are on our own. Don't talk to me unless you absolutely have to, and do not get in my way. Pretend as if you're living your life without me in it."

Jimmy nods his head and runs his hands through his dark hair, which matches the scruff on his face. "I thought you'd never ask."

I roll my eyes at him.

"Are you going to call in that order?" he asks, nodding his head toward the take-out menu on the counter in front of me. "Oh, and why was my sister crying earlier tonight?"

"Nope, we aren't friends, and my loyalty lies with her," I say as I roll my eyes at him and disappear into my room. I do end up calling in the order, and I even order his broccoli and beef with a side of steamed carrots.

3

JIMMY

I wake up the next morning to my phone ringing on the end table above my head. After eating the food Blaire graciously ordered me last night, I fell asleep on the couch watching TV. She offered me the guest bedroom next to hers while I stay here with her, and I planned on taking it, but exhaustion from the day beat me to it. Plus, I figured the living room would be a better place for me to sleep anyway. In case someone did try to break in, I'd hear it out here before I would in the guest bedroom.

I grab my phone to silence it so it doesn't wake up Blaire and answer the call from Luka, one of my Army brothers and a founder of the security firm.

"What do you want this early in the damn morning?" I ask him in a low whisper.

I hop off the couch and try to quietly open the sliding glass door to Blaire's balcony that overlooks the city.

"Jesus. Who pissed on your head this morning?"

I rub my face with my hand, feeling tired from not sleeping well on the stiff couch.

"Sorry, man," I say. "Rough night's sleep."

"This bitch wearing you out yet?"

I snicker. "Not yet, but it's only been a day."

"I still can't believe you have to watch Blaire fucking Hanson of all people. The world hates you, Jimmy."

"For some reason." I collapse in one of the chairs on the balcony and sink into the comfortable padding. My eyes close to block out the sun from the morning while Luka continues to talk.

"I just called to see how things went last night. We were all wondering if you got it in again, actually."

He says the last little bit with a laugh, and I huff at him. The guys know all about my run-in with Blaire Hanson months ago and how big of a bitch she is. This whole situation is ironic in so many ways, but the biggest would be the fact that Blaire and I absolutely despise each other and are now practically living together indefinitely.

"That's never happening again," I tell him, although I would like to fist that blond hair of hers again and grip her fragile waist. The woman's got a smoking hot body and fucks like an angel. It's just too bad she's a spoiled brat and a piece of work.

"Cut the shit, Jimmy," Luka says. "You two are basically married now. You can't avoid that, and you know it."

He's right. It's not like the thought of being inside of Blaire hasn't crossed my mind before. I just try not to think about it. My main focus is making sure no one hurts Blaire and booking my ass far away from her when this mess with her father is all said and done. Beautiful or not, I can't let Blaire distract me in any way. She's not right for me, anyway.

"Ah, man, I'm getting another call," Luka says. "Talk to ya later, asshat."

"Bye, Luka."

I hang up the phone and head back inside, where I'm instantly greeted by the smell of breakfast. I look up to see Blaire in the kitchen. A griddle on the counter is covered in crackling bacon, pancakes, and eggs, sunny side up. Blaire's back is to me, and her hair is in a big bun on top of her head. She turns her head to face me when she hears the door close and then turns her head back around.

"Did I wake you?" I ask, stepping farther into the kitchen.

"No. I've been up for hours."

I glance at my phone. "It's not even eight yet."

Blaire slides two pancakes from the griddle onto a plate, accompanied by bacon and eggs, and hands it to me. "I'm an early riser."

I take the plate from her, eyeing her skeptically as she goes back to pouring more pancake batter onto the griddle. "I'll keep that in mind," I say, walking my plate to the counter.

"There's fresh coffee made, too."

I stare at the back of her with wide eyes.

Breakfast and coffee in the mornings? This might not be bad after all.

I slide out of my seat to make myself a cup.

"Where are your mugs?" I ask.

"In the top right cabinet next to the fridge."

I move to the cabinet at the same time she steps in that direction. Our bodies collide and click together like they're magnets, forcing me to feel her perky breasts poking through her shirt as they press against my chest. My God, she's not wearing a bra. Her doe-like eyes find mine, and her lips lightly part as she feels my body pressed against hers.

I wonder if she feels what I just felt, the spark and intensity as we touch.

My eyes skim her face and down to her full lips, and I feel a pull in my groin. I remember kissing those lips and how soft they felt. I didn't want to stop kissing her, and I feel the push to kiss her now.

Shit. Who am I kidding? Now that she's my client, that fantasy is off the table.

Snapping back to reality, I back away to let her pull down a mug for me. Blaire keeps her eyes on me for just a few more seconds before giving the cabinet her attention. Her slim arm reaches to the top shelf to grab a white mug, and she sets it on the counter, turning away swiftly. I can practically see the embarrassment on her face. It makes me smirk. I know what's running through her mind.

"Thanks," I say, pouring coffee into the mug.

Blaire keeps her focus on the griddle. "Mm-hmm."

I start eating what's on my plate and am nearly done when Blaire turns to start on hers. She stands at the end of the island across from me, and we eat in silence. It's awkward, but neither of us knows what to say. There's not even much *to* say.

"So, what are your plans for the day?" I try, even though I'm not really interested.

Blaire looks up to me with a scowl, and it's then that I notice she has no makeup on. And damn, is she still beautiful.

"What?" I ask in regard to the look she's giving me.

"Don't do that."

"Don't do what?"

"Don't ask questions just to ask them."

My eyebrows shoot up. Is this chick for real? Puzzled over the offense she's taking to my innocent question, I narrow my eyes at her. "You're really getting mad at me over asking you what your plans for the day are?"

Blaire huffs, and her fork falls out of her hands with a loud *clank* as it lands on her plate. "You know what I mean, Jimmy."

"I'm just trying to make this the least awkward it can be."

Blaire rolls her eyes and pats her mouth with her napkin. She discards the remains of her breakfast into the trash can before storming off to her room.

"I have a flight to get ready for," she mumbles. This makes the hair on my arms stand up.

"What was that?"

Blaire freezes, keeping her back to me. She doesn't respond as I keep my eyes on her.

"What did you just say, Blaire?" I repeat, this time in a more threatening tone.

Blaire turns slowly on her heel, facing me with a chilling look. "I said I have a flight to get ready for."

"Where are you going?"

She huffs, not wanting me to know. "Miami."

Now I'm off my counter stool and striding to her. I feel anger start to rise in my chest at the sudden knowledge of this trip. She wasn't going to tell me. That's clear to see in her body language and her face. What this bitch doesn't know is that her little stunt could have cost me my job.

Blaire shrinks as my body towers over her once I've closed the distance between us. Her eyes look to the floor as I pierce mine onto that pretty little face of hers, reveling in the fact that she's intimidated by me.

"When were you going to tell me?" I ask in a low voice. I just want to watch her mouth admit that she was going to leave without me knowing.

"I wasn't," she chokes.

I blow a deep breath out of my nose. I can't lose my shit on her. She could use it against me and tell her father I lashed out at her, and that would be the end of it. I'll be damned if I let Blaire Hanson take me down.

"When does the plane leave?" I ask.

"Five."

Alright, I have enough time to make adjustments at the firm and get things together. I lose some steam, and I start to run through my routine for the day until it's time to leave.

I sink on my heels and take a step back. Blaire exhales as she releases a breath once I'm out of her presence.

This girl is going to be the death of me.

4

BLAIRE

The plan almost worked. It was so close to working that I could practically feel the freedom inside of me, ready to claw out. A few days in Miami without being under the supervision of Jimmy Maxwell sounded like a dream come true. I could get business done, have a little fun, and live my life as normal without him being up my ass the whole time.

I can't believe I spilled the secret myself.

Once I finish packing, I decide to head to work for the little time I have to be there today. When I come out of my bedroom, the quietness of the apartment alarms me. Pausing in the doorway, I peek my head out into the hall. The TV is off; the lights are still on in the kitchen, and it's as if life has carried on as usual after breakfast without the sight of Jimmy. I step farther into the kitchen and glance to the balcony and see the door is closed. There isn't the faint rumble of someone talking outside.

"Jimmy?"

No answer.

I narrow my eyes. "Jimmy?" I try again.

There's no answer once more. I walk around the apartment and check all the rooms to find them vacant. I don't even remember hearing him leave.

A wide smile starts to spread across my lips at the thought of being in the apartment alone. It's... refreshing, even though it's only been a day.

I quickly get ready for work and make sure my bags are packed before zooming out of the apartment.

A new plan hits me.

I pull my phone out of my purse and press a few buttons before waiting for my assistant to pick up.

"Hey, it's Blaire," I say once she's answered. "There's been a change of plans."

THE CAB PULLS UP to the airport in a swift glide. I tip the driver a crisp twenty-dollar bill before moving briskly to get my bags out of the trunk and into the busy airport.

My body fills with jitters. *I can't believe I'm doing this!*

The sliding doors open, and I step into the building like a spy on a mission, hiding behind my oversized Prada sunglasses. I resist the urge to turn my head around to make sure Jimmy hasn't followed me, and I scan every possible hiding place my eyes can spot as I walk through the airport. My movements are fast. I keep my head down and my pace fast so I can board this plane as soon as possible. Buying the new ticket for the earlier flight time was a genius idea, and I'm ready to put it into action. There's no way Jimmy could get here in time *and* find me in Miami.

My eyes still search the swarm of people as I take each step closer to boarding the plane. I make it to the security check, the last stop before handing over my ticket and crossing into freedom. *The plan is actually working!*

Once I pass through security, I book it into high gear to board the plane. My grip on my purse strap is tight, and my head is tucked between my shoulders as I weave in and out of people before making it to my gate. I finally board the plane and fall into my seat with a deep breath of relief.

In just a few short hours, I will be Jimmy Maxwell free in Miami, and life will be normal.

I settle further into the seat and lean my head back on the headrest. I close my eyes as I wait for everyone else to board before taking off. My mind starts to drift off to these next few days in Miami. The warm beach, exhilarating nightlife, successful business projects...

I feel the seat beside me shake with someone sitting down in it. I don't open my eyes right away until I hear a chilling voice.

"This seat taken?"

My body freezes.

It can't be.

I turn to the left to see Jimmy, sitting with his arms crossed and smiling his famous smirk. His arms are folded across his chest in a tight black T-shirt, making his biceps bulge out of the sleeves. I hate the way I find this man attractive. His hardness and masculine features are what I found to be irresistible that fatal night I gave in to him. What I wouldn't give to take that night back. His pink tongue darts out and lazily drags across his bottom lip, causing my belly to flop.

"How did you—"

"Let me stop you right there, princess, and remind you that it's my goddamn job. I was part of the Special Forces. I can kill a man fifty different ways and get away with it. You think you can outrun me? Outthink me? Outmaneuver me? You can't."

Jimmy shifts in his seat to lean in closer to me, pinning me to the back of my chair with his close proximity, and I smell the scent of him —cedar and pine, laced with Jimmy. An intoxicating smell proven to be dangerous. The man has the pheromones of a sex god.

His icy eyes grab a fierce hold on mine and signal their own dangerous warning before he opens his lips. "If you even *dream* about sneaking off while we are in Miami, I will make your life a living hell."

His voice is low and chilling, but I don't give him the reaction he wants. Instead, I mirror his expression and lean closer into him.

"It already is," I whisper.

Our eyes lock as the flight attendant comes over the intercom to let us know it's time for the plane to take off. I sink back slowly into my seat to buckle in and slide my AirPods into my ears.

I guess my plan wasn't that successful.

⊏═══⊐

WHEN THE PLANE lands and we collect our bags, the ride to the hotel is silent. I sit as far away from Jimmy as I can on the other end of the cab seat, and I keep my face pointed to the window. Every now and then, I can hear the faint tapping of Jimmy's fingers as they go to work on his phone screen with him staring at it intently. The man is a mystery I can't crack.

The driver pulls up to the entrance of our hotel, and we collect our bags before walking in. I pull my suitcase behind me as I approach the woman dressed in a navy blazer with a neat bun placed high up on her head. She gives me a tight smile before turning her gaze on Jimmy, sending him a softer smile with dreamy eyes as her eyes land on him. It makes me roll mine.

"How can I help you?" she asks, returning her attention to me.

"I need to check in. Hanson is the name."

Her hot-pink-tipped fingers type my last name into the computer. "Blaire?"

"Yes." I nod.

"Room for two? I'll just need to see your credit card and a form of ID."

Um, did she just say...

"I'm sorry, what?"

The lady, whose name tag says Melanie, draws her eyebrows

together and cocks her head to the side. "Room for two under Blaire Hanson, correct?"

"Blaire Hanson, yes, but I could have sworn I booked a room for one."

"Let me check." Melanie goes back to typing on the computer before falling silent for a brief moment. Her eyes move back and forth as they scan the words on the screen before saying, "No, you booked a room for two. I'm seeing here in my records that you booked a suite for two on March fifteenth."

I hear a faint chuckle from Jimmy behind me as I stare at the woman in shock. My insides begin to boil at his satisfaction.

I know this isn't the room I booked.

To avoid causing a scene, I begrudgingly hand over my credit card and driver's license before initialing the papers.

Melanie hands me a small packet with our keys and says, "Your room is on the ninth floor, room 912. Enjoy your stay, and let us know if you need anything. The bellman will grab your things."

Her voice says this to me, but her eyes say it to Jimmy.

"We've got it, thanks." I lightly huff and grab my suitcase to begin walking with the monumental man behind me to our now shared room. As we load into the elevator, I replay the day I booked the room in my head. Once I found out about the conference, I booked the room immediately, the penthouse—for one. How could this happen? Whatever. At least there are two queen beds in the room so we won't have to sleep next to each other. I'd rather cut my arm off than lie beside him.

The elevator dings once we've reached the ninth floor, and we walk to the room in silence. All the while, I feel Jimmy's eyes on my back. I know he's having the time of his life with this little hiccup, so I play it off like it's not a big deal. I'll just have to be extra careful when I venture off at night outside of work.

Stepping up to room 912, I slide one of the keys into the lock and open the door. When we first step in, we enter the little hallway with the bathroom and closet on the left before coming up to the bed.

Jimmy turns on the lights behind me and I freeze, a loud gasp escaping my throat.

What. The. FUCK!

This *seriously* cannot be happening to me.

I gawk at the single king-sized bed sitting in the center of the room. It's like the universe hates me now for some unknown reason.

While I'm frozen in place, Jimmy moves around me to the bed.

"Taking the side closest to the window. Hope you don't mind."

I narrow my eyes at him. "You think this is *so funny*, don't you?"

"Actually, yes, I do."

I roll my eyes at him. "I'm going downstairs to get another room."

I turn to walk out the door when his voice stops me. "Blaire, wait. I'll sleep on the couch."

While that doesn't fully solve my problem, I turn to look at him.

"I don't want to sleep next to you anyway," he says.

"Feeling's mutual."

I start to lay my bag on the bed and unpack. It's going to be weird to share this space with Jimmy for a few days, but unfortunately, I don't have a choice.

As I unpack my clothes, Jimmy collapses onto the couch. His fingers start to type furiously once more on his screen, and I watch him, wondering what goes on in his life. When I first met Jimmy Maxwell a few months ago, he was a closed book. He still is. He wouldn't open up much about his life when I asked. All I know is he's ex-military and all business. I could tell from my brief encounter that there are things in Jimmy's life he doesn't want to share. Even Harper doesn't disclose a lot of information about her only brother. But there was something about him that drew me in. Maybe it was the mystery of him and curiosity got the best of me, but whatever it is, there's something about Jimmy that intrigues me, and I want to know more. But then he opens his mouth, and I remember why I hate him in the first place. Arrogance isn't a personality trait I find endearing or even mildly charming. Especially when he uses it to get what he wants from me, then tosses me aside.

Jimmy looks up from his phone, his vibrant green eyes finding mine. For the first time, I feel speechless around him. He sits on the couch with his elbows resting on his knees, his eyes staring at me with such intensity, I can feel it in my core. It leaves me breathless, and my lips slightly part.

"Something you want, princess?" His voice is low.

"No," I whisper. He may be a testosterone-fueled ape, but the man can read my mind like a book and it's irritating as hell.

Jimmy stands up, his immense body already towering over me from a few feet away. He runs a hand through his thick dark hair and stretches his limbs in a way that lifts his shirt above his torso. My eyes follow the lines of his taut abs, all the way down to the sexy V that tapers at his waist and I have to peel my eyes away from him in order to not get caught.

"I'm going to step out for a minute. I need to make a call," he says.

I nod my head, expecting him to leave, but then he closes in on me. Jimmy reaches a hand to cup my chin and tilts my head upward. I can feel his breath on my skin as his intense gaze keeps me captivated.

"If I come back in and you're gone," he whispers lowly, "I will hunt you down and punish you. Understand me?"

My mouth goes dry at his promise and I slowly nod my head. The look in his eyes is enough to let me know his warning is real, and I swallow the dry lump forming in my throat. I don't say anything as Jimmy releases my chin to step outside onto the balcony for his call.

What the hell was that, and why did I like it?

I feel a weird pull between my legs at Jimmy and his words, but I quickly push it away once Jimmy closes the balcony door. I wait until I hear his voice speaking to whoever is on the other end of the line before I quickly open up a drawer and run to the bathroom to change.

If Jimmy wants to hunt, I'll give him something to chase.

5

JIMMY

I step onto the balcony of our hotel in Miami and dial the number I was told to call. Charles gave me his private cell number and instructed me to call him once we made it to the hotel. Man, watching Blaire squirm in the lobby was fucking priceless. Even though she pissed me off with her little stunt to get out of town quick, she was no match for the tracking device I had placed on her with her father's permission. I'll give it to Blaire, she's a smart, intelligent woman, but even she couldn't get past me with her quick little plans. If it wasn't my job on the line, it would even be funny that she thinks she can outsmart someone who was once paid to be invisible.

"Jameson, is everything okay?" Charles asks once he picks up my call.

"All is good. We're at the hotel here in Miami."

"Excellent. And how is Blaire?"

I choose my words carefully. "Cooperating," I lie.

"Wonderful. Good to hear. The conference will only last two days, mostly during the morning and afternoons, but it's the evenings I'm concerned about. Did you install the device?"

"Yes, it's in her cell phone and working perfectly."

"Excellent. Now, listen, Jameson. Blaire will do anything she can to impress the board. If she ventures off at night for meetings or drinks, please watch after her closely. I don't trust that city at all, and we're still investigating here at the office. Seems like the IT security team has found where the breach came from; they've traced the IP address."

"Understood, sir." I nod.

"Thank you, Jameson. Be safe and keep my daughter safe."

"I will."

Charles and I say our goodbyes, and I slide my phone back into the pocket of my pants before digging it out again once it vibrates. Holding the phone in my hands, I read the alert from Blaire's device. It only notifies me when she's out of the half-mile radius I programmed as the default.

I read the words on the screen that tell me Blaire is in a cab and heading west toward the strip, and rage begins to take control.

That fucking bitch!

I bolt back inside of the room for the hotel keys before booking it out the hotel room and to the lobby. I skip the elevator and shoot down the stairs to make it to the bottom faster and hail a cab once I'm standing beside the busy street. I keep the tracking system map pulled up on my phone so I can watch where Blaire's going and give the driver directions.

As the system shows every turn Blaire's cab makes, I look for shortcuts to catch her but miss her every time, until her blue dot stops on the map. My thumb and pointer finger zoom in on the screen to read where she's at, which, thankfully, is only ten minutes away.

"Stop at The Avenue Club, please," I say to the driver.

He pulls up next to the bar a few minutes later, and I sling his tip at him before hopping out and zooming into the club. Even for midafternoon, the small bar proves to be a popular joint as there's already a small crowd gathered outside, waiting to get in. I approach the bouncer and show him my business card and my security ID to be allowed in.

Once I'm inside, the loud music mixed with the crowd makes it difficult to find her quickly. I begin to search around for Blaire as I stand in the sea of people packed into the small area. Every square inch of the bar is filled with customers and drinkers all partying and letting loose for the upcoming weekend. My eyes scan the room back and forth until I spot the back of Blaire's blond hair several feet away at the bar.

I fight the crowd as I squeeze through it to get to her before tapping her on the shoulder. Blaire turns around, and I study her face only to realize it's not Blaire. It's some other woman.

"Hey there," she says, slurring her words. I can tell the girl is already wasted at twelve o'clock on a Friday afternoon.

I leave the girl as fast as I approached and continue to look around the room for Blaire. I'm going to kill her once I get my hands on her.

I feel a light tap on my shoulder, and I turn to see Blaire, eyeing me with anger. "What are you doing here?" she asks.

"Funny. I was wanting to ask you the same thing."

She rolls her eyes at me and proceeds to sip the fruity drink in her hand. My eyes skim her body in her tight white dress with a cross halter top. Her long tan legs look like silk as they slide out of the bottom of the dress and into her sandaled heels that lace halfway up her calf. "What the fuck are you wearing?"

"You like? It's a going-out outfit," she says, twisting so I can see all angles of her angelic body.

The dress highlights her delicate curves gloriously as the fabric hugs her like a second skin in all the right places. Her hips sway to the music. My dick twitches, urging me to take the dress off her and spank her for leaving the room the way she did and making me come after her, but I know what she's doing. She's testing the limits. This is a game to her. Who comes out to a club at lunchtime on a Friday dressed like that? Nobody but party kids, which are exactly the other customers in the bar with us right now.

If Blaire wants to play, I'll play. But she's going to suffer for it later.

"It's alright. I've seen better," I tell her.

Blaire rolls her eyes, and her lips bite down on the thin black straw in her drink.

"What is that?" I ask.

"Sex on the beach. Have you ever had sex on the beach, Jimmy?"

Her voice and question make me study her harder. Has she been drinking for a while?

"How many of those have you had?"

"Three," she says proudly, holding the drink up.

"Blaire, it's twelve noon and you've only been here maybe twenty minutes. What are you doing?"

"I'm having fun. What does it look like I'm doing?"

Blaire begins to tuck her body back into the crowd, and I lunge after her, grabbing her arm and pulling her back to me.

"Ow, let me go!"

"Where are you going?"

She jerks her delicate arm out of my hold and gives me a glare. "Why can't you just *leave me alone*, Jimmy!"

"Because your father ordered me not to."

Blaire barks out a laugh and leans her head back, no doubt feeling light and carefree from what she's been drinking. "Screw my father! I'm thirty-one years old, for crying out loud. I'm an *adult*. I did not consent to having a bodyguard. You know I have a law degree, right?"

"An adult that's acting like a *young* adult," I point out.

Just like that, Blaire's attitude changes. Her smile instantly fades into a straight line, and she holds my gaze for a quiet moment. "Why do you have to be such a stickler? Be a man for once, Jimmy, and just relax. Make the best of this situation and have some damn fun. You do know the word fun, right? Outside of being the fun police?"

I can tell she's reaching a limit. To be honest, I don't know what Blaire's limit is, but it's fast approaching. I reach out to grab her arm, but she disappears into the crowd, and the sea of people engulfs her.

Dammit, Blaire.

I keep my phone's tracker system pulled up in case Blaire gets too far. I try to follow her footsteps to reach her, but keeping my sights on her is impossible. God, Charles is going to kill me if anything happens to her.

For ten minutes, I keep walking around the place to find Blaire, my eyes bouncing back and forth between the bar and the tracking system. I watch the customers in the bar for any possible dangers they could pose to Blaire, her being a gorgeous girl in a place like this and all.

A few minutes later, I spot her across the room. The image of her in the distance with that tight white dress on her creamy skin is a sight to behold. I watch her body move to the beat of the music. Her hips dip and twist, and I find myself staring at them, wanting to feel that twist and dip on me... until I see the random prick to her right slink his arm around her flat waist and pull her into him.

Blaire, intoxicated, smiles and continues to maneuver her body to match the rhythm of the music playing through the speakers. Her body grinds against his, and I clench my fists together tightly, narrowing my eyes at the man I'm about to murder. That's it. I've had *enough*.

I march over to where they are on the floor and stand in shock at what I see.

Blaire's body moves like a slinky on this guy, and her fucking hands slide up to fist his hair. Obviously, this asshole loves it. He looks like he's in heaven as his hands grip her waist tighter, and he leans in to whisper something in her ear. Blaire giggles but then shakes her head as she continues to dance. The guy whispers something again with more force, and Blaire's smile fades into a concerned, pissed-off look. I stand by, waiting for the right time to swoop in when I'm needed based on this guy's movements. If Blaire wants to act like a fool, I'll have her learn a fool's lesson.

Blaire's hands fight to pry the guy's arm off her, but he doesn't budge. He yanks her, pulling her against him, and angrily whispers in her ear. It's then that I can see the look of fear in her eyes.

I step in and wrap my hand around Blaire's free hand, giving the guy a look. "Let's go, Blaire."

"Beat it, pal. This one's mine," the guy says.

I glare at his sunken eyes, swollen with liquor, and scowl at him. I size him up, noticing his smaller body frame and applaud him for feeling brave. I could knock this guy out in a second flat.

"No, she's not. Now let her go before I make you."

Blaire looks at me with pleading eyes. I glance at her, my gaze soft to let her know it's going to be alright, before turning my attention back to this prick.

My hand closes on his, and I dig my fingers into his hold to break Blaire free from his grasp. That's when I feel the hit to my face.

I stumble back—*barely*—at the sudden assault. *Did he just...*

When my vision settles, I see him dragging Blaire behind him, trying to make it to the exit. I quickly start darting in between the other bar patrons until I reach Blaire and extend an arm out to her. When she feels my touch, her head swivels, and I see the tears streaming down her cheeks.

"Help me!" she begs, loud enough to hear clearly over the music.

I pull her out of the guy's hold, and she grabs on to my shirt, burying her face into my chest. The guy turns his dark head back around, and I send a punch so hard, I can hear the smack over the music. The guy falls to the ground, taking down a few other people in the bar, and I rush Blaire out of the bar. Her body is limp in my arms and growing weaker with sobs by the second.

As soon as we're out in the fresh air, I settle us on the sidewalk to call an Uber to pick us up and take us to the hotel. Once I put my phone back in my pocket, I look at Blaire and give her a shake to keep her awake.

"Blaire, stay with me," I say, inspecting her. Her eyes are closing and she begins to laugh but she's not coherent enough for an actual conversation. "Blaire, can you hear me?"

"Mmm."

"How much did you drink?" I ask.

Her noodle-like body grows more limp in my arms, her own arms flung around my neck as I hold her upright on the sidewalk. Blaire mutters her response, something I can't make out, and luckily, our Uber makes it before she passes out.

I'm not getting paid enough for this shit.

I help settle Blaire into the cab and give the driver instructions on how to get to our hotel. Once he starts taking off, I look to Blaire in my lap and try to keep her awake. I shake her gently to keep her eyes open.

"Stay awake, Blaire."

God, she is getting it once we get to the hotel.

Our driver pulls into the parking lot ten minutes later, and I gather Blaire in my arms and carry her into the building. Once we're off the elevator and in the hotel room, I place her body on the bed and slide her up to the pillow. The bottom of her dress slides up to her stomach to reveal the white G-string she is wearing underneath. The sight of it makes my breath hitch. Her tan skin contrasting against the pure color sends shivers down my spine. Her skin feels like silk in my hands as I reach up to pull her dress back down. I can't help but look. God, she's so sexy, and watching the way she moved on that dance floor really made me itch to touch her, to feel her move against me. Even as she lies in the bed right now in another world, a consequence for her selfish actions, she looks like a dream.

My hands slide up her legs to drag the dress back down even though the last thing I want right now is for her to be covered. I want to remove this dress, remove the white string, and bury my tongue in her. Then devour her and drive her crazy until she's on the verge of coming and then stop to torture her like she's tortured me today. God, I want to *taste* her right now. To punish her like I told her I would.

No.

This is fucked up.

I dismiss those thoughts from my head and yank the dress down.

There's no hope in keeping her awake. She's just going to have to suffer the consequences later.

I remove her shoes from her feet and pull the bedcovers over her before crashing on the couch. Obviously, I can't go far from her, or she'll take the opportunity to run. Fuck her no smothering policy. She needs to be smothered. One more stunt like this and it's all over for her.

As Blaire sleeps in the bed, I turn on the TV as background noise. I pull out my phone to check in with Luka and the other guys while I wait for her to wake up before drifting off on my own.

What the hell have I gotten myself into?

6

BLAIRE

I wake up several hours later with the *worst* headache of my life. The first thought I have is, *what the hell did I do?* But it's quickly tossed aside when I shoot up in the bed and lean over to the side, puking my brains out.

There's sudden movement on the couch. I totally forgot that Jimmy was in the room with me. Wait, how did I *get* to the room?

Another wave of nausea hits me, but this time, the vomit lands in the small trash can Jimmy places before me. I think all of my dignity is in the trash can, too. I fall onto the bed, panting for air, trying to tell myself none of this is happening. I'm not throwing up in front of Jimmy Maxwell. I didn't make a fool out of myself in front of him either. No way.

"Here," he says, shoving something in my face.

My eyes groggily open, and I register the cup of ice water Jimmy is handing me. I muster up the little strength I have to sit up in the bed and take the cup from him. Every move I make only forms a deeper pounding in my head.

I see Jimmy try to stifle a smile with his hand as he pretends to scratch at his chin. I narrow my eyes at him and set the cup of water down on the table beside me. "What time is it?" I ask.

He glances down at his watch. "Ten."

My eyes widen. "At *night?*"

He nods his head. "Yeah. You've been out for hours."

"And you didn't think to wake me up?"

"You needed to sleep it off. You wouldn't have woken if I tried."

I scoff and bring my hands to my head and rub my temples. "Great. Now my whole night is thrown off."

"Are you hungry?" Jimmy asks.

At the sound of his question, my stomach grumbles. After the little bit I ate this morning, I didn't eat anything else before going to the bar. Thinking back on it, I'm not sure what I was trying to accomplish with that.

"Actually, yes," I say, sliding off the bed.

My legs give out the second my feet hit the floor, and I nearly fall to the ground. I'm saved by Jimmy's hands wrapping around my weak frame and keeping me in place. He pulls me close to him, and my body collides with his rock-solid torso. There's something about Jimmy's touch that sets my skin on fire, and as I look up to him and see his eyes peering down at me, I feel that fire everywhere in my body.

For a second, I can see the desire in his eyes. I watch his green eyes turn dark with lust as his eyes rake my face. It fuels me. The way he looks at me kills me. *Empowers* me. I don't know what it is about this man that makes me feel like such a powerful woman even in my weakest and most embarrassed state.

"You need to take a shower," he whispers, letting me go with ease.

I lightly whimper at the loss of contact once he puts more space between us.

"You smell like vomit and cheap tequila." Jimmy turns his back to me and pulls his phone out of his pocket once more before collapsing onto the couch.

God, he's such an asshole.

I head into the bathroom to shower and take my time standing underneath the hot water, letting it soothe my skin. As I massage the shampoo into my head, I close my eyes and think of Jimmy in the shower.

Am I still drunk? I wonder what kind of shampoo he uses for his thick hair to keep it looking soft and fluffed. I wonder if he's a bar of soap or body wash kind of guy. I wonder if he's like the guys in the movies that lean into the water and plant their hands on the shower wall as they let the water run down their bodies...

A light moan escapes my lips, and my eyes fly open. I look down to see my fingers buried between my slick folds, rubbing circles against my sensitive bud. Had I started pleasing myself thinking of *Jimmy?* I'm completely losing it.

But I continue to please myself because it feels *so* good.

My fingers rub my clit slowly with pressure as I try to bring myself to climax. My free hand slowly slides up my wet stomach to my breast, and I cup it before pinching my nipple, a sensation I crave. The water beats down on my skin as I rub faster and harder, restraining myself from crying out. I close my eyes and think of Jimmy fucking me. The mental picture of his enormous chest covering me and his muscular arms by the sides of my face as he grunts, pounding into me, sends shivers through me. My legs wobble and I sink with them, my mouth forming an O as my orgasm starts to tense my body. I keep picturing Jimmy rocking into me, his hand reaching down to grab my throat as he whispers dirty demands. God, I'm about to come when—

The door to the bathroom opens, and Jimmy walks in to the sink. I gasp and scream. "What are you doing!" I yell, pulling the shower curtain to my body.

"Brushing my teeth," is what I can gather while the toothbrush works itself in Jimmy's mouth.

I watch through the side of the curtain as Jimmy bends by the sink to brush his teeth.

"You couldn't have waited for me to get out?"

"You were taking a while," he says after spitting. "Besides, it's not like I haven't seen you naked before."

He says this with sarcasm and shoots me a look in the mirror. I roll my eyes and dip back into the water, annoyed and sexually frustrated as I wait for him to exit the room. Jimmy leaves after a few more seconds, and I'm left feeling frustrated at my delayed orgasm. It was going to be a good one, too.

I finish my shower and wrap my body in one of the towels before applying my lotion and body spray. I ruffle my hair in another towel before brushing it and running my fingers through it. Other girls would be too self-conscious to walk out makeup-less with a guy as good-looking as Jimmy Maxwell. Typically, I would be, too, but since I hate him other than for his looks, I don't give a shit.

I brush my teeth before walking out of the bathroom with the towel wrapped around my body to find my clothes. When I walk into the room, the smell of garlic and something charred greets my nose.

"What's that smell?" I ask.

I find Jimmy standing by the small table for two tucked against the wall at the back corner with two silver plate covers sitting on the glass.

"I ordered some food."

Jimmy removes the plate covers to reveal gourmet meals of chicken and potatoes that look absolutely mouthwatering. The sight and intensified smell are enough to make my stomach rumble.

When Jimmy looks up from the table, his movement freezes. His eyes slowly skim my body, and I watch his Adam's apple bob with his swallow. I fight the smile trying to creep its way onto my lips. Still feeling somewhat confident from the alcohol earlier, I pretend to not notice his eyes following my every move as I walk to the drawers to pull out my nightclothes. First, I pull out a pair of lacy black underwear and a white T-shirt that I know is thin enough to showcase my nipples. Jimmy stands by the table as he continues to watch me, and I do my best to nonchalantly flaunt the black lace panties in my hands.

As much as I hate him, I love the way he fucks me. The one night

I spent with him was enough to prove to me that I will never have another man in bed as gifted as Jimmy. It had been forbidden and accidental, sleeping with my best friend's brother, but I'd be lying if I said it wasn't the best sex of my life. God, what I wouldn't give to feel that release one more time.

And that's all it would be—a release. Nothing more.

In the one night I spent with him, I grew to know Jimmy Maxwell. I know his turn-ons and what he wants. I know what he likes to see and what he looks for. So I decide to give it to him. Not for his pleasure, but for mine. Because I deserve to be pleased.

I toss my clothes on the bed to face him, still gripping my towel. Jimmy still stands silent, watching me from a few feet away.

"You know what I hate?" I start.

Jimmy's eyebrows draw together in confusion. "What?"

"Being interrupted when I'm trying to come."

"When you're—"

Jimmy's voice stops the second I drop the towel to the floor. I sit on the bed and keep my eyes on his the whole time. The adrenaline coursing through my veins right now is the most intense it's ever been. I've never been one to comfortably display myself naked in front of a man, but I *want* to in front of Jimmy. I want to feel his tongue on me, assaulting me so devilishly that I'm screaming with release and grabbing the sheets. I deserve it after this torture he's putting me through.

I spread my legs and slip a finger in my mouth before dipping it back down to my slick folds to rub circles on my clit once more.

"I *hate* being interrupted before a climax," I say, holding his gaze as I please myself. "Like I was in the..." My voice drifts off as my head falls back, and I close my eyes at the sensation beginning to tighten in my body. All the while, in my head, I'm begging Jimmy to take over and fuck me.

My fingers continue to rub against my nub, and the sounds of my wetness fill the air. I moan loud enough for Jimmy to hear, and I hear him gruff by the table. *Yes.*

I lift my head back up to look at him and see the lust in his eyes. I look down to see his length begging to break free in his jeans. I smirk at him and give him a seductive look, lifting my fingers to my mouth and sucking on them while still keeping my eyes locked with his.

"Mmm. Wanna taste?" I ask.

Jimmy swallows. His knuckles turn white from gripping the back of the chair, and he remains silent. He tries to maintain a poker face, so I go back to rubbing myself before saying, "Fine. I'll do all the work."

I shift to lie in the bed and spread my legs open farther so it's the only visible part of me he can fully see. My back connects with the sheets, and I use my free hand to cup my breast while my other continues to move in circles. My lips part, and my head digs into the bed as I arch my back. I try to keep the sensation under control and not finish before Jimmy comes in. I know I can get him to crack. Right now, he's playing hard to get, but underneath that hard surface, I know there's the beast in him clawing his way out.

"Get down here and fuck me, Jimmy," I whisper, arching my back even more before letting another moan rip from me.

My eyes close tight as I rub myself but then—

A warmth. A delicious warmth wraps around me. I feel Jimmy's hands push my hand out of the way before wrapping around my thighs and pulling my exposed flesh to his mouth. His tongue spreads wide on my clit as he laps me and sucks me, causing an animalistic moan to rip through my body. My hands come down to fist his hair and push him further into me. God, I love this. I love the way this feels.

I can already feel my body tensing and tingling with my growing orgasm. It's not going to take me long before I come, but I want to savor this. I shouldn't be doing this. This shouldn't be happening. It shouldn't be happening for a multitude of reasons. This is mixing business with pleasure. On top of the fact that I *hate* this man, I hate knowing that he's getting satisfaction from my satisfaction. But damn, if he were to stop right now, losing my mind would be an absolute understatement.

"Yes, Jimmy, yes," I moan.

I start to rock my hips lightly into his licks as he ravishes me with his tongue. He moans into me, and the vibration against my clit makes me shudder. His fingers dig into my skin to keep me in place, and I whimper at the pain.

"I'm going to come," I say, moaning as the sensation intensifies.

"God, you taste so good, baby," Jimmy says.

His words reverberate in my stomach, and I smile as the orgasm begins to take control of me, but Jimmy doesn't stop. My body tightens, and I arch my back as I feel all the pleasure, all the stress, all the relief hit me at once, and I'm seeing stars, screaming his name and fisting his hair as his tongue sends me straight into oblivion.

God, this man.

Jimmy continues to ravish me and take me with his mouth. My orgasm intensifies as I grow wetter and begin to leak down my thigh. I feel the droplets soaking my skin and the sheets below me as Jimmy laps me through my orgasm. My body starts to shake uncontrollably, and I'm at a loss for breath, feeling as if I can take no more when he removes himself in a quick movement. The loss of his tongue makes me feel empty. I lean up on my elbow to find him as I'm being pushed back down by his weight. A scream escapes my throat as his hard and impressive length slides into me, stretching me in the most painful yet delicious way.

"Oh, *God!*" I moan.

"God, you're so tight," he groans.

Jimmy pounds into me and fills me with his length. My hands fly to his back to rake my nails into his skin as he begins to move at a rhythm so forceful, it brings tears to my eyes. Beads of sweat start to form on Jimmy's skin as he fucks me with all his strength. He rocks into my hips, rubbing lightly against my clit, and I feel a second orgasm starting to bubble inside of me. The headboard slams against the wall over and over and I randomly think how grateful I am that our room doesn't have a shared wall behind it.

Jimmy shifts and moves to his knees. He continues to punish me with his thrusts while leaning down and cupping my neck with his hand. His eyes grow dark and dangerous as he glares at me, slowing his pace to fuck me with one hard and forceful thrust at a time.

"Don't you ever"—he slams into me again, causing me to moan loudly—"run away from me"—another hard thrust—"*again.*"

I tantalize his demand with my own game by smirking at him and giggling. "Or what? You don't control me."

For a second, I wonder if it's anger I see in his eyes or the need to correct me. Jimmy's hand around my neck tightens, and I gasp as he removes himself from me in a painful movement before swiftly picking me up and slamming me on the bed with my stomach on the mattress. I feel Jimmy stand off the bed and pull my ass to him, lifting it in the air and parting my legs with his knee. My hands reach to stretch above my head, but he gathers them in his colossal hands and holds them tightly in his.

"Or you'll wish you never did," he says before slamming himself back into my opening.

I scream into the bed as he fucks me in an animalistic way. He grunts with each thrust while he reaches around to rub my clit with his free hand. My body convulses under him at the powerful assault, and I love it. Jimmy's hand keeping my wrists pinned behind me tightens with every attempt of mine to break free. His fingers pinch my nub at the same time his length fills me, and I feel the orgasm rising.

"I'm going to come; I'm going to come," I whimper.

Jimmy thrusts into me once, twice, three more times, then pulls out and rolls me onto my stomach before I can reach my climax. He spills his contents onto me with a shudder before standing back up to go retrieve something to clean it up with.

"You *asshole!*" I shout at him.

Jimmy returns a few seconds later with a wad of toilet paper in his hands. He hands it to me with a sly smile, and I take it with a glare.

"Why am I an asshole?" he asks.

I wipe off his cum and hand him the paper. "You know why."

"Because you didn't get your second finish? My, you are one selfish girl—and naughty, too. Spreading your legs right in my face... damn. Didn't know you had that in you."

I narrow my eyes at him, feeling suddenly embarrassed of what I just did. I grab the sheets to quickly cover me.

Jimmy snickers and leans onto the bed with his hands. "Don't feel the need to cover yourself on my account, sweetheart. I've seen *everything*."

"You are *such* an asshole."

Jimmy winks at me as he stands, and damn, do I feel like pulling him back on me. After pulling his underwear back on, he moves to the table where our now cold food sits. That's *all* he puts on. And those black briefs on that body... Calvin Klein would design an entire line just for him if they could see the way he fills them out.

Jimmy takes several bites before wiping his mouth and looking at me on the bed.

"Question," he starts. "Does this mean I still have to sleep on the couch?"

7

JIMMY

THREE MONTHS EARLIER...

"Come on, Jimmy, just meet her. Please?"

I roll my eyes at Harper and her childlike manner. She's been begging me to let her set me up with her friend who's newly single and "totally hot," as she puts it. Being back in the States and near my sister after starting the firm with my Army brothers has been great, but I'm reminded of why I enjoyed being deployed in the first place—being away from the annoying tendencies of my family to constantly feel the need to set me up with any woman who breathes.

"I'm going out with the guys tonight, Harp. I can find my own woman."

"No, you browse. You look for a one-night air mattress instead of the king-sized bed that will last you years—decades, even."

I give her a sideways glance at the bar in her apartment. The sandwich I was about to stuff my face with pauses just before my lips. "Did you just compare women to beds?"

Harper smiles proudly and pops one of my chips into her mouth. "Yup. And it was a great analogy too."

"No, it was fucking weird." I bite down on my sandwich, hoping to end the conversation.

"You're not even giving her a chance! She's the most gorgeous friend I have. All of the guys loved her in school."

"Good for her," I say with a mouthful.

Harper huffs, growing more aggravated by the minute. "I've already told her you agreed to meet her, so you have to be at Murphy's by nine."

"That's your own fault for giving her false information. I'm not going anywhere tonight besides out with the guys like I said."

"Would it help if I showed you a picture?"

"No! Harper, I don't give a shit about your friend. I'm fine on my own right now."

What Harper doesn't know about is the loss I'm dealing with from the client we just had. Miranda Shiplay was the most beautiful woman I had ever seen. Her long brown hair always had a particular shine to it that glowed in the sunlight, and her smile was the most picture-perfect smile I had ever seen. Miranda had a heart of gold, and I was falling madly in love with her. Until everything happened.

The thought of Miranda still stings. It's only been a couple of weeks since things went down, and I'm not ready to put myself back out there. I've never been one to be "out there" to begin with.

Harper stands up from her seat next to mine and slides the stool in with force. "Fine. Be a dick for all I care. I'm just trying to help you."

Harper disappears into her room and closes the door with a loud thud. She had called me over earlier to help with a pipe leak in the bathroom and repaid me by buying lunch from my favorite sub shop, which I had missed while being overseas.

I sit on the stool, feeling a little guilty and like a dick for the way I had just yelled at my little sister. In a way, she's right. I do need to think about the possibility of settling down even though that thought has never appealed to me. I'm thirty-three years old, former military, and a hard-nosed security firm man. Knowing the women my sister tends to attract as friends, I'm probably not even much of a catch to this chick.

But since I love my sister, I guess I'll meet her.

PRESENT DAY...

Damn, does that girl know how to fuck. When she came out of that bathroom and spread her legs on the bed and began touching herself... I could hardly control myself. In the moment, I couldn't ask for anything better, but now, as Blaire lies in the bed asleep and I'm out on the balcony, I know I'm in some *deep* shit. I just did the one thing I swore I would never do again, and that's mix business with pleasure. Granted, I had already tasted this pleasure—both literally and metaphorically—before this job, but now... This is different. I just *fucked* Blaire. I just slept with my client's daughter while I'm supposed to be protecting her. I'm supposed to watch over her and keep her safe, not get my fix as an added bonus. But damn, when she comes out and throws herself at me like the way she did tonight, it's hard to say no to Blaire Hanson.

I try to let the nightlife of Miami lull me to sleep as I sit on the balcony of the hotel. I'm nowhere near being tired, but I watch the lights and cars as a way to pass the time and hope to feel some sort of drowsiness. While I sit out on the balcony, I pull out my phone. I open my Facebook app, something I no longer use but can't make myself delete because of the memories captured on it.

My stomach sinks.

The first thing my eyes land on is the blown-up picture, taking up the majority of the screen, of a memory from a year and a half ago. It's a photo of Miranda and me, our faces smushed together as we smile for the camera that ended up being practically up our noses. I remember the photo and where we were when we took it. We were at the house where I was keeping her, and I had just got done setting up the porch swing. My Facebook page was private and the photo was so close up there were no details about our location or geotags on the photo. She'd told me she'd always wanted one when she was growing up. Once I finished building and staining the wood and connecting it to the roof, I led her out on the porch blindfolded to surprise her.

The look on her face was priceless. I'd never understood the expression of "eyes lighting up" until that moment Miranda saw what I had made for her. We sat down on the swing and took that picture, and every night after dinner, we would sit outside with glasses of sweet tea and talk about life outside of our current circumstances.

"Do you think when this is all over, you'll still want me?" she asked.

Her head was resting against my shoulder as we swayed softly on the swing. I chuckled at the question. It was pointless to ask. In the short time that I had spent with her, I knew I wanted to spend the rest of my life with her. She was the first woman I had ever felt that strongly for, and I had already been thinking of ways to propose to her when this mission was over.

"Absolutely." I kissed her hair. "I'll never stop."

She peered up at me with her soft hazel eyes. "Thank you for building me this swing." Her voice almost a whisper.

I smiled at her and squeezed her tighter against me. "Anything for you. I wanted to make your dream come to life."

"I'm so lucky to have you here protecting me, Jimmy."

It was in that moment I knew that I truly loved her. She didn't even have to say it; I could see it in her eyes clear as day. It was a word we hadn't yet spoken to each other, but every day, we knew it was there. We both knew how we felt about each other, and I had been waiting for the right moment to tell her. I knew from the first moment my lips touched hers that I never wanted to kiss another woman's lips. I was ready to let Miranda know that and finally had my moment.

"I love you," I told her.

Miranda's eyes softened. A smile spread across her lips, and I felt her body melt into mine as she held my eyes. "I love you too."

I bent my head down to press my lips to hers and experienced the most gentle and loving kiss I had ever felt. It was also the same night that I made love to her for the very first time. The connection I felt with Miranda as our bodies connected in the most special way was the closest to heaven I would ever be. With Miranda, it was never about pleasure. It was about the connection and being close to her without being close enough.

And now, as I sit here on the balcony, staring at one of the last photos we took, I wonder if that feeling will ever resurface. What I did tonight was something I had never experienced with Miranda. We never had the rough *I'm going to devour you this very instant* sex. The kind of raw passion and desire that takes over to the point of losing control. Miranda and I made love. I *felt* love with her.

I shut my screen off on my phone and slide it back into my pocket. That's enough social media for the night.

I walk back into the room as quiet as I can so as not to wake up Blaire and get ready for bed. When I slide the door closed, the first thing I see is her rolled over and sleeping peacefully in the bed. For a split second, I observe her. Her hands are folded together and tucked under her head, and she looks like a sleeping angel. I notice her breathing, slow and steady, and I can tell she's in a deep sleep. I tiptoe around the room to brush my teeth before stripping down to my briefs. Coming out of the bathroom, I walk over to the couch where a folded-up blanket sits on the back, and I claim my sleeping place for the night. I was never going to actually sleep in the bed with Blaire. It was just fun to watch her squirm when the thought crossed her mind. After what we did earlier, I don't need to sleep in the bed. I don't trust myself around her. With Blaire, things are different. It's almost like an escape with her, and that's how it's been from the very first moment I met her.

Blaire is different from the other girls I have acquainted myself with, and she is certainly a complete one-eighty from Miranda. Miranda needed saving. She had an innocence to her that contrasted against my brutality.

But Blaire, Blaire's tough as nails. It's not a matter of if she needs me; it's if she *wants* me. Blaire Hanson has enough strength in her to save herself, and her confidence is something I've never seen before in anyone. It's a trait I find sexy and compelling. I noticed it the first time I met her. There was something that made me feel at ease talking to her. In a way, I saw myself in her. I saw right through her stubbornness and her walls—walls that I knew how to crack. Harper was right; Blaire is the total package for me. She's strong, capable, and gorgeous, like Harper said.

But she is no Miranda. And as much as I find myself drawn to Blaire, I know I can't let the same thing happen to her.

I glance at her for another moment longer before settling on the couch for the night. My eyes close within a matter of seconds, and I drift off to sleep, seeing Miranda *and* Blaire in my dreams.

I need this job to be over soon before I find myself in deeper shit than I am now.

8

BLAIRE

When my alarm goes off at five the next morning, I feel worse than I did the last time I woke up. My stomach feels like slush, and my head feels like it's been hit by a freight train. I roll over with a groan and bring a hand to my head. As if that's going to ease the pain. *What* did I *do* yesterday? The memory of slinging my body off the bed to empty myself of what I drank flashes in my mind, and I groan once more at the embarrassment.

Jimmy stirs on the couch, and I watch his massive frame shake awake. He shoots up on the couch and blinks his tired eyes before coming into focus with the new morning light.

The morning looks good on him. The bright sliver of sun shining through the curtains settles on his tan, ripped body. Even after a night on the couch, the man looks like he spent an hour getting ready for a photoshoot. It's almost heart-stopping.

This man devoured me yesterday, I think to myself. Then I remember how exposed I made myself to him, and I feel my cheeks redden. That woman last night was someone I don't recognize.

"You don't have to get up yet," I say with a crackly voice.

Jimmy groans and rubs his face with his hands. I sling the covers off me and start my morning routine before the conference. While Jimmy stays in the room, I quickly shower before brushing my teeth and dressing in my sensible business attire—a blazer, slacks, and a white blouse. I style my blond hair in waves and apply my makeup, then step out of the bathroom. Jimmy is nowhere in sight.

My heart and stomach sink at the loss of him. I feel safe when he's around. The sound of the key activating the door lock behind me causes me to jump as Jimmy pushes the door open with his foot and steps into the room with two coffee cups in his hand, stacked one on top of the other, and a plate of breakfast foods in the other.

He walks to the small table and sets everything down before looking at me. "I didn't know if you were hungry, but I brought you back some food and coffee," he says, extending one of the Styrofoam cups to me. I take it reluctantly and sip the hot liquid, marveling at its sweet and precise taste. It's just the way I like it, creamer and all.

"Thank you," I say. "You got the creamer right."

He shrugs nonchalantly and picks up one of the biscuits. "I saw how you made yours the other morning and went off that."

I hide a smile by bringing the cup up to my mouth once again. Pulling out one of the chairs at the table, I take the seat facing Jimmy and tear at the stack of pancakes he piled on the plate. We eat together in silence, and it's not the most awkward it's ever been between us, surprisingly. I wonder if he's thought about last night and what we did... more like what I did by touching myself in front of him.

I'm hesitant to bring it up, but for some reason, I do.

"Jimmy..." I start.

He silences me by bringing up a hand. "Don't go there."

"We need to talk about last night."

"No, we don't."

There's a hardness to his voice that matches his eyes. The intense way he's looking at me with his mouth in a thin line lets me know whatever last night was to me, it meant nothing to him. It was purely just carnal lust. My insides twist in disappointment at the thought.

"Well, we can't act like it didn't happen," I suggest, growing defensive.

He ignores me and looks down at the food. "It's not like we haven't had sex before."

I narrow my eyes at him. "Are you serious, Jimmy." It's more of a statement than a question.

"What?"

I scoff and toss the pancake down on the plate with a little *plat*. The chair underneath me slides out with force as I stand from the table and move to grab my purse off the entertainment center.

"Sometimes," I start, slinging the strap on my shoulder, "you are the biggest asshole I've ever met."

With one last glare, I snatch one of the keys and slide on my pumps before walking out the door. I know he'll follow me as it is his job, but at this point, I don't care. I just want to be out of his presence. Jimmy is a man of pure business and his own desires. He never steers off track. Even if he does break a rule, he acts as if he didn't, not caring if that means hurting feelings in the process.

The elevator dings as it opens on our floor, and I step in it at the same time Jimmy jogs to catch up to me. I glare at him as he stands beside me, and we ride the car down to the lobby in silence. We stay like this for the rest of the afternoon.

THREE MONTHS EARLIER...

I walk into Murphy's a little later than I was supposed to get there. Thanks to work tying me up with new contracts, I had to stay late to make sure everything was in order for our new clients. Who am I kidding? I stay late every night at work. My friends find it annoying and unnecessary, but I take my work seriously. Being a woman in the corporate world, it's hard to prove yourself to a bunch of men, even when your father owns the company. It's either nepotism and you got the job because of daddy or it's sexism and you got the job because of who you slept with.

I look around the bar for the man I'm supposed to be meeting—my friend Harper's brother, whom she's been dying to set me up with—and try to find anyone that matches the description she gave me: tall, muscular, and dark hair. "He looks like a brown-haired Liam Hemsworth on steroids," she said.

No one in the bar matches that description. I take a seat at one of the empty stools and order myself a glass of red wine as I wait for him to show. I wonder how Harper described me to him and if I will meet his expectations. In all my years of knowing Harper Maxwell, I've never seen nor heard much of her brother other than he's former military and owns some high-end security firm. When I pressed her for more information, she told me that if I wanted to know, I was going to have to get to know him.

"It'll be like a hot new meetup," was Harper's defense.

The bartender sets my glass of wine down in front of me, and I thank him before pulling out my phone to check my notifications. There's a text from Richard from work asking about the new account we just got, and I start to type back a message when I feel someone sliding into the seat next to me. He orders a whiskey, and I steal a glance from my peripheral vision to see if it's Harper's brother. My eyes meet the sight of an imposing man who fills out his white shirt gloriously. His sleeves are pushed up just below his elbows and his bulging muscles are nearly busting out of the soft fabric. I study him closely, trying to find any hint that this might be the man I'm supposed to meet, and it's then that I see the dog tags hanging from his neck.

God, this man is beautiful.

He doesn't notice me as he plays on his own phone, and I wait to see if he starts to look for me. I study him more and try to think of what to say.

I bring the glass of wine to my lips and respond to Richard. Every now and then, my eyes steal glances in his direction.

After sipping his whiskey, he sets the glass down and runs his fingers around the rim, staring at it intently.

"Are you waiting for it to say something?" I ask, starting the conversation.

He snickers and looks over to me, making me feel fully held by his gaze. His eyes are vibrant green, the purest shade I've ever seen in a pair of eyes, and I feel fully and totally captivated.

"I'm actually waiting for someone," he says.

I decide to play with him, to test his loyalty and faithfulness. "Who's the lucky lady?"

He shrugs, giving me a look I can't read. "Some chick my sister is friends with."

I don't know if I'm more alarmed by the word "chick" or the way he says this as if he has no interest in meeting me. I mask my expression by giving him what I call my signature flirty eyes and hold my glass in my hands. I cross my right leg over my left, exposing my skin as my pencil skirt slides up my thigh. Just as I expected, his eyes dart down to my exposed skin.

"Sounds like you're really interested in meeting her," I say in my most sultry voice.

"Eh, more interested in getting my sister to stop whining."

He's giving me instant asshole vibes but I try not to let that ruin the moment. I know this man has seen some shit and been through some shit. Maybe he's just guarded.

"What do you know about this chick your sister is setting you up with?"

"Not much. Don't even know her name, to be honest."

"Do you know what she looks like?"

"Nope. Harper just said she was nice to look at. Blond hair." He pauses. His gaze shifts from casual to studying me hard. "Same as you," he says.

The corners of my mouth twitch upward in a smile, and I know I'm going to crack. He's figured it out. "I'm Blaire," I say, extending a hand to him. "Harper's chick friend."

His eyes widen as he looks me over once more, and not a shade of embarrassment flashes on his face. "Jimmy," he says.

"Nice to meet you." I flash him a flirtatious smile.

The more I look at Jimmy's face, the more I see features of Harper in him. Jimmy's older by a few years, but he's a complete contrast to Harper. Harper is more fragile and delicate, someone who people love to take advantage of, while Jimmy screams trouble, like he's the one taking advantage of people like her. His body is built like a rock, and his face is covered in scruff that matches his thick hair. He's a fantasy in real life and I'll be damned if I'm not finding myself staring at those lips.

My eyes travel down to his hands cupping his glass, and I study the size of his palm. Even his fingers look strong and muscular, like every other square inch of him. This guy is certainly not human.

We spend a few more hours at the bar getting to know each other before deciding to head to my place. At Murphy's, I find out things about him, like how he used to be in the Special Forces and has since started a security firm with three of his Army brothers once they got out. He just moved back to New York after living in Florida for a year which was after he returned home from overseas, and he lives alone in his apartment, which is only a block away from Harper's.

After convincing him to finish the night at my place over a bottle of great wine, I find myself nervous in his presence. My apartment is only a short walk from Murphy's, and I feel like an ant as I walk next to Jimmy. His height and strength are definitely intimidating, and while I feel nervous next to him, I feel safe at the same time.

When we make it back to my apartment, Jimmy settles himself in one of the stools at the marble island in the kitchen. I grab two glasses from the top cabinet and make sure to show off my ass as I reach up on my toes. I see the way men look at me as I walk outside. I'm not blind. After being featured in Forbes *and* Vogue *as being one of New York's sexiest businesswomen, I saw the way men started to gawk at me when I was near. A small part of me wonders if Jimmy knows who I am. My father, Charles Hanson, one of the wealthiest businessmen in the* world, has definitely made his way into the news, alongside numerous mentions of me, as I'm the one who will be taking over the company once he passes it on. My position in my father's company is something I'm proud of. It's something I'm known for, in addition to my knowledge of business, and it's landed me in the eyes of the media several times, especially since I'm young and single.

I grab the bottle of chilled Moscato from the fridge and pop the cork off with my wine opener before pouring us each a glass. I can feel the intensity of Jimmy's eyes watching my every move, and his stare sets my skin on fire. There's something about this man watching me that I find pleasurable. I like his eyes on me, and it's something I want to feel often.

I slide a glass to him, and we clink our glasses before we take a sip. The wine earns an approving look from Jimmy.

"Pretty good," he says.

"I'm guessing you're not a wine guy?"

He shakes his head. "Not at all, but I like this."

I keep my distance across from Jimmy on the other end of the island. I take one more sip of my wine before removing my blazer, thankful I decided to wear the white silk blouse that highlights my breasts. The white push-up bra was another excellent choice for the night.

Little did I know that I would be regretting those decisions in just a few short hours.

9

JIMMY

PRESENT DAY...

Wdrop

While Blaire attends her conference, I stay close by and keep her tracker open in case of an emergency. There's a gym across the street from the building Blaire's conference is in, and I bring a change of clothes to work out in as I wait for her to finish.

This morning went just as I expected. I knew as soon as my head hit the pillow last night that she would wake up this morning with our night together fresh on her mind, wanting to discuss it and find some sort of explanation. However, it was not something I wanted to rehash. As long as I am working for her father, Blaire and I are never going to fuck again. That I promised myself, no matter how much I want her or if she throws herself at me again. I've got to keep my mind focused on the mission—watching her and her surroundings at all times. If Charles found out about what happened, my ass would be screwed. His daughter is like forbidden fruit, and I've fallen in love with the taste of it.

Literally.

When Blaire's workday at the conference is over, it's nearly five thirty in the evening. I wait on the crosswalk as she exits the building, and she gives me a tight smile as she approaches. Her small fingers are gripping the straps of her bag tightly.

"How was your day at school, sweetheart?" I mock once she reaches me.

She rolls her eyes and stays quiet.

"The Uber should be here in a few minutes. Do you want to go out to dinner tonight?" I ask.

Blaire crosses her arms over her chest and keeps her eyes on the parking lot. "I'm not hungry."

Now I roll my eyes. "That's a lie. Where do you want to go?"

No response.

I huff. I guess I'll be the one to choose.

We stand in silence for the next five minutes until the Uber pulls up. I open the door for Blaire to slide in, ignoring the fact that she doesn't tell me thanks, and follow in after her.

"You want somewhere specific?" the driver, a middle-aged white-haired man, asks. "App just says uh..." He squints at the screen, trying to decipher what I typed in as the end destination.

"Just take us to anywhere on Fifth Street," I tell him. Blaire's head snaps in my direction.

"Fifth Street? That's all sit-down restaurants."

I shake my head. "I know."

Blaire's eyebrows scrunch together, but she quickly turns her attention back to the window. Whatever her deal is, she needs to fucking snap out of it. I'm not going to put up with her bratty attitude this evening.

As we ride the way to Fifth Street in silence, I pull my phone out when I feel it buzz in my pocket from an incoming text. Harper's name flashes on the screen.

Harper: *Hey! Where are you? I stopped by the apartment and knocked, but no one answered. Wanna meet at Murphy's?*

Before I respond, my eyes dart over to Blaire's seat. Her gaze is now down on her own phone in her hands, and I look back to mine to send my sister a response.

Me: *Can't. In Miami for a client. When I get back.*

Harper's response is fast.

Harper: *Ugh!!! Okay. Have fun! Keep whoever it is safe from the bad guys :)*

I go to slide my phone back in my pocket at the same time our driver pulls up to the curb on Fifth Street. Even at six in the evening, the street is filled with locals and tourists. I tip the driver and file out of the car with Blaire behind me. We walk aimlessly down the street in silence, and I scan the signs of the different restaurants. I used to live it up down here when I would get home from deployment. Now I can't remember shit about this place.

"Anything look good to you?" I ask her.

Blaire keeps her eyes on the street and shrugs.

That's it.

I grip Blaire's arm and push her into the alleyway next to us, but not without a fight from her.

"Ow! Get off me! What the hell are you doing!" she yells as I push her against the wall with slight force.

Both of her hands try to pry my grip off her, but she's no match for my strength. I give her a chilling look that causes her to settle, and she glares at me. I can feel the tip of her pert nipples skim my chest as her breathing causes her breasts to rise and fall. We're close, so close, and even though I shoved her here to threaten her out of her bratty mood, I can't help but think now how bad I want to take her right here and claim her.

I quickly force that thought out of my head before I act on it.

"I don't know what's crawled up your ass this morning, but you need to stop acting like a little brat. Do you hear me?" There's an edge to my voice as my eyes hold hers with an intensity that shrivels her glare. Blaire relaxes in my arms and softly nods her head in defeat.

That was easier than I expected.

I make sure she reads my seriousness before letting her go. When she's out of my grasp, she stands straighter and smooths out her shirt, which I just wrinkled.

"Now, do you want to tell me what you want to eat?" I ask again.

She shrugs. "Anything is fine with me."

I try to remember what's around here and quickly think of an Italian place Harvey used to love. "Do you like Italian?"

She nods her head.

I lead us out of the alley and back onto the sidewalk. We walk a few more yards before we step into Lucendo's. Lucendo's used to be the place we always came to on the nights Harvey picked where we ate for dinner. He loves the olive oil bread dip that comes with the complimentary baked bread they give each table while you wait for your meal. It always smells of fine cheese and garlic in Lucendo's, and tonight is no different. Thankfully, there's no wait.

The hostess leads us to a table for two in the center of the room. Blaire and I sit down facing each other, and a server approaches to start preparing the dip before setting down the basket of fresh bread. Another server appears, a younger woman with brown hair tied in a neat bun on top of her head, and asks for our drink orders. I notice the way her eyes linger on me while she barely looks at Blaire, but I don't make a scene about it. I know Blaire will more than likely make a comment about it once the server leaves... if she feels like talking.

Blaire orders a glass of wine and I order a water. The server, giving me a gleaming look, takes our dinner orders and throws me a wink after collecting our menus.

"Let me know if there's *anything* I can get you," she says before walking away. Out of the corner of my eye, I see Blaire roll hers. I have to bite my bottom lip to keep from laughing at her obvious jealousy.

When the server leaves, an awkward silence falls over the table.

I pull out my phone to pass the time as we wait for our food while Blaire sits on her side of the table, pouting over God knows what.

"Oh my God, why are you always on your phone?" Blaire asks with obvious frustration after a few minutes of silence.

I look up at her with raised eyebrows. "It's work," I say, flashing her my screen of emails.

She rolls her eyes. "Whatever. You're just always on it."

"Why does it matter? We're not supposed to talk, remember? Your rules."

"Yeah. I'm also not supposed to be smothered, but here you are ordering me to eat dinner with you."

This chick has lost her damn mind.

My eyes widen at Blaire. "I mean, if you wanted McDonald's, all you had to do was say so. I was hungry, too, and we were already out. Sorry for taking you into consideration."

I can see Blaire growing flustered by the second. Our server interrupts our banter by placing our drinks in front of us and setting down another loaf of bread before disappearing again. The second she's gone, Blaire starts back up.

"I don't need you to take me into consideration. I'm not your girlfriend."

"Yeah, I know. Yet you're acting like one."

Her mouth drops. "How am I acting like your *girlfriend,* Jimmy?"

"Complaining about me being on my phone and shit! You have an attitude for some reason. Before we came here, you wouldn't even talk to me. Now you're upset about me bringing you out to dinner. Need I go on?"

Blaire's mouth presses into a hard line. She folds her arms across her chest again, which pushes her breasts up and into view in the slit in her blouse. God, to have those in my mouth right now...

"I just... Never mind," she says, shaking her head.

I narrow my eyes slightly at her. "No, go on."

Blaire hesitates and looks up at me with unreadable eyes. They're a mix of sadness and anger, and the power they hold is threatening. "I guess I'm just upset at how you quickly dismissed me last night," she says, her voice small.

It's not her words that shock me. It's the way she says it with sadness and betrayal. What we did last night was amazing and satisfying, but it didn't mean anything. She knows that. It was sex. Pure sex and nothing more. We shouldn't have even done it in the first place, no matter how bad we both wanted it and how good it felt.

I take a deep breath and sigh, scratching the back of my head as I look for the right words to say. I can see how upset she is, so I need to tread lightly. Before I can respond, our server sets our plates of pasta down in front of us, breaking the tension, but it comes back the second she's gone. I look to Blaire, and the moment I see her, I start to question everything I'm about to say. Was it just sex with Blaire, or could it be something more? Damn. Never would have thought that I'd be asking myself that.

"You tell me what it was to you," I ask calmly.

Blaire's features soften. Her arms fall from her chest down to her lap, and I watch as her eyes study me. The silence between us is palpable, and I forget all about the food that's sitting in front of us. Blaire's incredible eyes glisten, and she opens her pretty mouth to speak.

"I thought—"

The loud sound of a ringtone slices into the air around us. It shuts Blaire up immediately, and my eyes scan the mostly vacant restaurant to find the perpetrator.

"Jimmy, it's yours..." Blaire says at the same moment I realize it's my phone.

Fuck!

I fish my phone out of my pocket and read the caller ID. It's Blaire's dad. *Damn this man and his endless calls.* My eyes flash to Blaire, who's trying her hardest to not look frustrated about being interrupted by picking at her nails. She senses me staring at her, and I hold the ringing phone up for her to see. "I've got to take this."

Blaire shrugs nonchalantly and starts to twist some of her spaghetti onto her fork. I shoot up from the table, the chair sliding across the ground and making an awful sound. I walk toward the back of the restaurant where I can still see Blaire.

"Mr. Hanson, how are you?" I say into the receiver. I'm greeted with uncontrollable coughing and the sound of sirens in the back. "Mr. Hanson, are you okay?"

"Yes." He coughs into the phone. "I'm fine." There's another loud burst of ragged coughing. "There's been a fire at the office, and it's believed to be arson."

My eyes immediately flash to Blaire at our table. She's glued to her phone as she lifts a fork of spaghetti to her mouth. Charles continues.

"I'm going to lay low for a few days, Jimmy, while I discuss options with my lawyers and increase security measures. Please don't let my daughter out of your sight. I don't know what is going to happen next."

I can hear his concern for Blaire in his voice, and my eyes don't leave her as I stand against the wall. "I won't, sir."

"And Jimmy?"

"Yes?"

"Don't tell Blaire. I don't want her worrying and begging to come home."

Something about not telling Blaire her father's office was set on fire doesn't sit well with me. One of the aspects about this job I hate is the order to obey and do anything our client asks of us, minus the lines you draw yourself in order to do what's right. Clutching the phone tightly in my hand, I nod my head. "Will do."

"There's just two days left of the conference. I'll tell her in person when she gets home."

"What about the media outlets?" I ask.

Charles grunts. "I'll deal with them. All I want you focused on is keeping my daughter safe."

I hang up the phone a few seconds later and walk back to the table. Blaire doesn't look up as I sit back down, and I study her for a few seconds. Only two more days with this woman and we'll be back home.

"Everything okay?" she asks with disinterest, keeping her eyes focused on her phone screen.

I twirl some of my pasta on my fork even though my appetite has fully vanished. "Yeah. Just work."

I sit in anticipation, watching her, wondering if we're going to finish the conversation we started before Blaire's dad interrupted with his phone call. I imagine the thoughts are still swarming in her head, but to my surprise, we sit at the table for ten more minutes in silence. When Blaire's back connects with the chair, and she folds her arms across her chest, I can tell by the tightness of her lips that all hopes she had of hashing out our business is gone. I can't help but let out a sigh of relief. I know I'm not out of the woods yet.

Our waitress drops off our check, and I pay the bill before we leave. The Uber I order takes us back to the hotel, and the whole time Blaire and I are in the car, we're silent. I wonder if the driver can sense the tension between us as we both sit against the far sides of the Honda. Blaire keeps her eyes directed out the window while I keep mine between my phone and window. The tension lingers even once we're back at the hotel, and I let Blaire do her thing while I go sit on the balcony.

It's going to be a long two days.

10

BLAIRE

The last two days at the conference go by in a flash but not without the awkward tension between me and Jimmy. Ever since that dinner, we haven't spoken a word to each other. While I'm in my meetings and presentations, Jimmy will text me and ask what I want for dinner, and I'll tell him takeout so I don't have to sit down with him again. I think he got the hint that I don't want to speak to him and rightfully so.

The man is an obtuse asshole with no regard for women's feelings whatsoever, and I wish there was a way my father could switch out the man he had protecting me. I swear, sometimes, I feel as if I could run this business single-handedly and do a fantastic job.

On the last day of the conference, I walk out of the building to see Jimmy sitting in his usual spot on the bench outside. He's once again tapping away at his phone, and I approach him to wait for our Uber. Jimmy says nothing for a few seconds as I join him but then slides his phone into his pocket and looks in my direction with feigned interest.

"How'd it go?" It's the question he always asks just to be polite.

"Fine."

He nods, relaxing against the bench. He extends his bulging arms, stretching them out before placing them behind his head, flexing them in the process. Jimmy looks cool and unbothered as he sits on the bench waiting for the Uber, and I study his features as if I've never seen them before. I wonder what girls think when they're graced with his presence. Jimmy Maxwell is certainly a man who knows the power he has on women, and he uses it to his advantage, just like he did with me the first night we met before I found out what a giant ass he was.

Jimmy stands up and turns to me. "Uber's here."

I follow him to the van and climb into the vehicle once Jimmy opens the door. We ride in silence—it's become our new thing—back to the hotel, and this time, I spend the twenty-minute ride scrolling through emails and responding to texts. Jimmy orders us Chinese when we're back in the room, and I take the time waiting for the food as extra time to work. I change out of my professional attire into some lounge leggings and a loose gray sweater. After throwing my hair into a messy bun and exiting the bathroom, I walk by Jimmy, who's lounging on the couch, to grab my laptop and sit beside him.

"I'm going downstairs to work," I say.

Jimmy's head shoots up. His eyebrows are scrunched together. "Come again?"

"I said I'm going downstairs to work. Text me when the food is here."

I slide my feet into my slippers and grab a room key. As I start to walk to the door, I hear quick movement behind me, and the door quickly shuts when I try open it as Jimmy's massive hand slams it closed. I can feel his chest barely skim my back.

"Like hell you are," he says.

I don't turn around. I'm scared of what will happen if I'm within close proximity of him again. As much as I hate him, the man is dangerous to my self-control.

"Let me go, Jimmy. It's just downstairs."

"Fine. If you want to go work downstairs, I'll go with you."

I take a deep breath and sigh, keeping my back to him. "I think I'll be fine alone for a few hours."

"Leaving you alone is not in my job description, and you know that."

I quickly turn on my heel, my face mere inches away from his. I size him up and my eyes lock with his. We're so close, I can feel his ragged breath on my neck. Jimmy's eyes are hard as they look at me with authority, and I match him with my own. "Oh, but fucking me is?"

Jimmy's head shakes subtly. "Why do you have to be so stubborn?" he whispers.

"The same reason you have to be so closed off."

The hand Jimmy had planted against the door falls to his side, and he starts to back up. "You begged me to."

"Don't act like you weren't already thinking about it."

"So what if I was? What point are you trying to make here?"

I hold his gaze. I'm not really sure why I'm making a fuss over this. I knew in my mind this was more than likely going to happen at some point. I told myself the first night in my apartment when I went to sleep knowing Jimmy was twenty feet away from me that it would be mindless and nothing more. But now that it's happened...

"I just don't understand why we can't talk about it." I register the sadness in my voice and hate the way it sounds so whiny. I don't want Jimmy to get the impression that I have feelings for him because I absolutely don't, but I don't want him to think of me as a walking Fleshlight either.

"Why do you want to? Honestly, Blaire, it was just sex. Really good sex. That's all it was and all that it will ever be between us."

His words feel like a blow to my stomach. I feel the breath in my body hitch at his audacity to say those words to my face, and tears begin to swell in my eyes. Dammit, I didn't want him to see me cry.

I blink my eyes fast and do my best to not look so hurt. I knew all of this, too, but hearing Jimmy say it so dismissively feels completely different than when I say it myself.

With my laptop in hand, I yank the door open. I need to get out of this room fast. Jimmy gives me a questioning look, and I silence him before he even gets the chance to speak.

"Follow me and I swear to God I'll find some way to sue you for everything you own."

The door slams shut behind me with Jimmy still in the room.

———

THREE MONTHS EARLIER...

Jimmy swallows the rest of his wine and sets the empty glass on my counter. I'm still nursing my full glass as I sit on the counter, looking down at him perched on one of my stools. The wine is giving me the extra boost of confidence I need to be under the gaze of this man, and the way his eyes are staring at my breasts sends fire blazing down my skin. I never knew Harper had such a freaking hot brother. I feel like there is some kind of "girl code" that says I should leave him alone, but I want to do quite the opposite. Besides, she set us up. It's fun feeling like a sexy goddess in front of a man this gorgeous. I feel as if I'm in the presence of some Greek god mixed with a superhero. He's built like no other man I've seen.

My eyes travel the length his rock-hard body, buried beneath the clothes I want to rip off him, and I imagine the endless activities we could do right here on my kitchen island. Damn... this wine is really getting to me.

"What are you thinking about?" Jimmy asks with a smirk. "Your eyes look like they're in a whole other dimension right now."

Oh, they are...

"Nothing," I say with a smile. "I was just thinking how Harper never mentioned you."

He scoffs. "Yeah, she never mentioned you either."

"How did she describe me?"

Jimmy playfully shrugs. "She said you were alright."

I swat at his shoulder and try to conceal the wince I want to make at the sting in my fingers. God, this man's body is tough.

"She said you were beautiful and the most gorgeous friend she had and that all the boys in your class wanted you," he adds.

I beam at Harper's compliment. "And?" I push.

Jimmy's eyebrows scrunch together. "And what?"

"And what do you think? About me?"

I dangle my legs off the counter, nervously kicking them in and out. Jimmy stands from his stool, his eyes growing dark, and he grips my knees to push my legs apart and inserts himself between them. My breath hitches.

Jimmy's fast movement wafts his scent into the air, and I smell the glorious aroma that is Jimmy and cedar. My stomach starts to churn. Being this close to Jimmy feels oddly erotic, and yet we still have our clothes on.

"I think, if I went to your school, I wouldn't have been able to keep myself off of you."

My mouth parches at his words. I want to feel him all over me now, right on my kitchen counter. I reach down and pull my shirt open slowly.

"What about now?" I whisper breathlessly. Suddenly, the air between us feels thick and laced with passion. I can see the wild in Jimmy's eyes as they bore into mine, and I want him to please me. I want to know what it feels like to be taken by this man anywhere in this apartment. Jimmy's jaw clenches, and I feel myself start to become a puddle between my legs.

I wonder what his mouth would feel like...

I watch Jimmy's eyes rake down my face to the exposed skin of my breasts in my push-up bra, and my nipples harden at the thought of Jimmy's touch. If he doesn't make a move soon, I might explode.

"Right now, I want to devour you with my mouth until your entire body is shaking and you're begging me to stop. Only, I don't stop, and I make you come so hard right here in your kitchen that once I'm through with you, it looks like you spilled an entire glass of water."

Speechless.

Utterly.

Completely.

Speechless.

I've never had a man talk to me that way, and all I know to do is gape at him. His words alone are powerful enough to make me soaked between my legs, and judging from the darkness in his eyes, he intends on living out what he just said. I sit on the counter with Jimmy standing between my legs, and I want nothing more than for him to claim my mouth and all of me. There's a delicious, nagging pull in my stomach to reach for him, so I do, and I clench my fist around his shirt and pull him to me, crashing Jimmy's lips onto mine.

It's what I've been waiting for all night. Every second sitting in the bar, crossing my legs over the other to expose my thigh, perching myself up on the counter to arch my body into his view has led us to this moment, this fulfilling moment where I taste Jimmy and he tastes me, where he fucks me and licks me and carries out whatever else he would like to do to torture me while I scream his name into oblivion.

My lips move in harmony with Jimmy's as if they already know him. I'm surprised how naturally my body melts and reacts to him, and pretty soon, I'm arching myself into his touch, needing to feel Jimmy's hands on me.

Our kiss is rough and animalistic. My lips search his as if they've been starved for him for years and are finally being reunited. My fist that was bunched into the collar of his shirt slides up to the back of his thick hair where I pull and tug at the soft strands. My other hand grasps onto his large back and pulls him closer to me until our chests touch. The connection of his chest to mine makes me moan into his mouth.

I don't recognize myself right now. I've never felt this... this... confident when it came to hooking up with a man. I've never kissed another human being with this amount of urgency and need. I've never reveled in the touch and pinch of Jimmy's fingers palming my breast through my clothes and the dying need to rip my clothes off so he can have access to my bare skin. I quickly pull my lips away from Jimmy to briskly tear off my shirt. A few of the buttons pop at my urgency, but I don't care. I can buy another shirt, but I can't buy another Jimmy Maxwell. He chuckles as he watches me sling the white fabric to the floor, and my fingers quickly reach to the hem of his shirt and pull it over his head.

God... this creature.

This isn't a man. There's no way. The definition and perfect cut of his beautifully sculpted abs leave me speechless. I've seen this in movies, read about it in books, but never experienced it in real life until now. Who am I in the presence of?

Jimmy claims my mouth with the same hunger, and the heat of his skin burns into mine. I let out a loud moan, feeling the tingling connection of our bodies pressed together, and I reach around to unclasp my bra. I toss it to the floor and let my whole chest press against Jimmy's, letting him feel my small frame compared to his massive build. Jimmy's arms slide around to my back to hold me firmly against him. My legs wrap about his waist to pull him closer, and I can feel the growing bulge in his jeans pressed against my entrance. Without breaking the kiss, Jimmy's hand reaches down to my bare breast to pinch my nipple. I moan into his mouth, and he takes the opportunity to slide his tongue into my mouth to lap mine, and he hums in appreciation. Jimmy pulls his head back to stare at my bare chest, and I see his eyes widen.

"God, you're beautiful," he whispers.

I feel my skin heat at his compliment, and I gently kick him away. I decide to give him a view of my most delicate place as I hitch my skirt higher up my thigh. My fingers dig into my skirt to hook with the lace panties I'm thankful I wore, and I slide them down my legs slowly, giving Jimmy my most sultry look. He watches me pensively, desire darkening his eyes, and I toss them to him once they're completely removed. I lean my back down onto the cold surface of my kitchen counter, and I spread my legs open for him to take me. Jimmy wastes no time charging to me and devouring me like he said he would. The moment his warm tongue latches on to my wetness, my back arches off the counter. My head digs into the white granite as my hands reach down to push Jimmy's tongue farther into me.

"Oh... God..." I moan, gasping for air as Jimmy sucks it out of me.

His tongue moves in circles around my sensitive bud, and I can hear how wet I am with every lick. Jimmy continues this assault as he slides in two fingers to hook around my sweet spot, and I gasp loudly at the marvelous sensation. He falls into a rhythm with his fingers and his tongue, and I slowly start to rock my hips to match his pace. My body begins to tighten at the growing orgasm, and my legs start to shake. Jimmy hums, and the vibrations circle my clit, making my stomach clench with pleasure, but a moment later, he removes his mouth.

"You taste so good, baby. Like fucking candy."

"Keep... going..." I say breathlessly at the assault of his fingers. The amount of pressure he's applying is perfect, and the need to release continues to grow. I moan loudly, not caring if the neighbors can hear as I experience the best oral orgasm in my life. I come hard in just a matter of seconds as Jimmy's fingers push against my G-spot and his tongue flicks my clit with precision. He makes good on his promise to not stop once I orgasm, and he continues to pleasure me with his mouth and skilled fingers until I'm screaming his name.

"Jimmy! Oh, God!"

My body convulses, and another orgasm more powerful than the first starts to wash over me. I grow wetter around Jimmy's fingers, and I feel myself release on him, all while Jimmy licks my wetness right up.

And we haven't even gotten to the main event.

Jimmy pulls out and away from me, and I lie on the kitchen counter, breathless, feeling absolutely weak from the two most intense orgasms I've had to date. I hear the unzipping of Jimmy's fly and the clink of his belt hitting the floor as he drops his pants. I shoot up on my elbows to find his length, and my eyes bulge at how hard and long he is. It certainly lives up to the rest of his impressive mass. My mouth begins to water. I'd like to have him in my mouth.

I watch as Jimmy strokes himself softly, his eyes piercing into my skin. I rake my eyes up his body, feeling the need to collapse onto the floor and take him into my mouth like he did me. He's wearing a proud smirk as he strokes his hard length and stares at me on the kitchen counter.

"Get on your knees," he orders with authority.

Even though my body feels like Jell-O, I waste no time hopping off the counter and collapsing to the floor. I palm his hard shaft and open my mouth to accommodate his hard cock down into my throat. My tongue laps up the delicious, salty bead of cum on the tip, and I hum on him like he did me. Jimmy takes a sharp intake of breath, and his hands fist my hair behind my head.

"Fuck, that feels so good," he says.

I move my mouth up and down his long shaft to try and get his length all the way in me, but it's nearly impossible. I pump him in my hands in the same rhythm as my mouth, and Jimmy starts to rock his hips, fucking my mouth.

"That's right. Take me in your mouth, just like that."

His dirty talk heightens my desire as I feel wetness pool between my thighs. I hum against his tip and pump him hard in my hand before placing him back in my mouth fully and taking his thrusts.

"Play with yourself," he orders.

I widen my bent legs on the floor as I continue to take him in my mouth. I use my free hand to play with my clit. God, I am so fucking wet! My fingers move vigorously on my overly sensitive bud, and I moan into him, feeling completely and utterly desirable. I feel sexy in a way I never have before. This feels primal and wrong, but the wrong makes it feel so right.

"Make yourself come again at the same time I do. And you're going to swallow," he orders.

I move my fingers faster against me, feeling too tingly to enjoy it, but I power through as my body starts to tighten again. Jimmy curses my name, fucking my mouth more forcefully, and I swirl my tongue around him as another orgasm starts to birth itself inside of me.

"Not yet," Jimmy huffs at my moans.

I moan on his cock at my growing third orgasm and feel him start to pulse in my mouth. Jimmy's eyes are closed as he rocks his hips, cursing. "Fuck, you do me so good..."

My fingers continue to play with my clit, alternating between flicks and fingering my entrance, which is begging for his cock. I'm on the verge on convulsing when Jimmy gives me the green light. "Come."

I flick my pussy so fast that I shake and scream at my rippling orgasm at the same time Jimmy pulses his hot cum into my mouth. My scream is silenced by the liquid sliding down my throat, and I swallow before falling onto the floor. Jimmy bends down to scoop up my limp body and carries me a few feet over to the couch, placing me on my stomach. He positions himself at my entrance and wastes no time pressing his still-hard length into my slick folds, and I cry out in pain.

I stretch as his thickness widens me, filling my pussy so much it hurts, but it's the best kind of torture there is.

"Take it like a good girl," Jimmy grunts, slamming himself into me.

Gripping one of the pillows, I yelp at the pressure with each thrust Jimmy drives into me. The most guttural and throaty moan escapes my lips, and I relax my body by arching my ass farther into the air. It deepens Jimmy's cock inside me, and he hits my sweet spot with each pump. I'm screaming his name, burying my face into the couch, as Jimmy picks up his speed and force. He fucks me for several more minutes, insulting me with words I find so fucking sexy, it floods me with pleasure until I have another small orgasm that makes me clench around him. Jimmy pulls out to release his contents into his hand before walking away to clean it up by the sink.

The last thing I remember is the running of the water as I lie on the couch, completely exhausted by the number of orgasms I just had in such a short amount of time. It doesn't take me long to drift off to sleep, and when I open my eyes, it's morning. I realize I'm naked on the couch, no blanket covering me or anything.

And there's no trace of Jimmy in my apartment.

11

JIMMY

THREE MONTHS EARLIER...

Yeah, I left right after. So what? She completely passed out and neither one of us made any attempt earlier to say this was anything more than a hookup.

While she was good in bed—and the kitchen—there wasn't anything there. Not like there was with Miranda. I quickly realized that once we got back to Blaire's nice-ass apartment in Uptown Manhattan. There was something about being there with her that made me realize my attraction to Blaire was purely carnal and sexual and there would be nothing there emotionally between us. Ever.

I also came to the conclusion on my walk home that there might not ever be another connection like the one I had with Miranda. Miranda was the first woman to open my eyes and make me see that there's more to relationships than sex. There's hope and happiness and love. I've never been one to be in love or think love is real. Hell, the mere thought of pouring my heart out to someone made me want to run for the hills. But with Miranda, I wanted to do that stuff. All I wanted to do a few hours ago with Blaire was blow her mind with my dick and in return get off, and I did that. Mission accomplished.

When I wake up the next morning in my apartment, my eyes

fly open to the smell of freshly brewed coffee. I throw the covers off me and march out of the room in only my briefs, ready to kill whoever waltzed into my living space. As I step foot into the kitchen, I hear a sharp-pitched scream from the figure near the stove.

"Oh my God, my eyes!"

It's Harper being her typical dramatic self, and I roll my eyes. "Harper, what the fuck are you doing here?"

She's covering her eyes with her hands. "I came to hear how my brother's date with my best friend went. God, Jimmy, go put some pants on!"

I huff as I walk back to my room to find a T-shirt and sweatpants before returning to the kitchen. Harper slides me a cup of coffee at the dining room table and sets down a plate stacked with bacon and waffles.

"I told you not to break into my apartment again," I warn. She's lucky I smelled the coffee. Thanks to the Army, I have a sixth sense now and know when I'm not the only one in my apartment. I typically carry a gun with me to investigate when I get that feeling.

"Stop with the Army thing. I have a key, remember?"

"Yeah, but that doesn't mean you get to barge in whenever you want without asking."

Harper proudly smiles. "I didn't barge in. I texted and said I was coming over."

"And did you not stop to think that I was still asleep when I didn't respond?"

She shrugs. "I knew you'd wake up eventually."

I roll my eyes.

"What happened last night?" she asks.

My eyebrows draw together. "What do you mean?"

"Don't play stupid. I mean you leaving. I texted Blaire this morning to see how things went only to hear that she woke up confused and alone in her apartment."

I don't feel threatened by the look Harper is giving me. I also don't feel sympathy. She wants me to feel bad or explain myself, neither of which I have to do.

"Wasn't feeling it," I say.

She shakes her head in disbelief and whispers, "What happened to you?"

I know she's referring to how I've been since Miranda, and that's a discussion I completely ignore. She doesn't even know about Miranda. No one does except for the guys, and it's going to stay that way. "You know, most people would be disgusted at the thought of their friends sleeping with their siblings. Why can't you be like that?"

"Because you and Blaire would be perfect together."

This is annoying nonsense. I stand up from the table to go grab the syrup from the cabinet. Compared to Blaire's apartment, mine is nowhere near as elaborate. She had white and gray granite countertops with pure white cabinets and expensive chairs and glassware. My apartment is a typical bachelor pad, with oak wood cabinets, counter-tops that are a funky shade of blue, and a small round dining table. I eat off paper plates with plastic silverware, and my pantry and fridge stay stocked with only the necessities—beer, chips, microwave dinners, and a half-empty bottle of pancake syrup. As far as I'm concerned, Blaire Hanson and I are polar opposites.

"The woman is a rich brat," I tell Harper. "I've read all about her in the magazines and news articles. She's nothing but a trust fund kid and is too power hungry for her own good. Did you not see the article People wrote about her where she cussed out that teenage worker at Nordstrom? Over a pair of fucking shoes?"

Harper gives me a ridiculous look. "They weren't just a pair of fucking shoes, Jimmy. They were Gucci and what the article failed to mention was that the kid purposely and slowly poured his coffee onto her shoes because she wanted to try on a different pair. I was there; it was a shit show, but Blaire didn't do anything wrong."

I roll my eyes. "Furthering my point."

Harper sighs dramatically. "Well, I still think you owe her an apology. She said she really liked you."

I narrow my eyes at my sister. "Did she really?" I ask. I'm not buying her bullshit. Harper is really good at exaggerating the truth to get people to do what she wants, and I'll be damned if she does it to me.

"She did."

"I don't believe you."

Harper holds her arms up in surrender. "True story. I told her I'd get you to meet her back at Murphy's tonight for an apology drink. It's the least you could do."

I glare at my sister. "Why would you do that?"

She smiles and bites off a piece of bacon. "Because I can."

"Well, I'm not going."

"Thought you'd say that."

There's a knock on the door the second Harper finishes speaking. I look in the direction of the knocking before glancing back to Harper, who's wearing a proud smirk. I narrow my eyes at her and whisper, "What the fuck did you do?"

Harper stands from the table and takes a piece of bacon in her hand. "Magic," she whispers before tiptoeing to the back bedroom. "I'm going to go take a call. See you in thirty minutes."

There's another loud knock on the door, and I close my eyes to take a deep breath, cursing to myself before walking to face the music. I know it's Blaire behind the door, so I don't look through the peephole before yanking it open. Fucking Harper. This is the last time I let her set me up with a chick. Blaire goes to knock once more at the same time I pull the door open, and her fist connects with my chest. It barely feels like the touch of a feather.

For the early morning, Blaire looks impeccable. Her blond hair is freshly washed and falls straight down her shoulders, framing her perfectly made-up face. I can smell her sweet, expensive perfume, and I see that she's dressed as if she's going to court.

"Who's the defendant?" I tease, stepping aside for her to walk through. I don't pretend to not notice the glare on her face. Blaire struts into the apartment angrily, her heels clacking away on my hardwood floor. She turns in my direction with a scowl plastered on *those pretty little lips I had wrapped around my cock just the night before. Thinking back to the memory of Blaire on her knees, taking me in her mouth, makes my dick twitch. She crosses her arms over her chest to push her breasts further into view and cocks her hip out to the side.*

"I take it you're not here for a friendly visit?"

Her eyes narrow at me. "Harper said you wanted to see me."

I scoff. "Well, Harper's a liar if you haven't figured that out yet." I move by her to start cleaning the mess Harper made in my kitchen in an attempt to get Blaire out of here quicker. Instead, she stands in the middle of my kitchen with her arms still folded together and scowls at me.

"Is there something else you want to say?" I prod.

"God, what is wrong with you? You've officially become the biggest jackass I know, and that says a lot coming from me."

"Well, I'm honored."

"Oh my God, you are so not worth my time."

"Yet here you are at my apartment for some reason."

Blaire's mouth gapes open. It's kind of hot seeing her get bent out of shape so easily, and I find myself wanting to bend her over again right here in my kitchen. It's fun bantering with her and watching those expertly waxed eyebrows shoot up at my responses.

"You know what? You can kiss my ass, Jimmy Maxwell." She turns to head for the door.

"I already did after I smacked it last night," I say, just to get under her skin.

Blaire freezes with her dainty hand gripping the doorknob. Her hazel eyes shoot to me, full of hatred. I bask in it. "I hope I never see you again," she says in a voice that is supposed to affect me.

"Don't worry, you won't."

With one last narrowed scowl, Blaire slams the door closed behind her. I hear her heels clack away on the floor in the hall until they come to a stop. Harper emerges from the hallway, biting her lip. "Well," she starts, "that wasn't the reunion I was hoping for."

I shoot Harper a glance and walk by her to my room where I slam the door and change into joggers and my tennis shoes.

I need to go for a run.

━━━

PRESENT DAY

Blaire sits in the seat next to me, passed out. She's been asleep the last two hours of the flight home, and I've been killing the time taking off and on naps of my own and skimming through a magazine that was peeking out of Blaire's bag. I've grown accustomed to the silence between us since it's been like this for the last two days. I let Blaire go downstairs alone, or so she thought, but really, I went down and kept my distance. She had no idea I was there watching her while she worked on her computer.

What I saw down in the lobby as I watched her was something I know she wouldn't want me seeing.

Blaire *cried.*

Not full-on tears streaming down her face kind of crying, but crying enough to where I can see the sadness on her face and the two tears she quickly swiped away with her fingers before taking a deep breath and collecting herself. It doesn't take a rocket scientist for me to know I was the one that made her cry. While it didn't snap something inside of me to magically make me become a man who worships at her feet, I did surprise her with coffee and a bagel with cream cheese this morning. She eyed it skeptically and mumbled a thank you before showering. Since then, we've been silent all morning.

As the plane lands, I gently nudge Blaire awake. She jostles in her seat and blinks her squinted eyes to adjust to the light as she tries to wake up. We follow the flight attendant's instructions to prepare to exit, and when we do, my phone in my pocket begins to vibrate constantly against my leg. It's vibrating so much, it feels like one long phone call. Fishing my phone out of my pocket, I see several missed calls from unknown numbers and the firm, along with texts instructing me to call them as soon as possible. When my eyes scan the last text from Luka, my stomach sinks.

It's regarding Blaire's dad.

My eyes flicker in Blaire's direction, but she's glued to her own phone. I wait to see if there's any reaction from her. When I see her carry on like normal, I pause. Blaire looks at me skeptically, and I hold the back of my phone up to her. "I'm sorry. I have to make some urgent calls." Blaire doesn't say anything or make another face as she returns her gaze to her screen. I'm going to have to make this call as discreet as possible. My fingers move fast to unlock my phone and call Luka back. He answers on the second ring.

"What's going on?" I ask, bracing myself. I know whatever it is isn't good, judging by the number of missed calls, especially since it's about Blaire's dad.

"Is she near you?" Luka asks, being careful to not have Blaire overhear.

"Yes."

Luka sighs and then says lowly into the phone, "Charles has been kidnapped."

My grip around the phone tightens, and I close my eyes to take a deep breath. *Fuck. How am I going to break this to Blaire?*

"What happened?"

"I don't know. I thought Alex had a close watch on him. After the office fire, he said he stepped up his watch." While Charles didn't hire us to keep an eye on him, I told the boys to do just that. Something about his own security team felt off to me. I put Alex in charge of surveillance but made it clear to him not to act on anything, only report back to me.

Blaire still doesn't know about the office fire either. Damn, this is going to be a serious blow to her.

"Apparently, he didn't do a good enough job," I say, stealing a glance at Blaire.

"You need to stay with her, Jimmy. Shit's getting real, and they're coming for her. There's been another threat. Whoever it is wants the company."

"Well, they're not going to get it."

"What are we going to do?"

It's a question I've been asking myself since Luka spoke of Charles' kidnapping. "Let me call you back later," I say, keeping my eyes on Blaire. The last thing I want to do is break the news to her, but I've got to.

My stomach sinks. I hang up my phone and slide it into my pocket. "Blaire," I say. She keeps her head down, skimming her Facebook. I say her name once more time to get her attention, and she freezes.

"I need to talk to you."

Blaire's head doesn't look up from her phone. I feel myself start to bubble with frustration, and I sigh.

"For God's sake, Blaire, would you fucking look at m—"

My voice fails the second my eyes read her phone screen. It's a breaking news headline with a photo of Charles Hanson and the words CHARLES HANSON KIDNAPPED beside it. Blaire's body starts to crumple to the floor as she clutches her phone tightly in her hands, a wail escaping her throat. I sink to the floor with her, holding her in my arms and trying to calm down her hysteria. *Fucking media outlets.*

"They're going to find him, Blaire. I was just about to tell you."

"You *knew*?" Her voice is full of rage as she jumps out of my embrace.

"I just found out. It's why I was on the phone."

Blaire starts to cry, and I'm aware of the people staring at us as they walk by. I manage to get her off the plane and into the terminal. I continue to comfort Blaire until I see the swarm of paparazzi jogging toward us with their cameras.

"Blaire, we need to go," I whisper, pulling her off the floor. She groans and tries to refuse but quickly sees the paparazzi who are now snapping pictures as if they've just caught the hottest scandal.

"Blaire! Over here!"

"Have you heard about your dad?"

"What do you have to say to the kidnappers who took your father?"

I try to briskly drag Blaire out of the airport as we continue to be followed by the media. I shield her with my jacket to hide her crying face. I shoot the paparazzi a threatening scowl.

"Fucking leave her alone. Do you not have any respect?" I snap.

They continue to snap their cameras. A bulky man with a balding head smirks at me.

"Are you Blaire's boyfriend? Any comment on your relationship status?"

"Go to hell," I tell them.

Pushing through the pile of paparazzi is a difficult task, but we finally manage to get outside with our bags and file into the Escalade belonging to the security firm. Our driver, Marion, opens the door when he sees us approaching. I let Blaire file in first and shield her from the view of the media. I give Marion a serious look. "Get us out of here fast."

He nods his head once.

I climb in after Blaire, and Marion shuffles to the driver's seat to start the car and get us out of here. Blaire falls into the seat crying, and I twist in the leather cushioned seat to see if any of the paparazzi crowd tried to follow us. When I see they didn't, I turn back around to Blaire and reach out to stroke her. Seeing her this upset actually kills me. There's nothing I can do to comfort her at this moment, and I know that. Even stroking her soft blond hair like I'm doing now feels pointless. There's nothing I can say to make this remotely okay. All I can do is let her cry her heart out into the seat of the firm's vehicle.

Thankfully, Marion slides up the glass to give us privacy. I text him, telling him to take us to my apartment, and then slide my phone back into my pocket. I let Blaire cry the whole way to the building as I gently rub her back. Marion pulls up to my building twenty minutes later, and by then, all the crying has Blaire drifting off to sleep.

I look over to her and smile. Even with streaks of makeup staining her cheeks, she's gorgeous. Her silky blond hair lays perfectly against her shoulders, and the white crop tank top she's wearing under her open Nike jacket displays her perfectly tanned skin. Blaire is a wildly independent woman but right now she needs me and I hate seeing her in distress.

"Hey," I say softly, giving her a gentle nudge. "Wake up. We're home."

Blaire jolts at my touch and groans as she sits up. She rubs her face with her hands and blows out a deep breath. I see her lip start to quiver, and she shields her face from my view by turning her head in the opposite direction. She sits up straighter and turns to me with questioning eyes. "Where are we?" she asks.

"My apartment." I open the door. "Come on."

I don't give her time to say something about being at my place. I climb out of the car and open the hatch to retrieve our bags. Blaire files out of the Escalade timidly and follows me into the building. I wonder if she remembers the last time she was here three months ago when she stormed in and called me the biggest asshole she knows. I chuckle at the memory.

Blaire stays by my side and is quiet the whole ride up to my floor. I steal a glance at her and see her blank face. It's ghostly white. When the elevator car brings us to a stop and opens, I step off with our bags and walk down the hall until I reach my apartment. Blaire's head swivels back and forth as she checks out both sides of the hall, and I wonder what she's thinking.

"Not like Uptown Manhattan," I say, opening the door.

Blaire's head swivels back to me. "Huh?"

"The apartment. Sorry it's not like a scene from *Gossip Girl*." I don't know what I'm saying, just trying to lighten the mood if that's even possible.

Blaire makes no comment as she steps into my place. I close the door after glancing both ways down the hallway myself to make sure we haven't been followed. I lock the four locks on my door before turning to Blaire, who's planted in the same spot she was when she barged in a few months ago.

"Wait here," I tell her. I pull out the gun I always keep lodged in the back of my pants.

Blaire gasps and her eyes widen. "Jimmy! What the hell! Put that away!"

I ignore her as I scan my apartment room by room to make sure nothing suspicious happened while we were away. When I return back to the kitchen and tuck the gun back in the waistband of my jeans, I see the fear lodged in Blaire's eyes.

"Relax," I tell her. "It's for safety reasons."

"What safety reasons require a gun in your own home?"

"You'd be surprised."

She shakes her head. It's like a switch flips inside of her because her face crumples and tears start to fall down her cheeks like a dam just broke. Her body starts to collapse, and I catch her, leading her to one of the chairs at my dining table. Blaire's head tucks into her folded arms on the table, and she weeps, her whole body shaking. I drag the other chair at the table closer to her, and I do as I did in the car and rub her back.

"Is he going to die?" she asks through tears.

"No. They're going to find him."

"Who?" She sits up, sniffling and wiping her tears with her arm.

"The police. Our firm. His security detail. The FBI... Your father is a very powerful man and has an army of his own out looking for him."

I talk her through everything I know. I assure her multiple times that they have no interest in killing him; it would destroy their entire plan to extort him. I explain to her about the process of negotiating and proof of life. It seems to sink in, but I know I'm throwing an insane amount of information at her, information she never thought she'd have to process. Nobody is ever prepared to talk through proof of life negotiations.

She groans, rubbing her head with her hand. "He's all I have left."

My lips tuck together. "He said that about you too," I tell her in a comforting voice.

Blaire smiles a little, but it seems to calm her down.

"Do you have any idea who would want to kidnap your father?"

She shakes her head. "No. Not unless it's someone on the board wanting to manipulate his vote to get to his money."

"When the police ask you that, you need to give them the names of everyone in the office, even those you don't think would do this."

Blaire nods her head. "Will you go with me?"

"Where?"

"To talk to the police."

The way she's looking at me right now with wide eyes full of fear and hope pulls at something in my stomach. Looking at her right now, it would be impossible to say no to her. I'd go with her even if she didn't ask.

"I have to, remember?" I joke. It gets a smile out of Blaire, which gets a smile out of me. "I know you're upset, but you need to eat. Are you hungry?"

Blaire's nose crinkles. "Not really."

"We don't have to eat out. I can order something to go."

She shakes her head. "No, it's okay..."

I huff. "You can't go without eating."

"Jimmy, my father was just kidnapped. Excuse me for not being in the mood to stuff my face."

"That is true, but your father also ordered me to keep you safe, and that includes your health. Now, I don't think I'm wrong when I say he would want you to eat, would he not?"

Blaire's lips purse together. She finally nods her head and sniffles, looking down to her twiddling fingers on the table. "Yes."

"Exactly. Now what would you like?"

"What do you have?"

"Beer and chips," I say matter-of-factly to make her laugh.

Blaire lets out a soft huff, exactly what I was wanting, and it's nice to see her smile, even with her mascara-stained cheeks. "Really? That's it?"

I shrug. "Well, I also have some pancake syrup and a can of... something."

"You live life like a true bachelor."

"And I take pride in it."

She hesitates a moment, looking as if she shouldn't be worried about food at the present moment. "Do you have any pasta?"

I jump out of my seat and walk over to the cabinets where I keep my pantry food. To my surprise, there's an opened box of spaghetti noodles all the way in the back, tucked behind my now-stale bag of salt and vinegar chips. I pull it out and hold it up for Blaire to see.

"Apparently so," I respond.

She stands up from her chair to come over to the cabinet and begins to sift through it by lifting on her toes.

"What are you looking for?" I ask.

"Some sauce or something," she says with slight defeat, planting her feet flat on the floor. "You live more like a college student."

"Don't insult me."

Blaire pulls out her phone and starts to tap at the screen. I eye her skeptically. "What are you doing?"

She's quiet for a few minutes, tapping away before closing her screen and smiling up at me proudly. "Buying some groceries. They will be here in forty-five minutes."

"You bought me *groceries*? I'm not poor. I can shop for food myself."

"I bought *us* groceries—and relax, I only bought food we need for tonight... although it probably would have done you good if I bought something extra."

I narrow my eyes playfully and rub my tongue over my teeth. Blaire notices my smug look and grows a studying look of her own.

"What?" she asks.

"You said *us*."

"Yeah? Because we're *both* eating?"

I shrug. "I'm just saying. I don't think I'm comfortable being exclusive yet."

Blaire laughs and playfully rolls her eyes, followed by sticking her tongue out and making a gagging sound. "Don't make me sick!" she plays.

I know it's horrible, but watching her pretend to gag stirs something in me, and being the guy that I am, my tongue gets the better of me.

"Well, I know something else that can make you gag."

Blaire's eyes widen. Her mouth drops in shock at my crude remark, and I laugh at her face. It's so fun messing with her.

"You are so disgusting!" she says.

"Hey, I'm just trying to get your mind off of things."

A small smile creeps its way onto Blaire's lips as sadness takes over her eyes again. She holds my gaze briefly before dipping her head down to look at her feet. I know this is her way of shielding her tears from me. Blaire is a strong woman, and strong people don't like to appear broken. But given the current situation, I'd say she gets a free pass. Without thinking, I reach out for her and pull her close to me in my arms.

The second Blaire's small frame collides with mine, she breaks, full tears and sobs. Her hands reach around my back to hold me tighter against her, and her fingers bunch the fabric of my shirt. Her bony shoulders bounce in my arms as she sobs into my chest, and all I can do is rock her and let her cry. God, it's killing me to not do anything more.

"It's all going to be okay," I whisper to her even though I know it's going in one ear and out the other.

It's words I know Blaire doesn't care to hear right now, but I offer them anyway to comfort her. Plus, a small part of me likes this— holding her. I just wish it were under different circumstances.

I don't say anything else as I let Blaire continue to cry into my chest. We must stay like this for a while because when there's a knock on my door from the delivery person, Blaire is still full-force crying. The person knocks again at my door, and I gently pull Blaire away so I can answer it. I reach into my back pocket where my wallet is to pull out enough cash to cover the bill and tip and quickly shove it in the dude's hands before dipping back into my apartment.

I set the bags on the ground and lock the door behind me. Blaire's now leaning against the edge of the counter with her face in her hands, but she's stopped crying. Now she just looks lost, no doubt feeling low and helpless. I can see that on her face. No matter how hard I try to change things around tonight for her, there's no use. Her father was just *kidnapped*. It's perfectly right for her to feel the way she is.

Blaire drops her hand from her head, a sullen look on her face. I don't know why, but I feel the incredible need to comfort her again by pulling her back into me. Maybe it's selfish, but I liked the feel of her body against mine. I liked the way it felt to have her in my arms and to be the shoulder she cried on, literally. Even though we both seem to hate each other, I keep crawling back to wanting her in my arms.

This time, I don't wrap her into me. I stand next to her, our bodies leaning against the counter, and I gently reach out to stroke her soft hair.

"Blaire," I say softly, "you really need to eat something." I feel like a mother trying to force their child to eat after throwing a fit, but it's partially true. She can't slip into a depression the whole time her dad is being held hostage. We're going to find this son of a bitch and kill him, but we need Blaire strong in the process.

She shakes her head. Her lip quivers once again. "No," she says with a shaky voice. "I can't."

"So you're going to let all these groceries go to waste? Spaghetti was sounding really good to me. Let's see what we have here." I start to reach into the bags to pull out the ingredients Blaire threw into the virtual cart, and thank goodness I did. There's cold stuff in here.

"We've got *more* noodles." I set it down on the counter for her to see and pull out the next item. "Jar spaghetti sauce—mmm. Next we have... What's this?" I ask, holding up some white bulb-looking item.

It's wrapped in flaky paper that peels like an onion, except it's not an onion, and Blaire looks to me with a ridiculous look. There's a strong aroma coming from the white item, so I lean in to sniff it, instantly aware of what it is.

"Is that *garlic?*"

Blaire makes a face. "Yes. Have you never seen a garlic bulb before?"

I shake my head and hold the bulb in the air as if I'm inspecting it. "Can't say that I have. Every time I've seen it, it's been in chunks in my Olive Garden pasta."

Blaire scoffs and rolls her eyes. She yanks the bulb out of my hand and starts to unload the rest of the groceries onto the counter.

At least the plan looks like it worked.

"I take it you've seen a garlic bulb before?"

She nods her head. "Plenty of times. I love cooking with garlic."

I freeze next to her, my head snapping in her direction. Blaire can feel my eyes on her, and she turns to me, noticing my weird look.

"What?" she asks.

"Nothing, it's just... I didn't... expect you to cook your own meals, that's all."

Blaire's sass starts to come out. The forks she had pulled from my drawer *clink* as they fall onto the counter. Her eyes are shooting daggers at me.

"What is *that* supposed to mean?"

I can practically feel the defensiveness.

I shake my head to dismiss it and go back to putting away the groceries. "Nothing, it's nothing."

"No, it's not *nothing*. What did that mean?"

"I feel like you know what it means."

"Are you insinuating that I have a butler or a maid on hand who cooks me meals whenever I want them?"

My shoulders lift in a lingering shrug. "Yeah, actually. Your family is top one percent wealthy, Blaire. It's not like you guys are just upper middle class."

Blaire's mouth gapes open in horror, and she looks at me with wide eyes before swatting at my shoulder. "I do *not* have a maid on hand. I can do things for myself!"

She says this assertively and with a straight face to make sure I believe her. I scoff.

"Believe me, I read all about that on the cover of *Forbes Magazine* last month. I wasn't insinuating you couldn't, just that you *didn't*."

I say this to get under her skin, and it works. Blaire swats at my shoulder once more, this time with more of a punch, and I chuckle next to her. My eyes linger on hers in the close proximity we're in, and our breathing synchronizes the more our eyes stay locked. For the first time in this whole mission, I don't mind being around Blaire. It's not that I minded before. I just didn't like the spoiled woman that stormed into my apartment a few months ago and what she did after. The bitch almost cost me my job.

Blaire Hanson *is* a woman who can do things herself, but she wants people to know it. She wants people to fear her. But now, since seeing her vulnerability in Miami and seeing her crumble right here in my apartment, there's a different side to Blaire that I'm seeing and, to be honest, that I actually might like.

What is happening to me?

12

BLAIRE

THREE MONTHS EARLIER...

I feel like pulling my hair out the whole time I'm at work. I'm seething, gritting my teeth, snapping at my employees... It's not a good combination, and it's all thanks to that jackass—which is putting it nicely—Jimmy Maxwell. I'm so furious and pissed off that I can't see straight.

The numbers and letters on my computer screen look like a blurred mess, and it stays that way nearly the entire day. What also pisses me off is how this asshole is distracting me from work. That never happens. So not only has this prick taken advantage of me, embarrassed me, and neglected me, he's also distracted me from the most important thing in my life—my career.

As I'm sitting in my office with a gorgeous view that overlooks the city, I decide to take a break. A nervous habit of mine is chewing my fingernails mindlessly, which is exactly what I'm doing when my father buzzes in. His voice pulls me out of my trance.

"Blaire," he says, "my office, please."

"Yes, Daddy."

I do as he says and make my way to his massive corner office. I hope to have his office one day when he hands the company over to me.

I'm not power hungry. I think my father is an excellent businessman and is doing a wonderful job running the company, but unlike most kids I grew up with who want to venture out of the family business and pursue a life of leisure, I crave the work. And my first order of business to take care of when I get in this office is to totally redesign it. No more dark-wood, Mafia feel to the room. It will be modern, clean, and elegant.

I open the doors to his office and walk to his desk in the center of the room. I plop down in one of the chairs facing him and wait to hear what he called me in for. Daddy finishes writing on one of his papers before removing his readers and looking at me.

"What's going on?" he asks.

I scrunch my eyebrows together. "What do you mean?"

"I mean your attitude today, Blaire. Do you really think I haven't noticed?"

I feign innocence. "I wasn't aware that I had one."

"Well..." He sighs. "Then head home for the day."

My eyes widen. Is my father seriously sending me home?

"You're sending me home early?" I ask in bewilderment.

He nods his head. "Yes, I am."

"But, Daddy, I'm fine! Really, I am. There's an hour left until it's time to clock out and—"

"Then clock out now. Honestly, Blaire, just take the rest of the day. I don't know what's gotten into you, but I won't have you treat our employees the way you have today."

I sink back into the seat, accepting defeat. When my daddy makes a decision, especially one regarding his company, his mind is completely made up. I know no matter how hard I fight to stay here today, I won't win. So, with a huff, I give him a glare to let him know I don't appreciate this order and then head back to my office to gather my things. When I'm back in my office, my seething from earlier has stepped up several notches and in order to protect whoever I'll run into once I leave, I take a few minutes to calm down.

Reaching for my phone, I open up messages and click on the group chat the girls are in, and I send them a message asking who's down to meet at Murphy's in an hour for drinks. The ironic thing is that Harper is the first to respond.

Harper: *Me, me, me, me!!!! See you at five! :)*

Hate to say it, but seeing her name makes me feel a touch salty. She has nothing to do with the way her horrible brother treated me last night, but he is related to her so it still stings just a little. Thankfully, Juliette and Aspen respond just as fast and say they will be there too. After grabbing my belongings, I walk home to change quickly before heading out to Murphy's.

When I get to Murphy's, I'm the first to arrive. I order a gin and tonic before claiming a high-top table and waiting for my friends. Typically, I stick to wine when I go out, but tonight, I'm feeling something stiff will do the trick.

Juliette, Harper, and Aspen all come in together and instantly find me. Their smiles make me want to vomit. I'm not in the smiling mood today. Harper notices right off the bat and sends me an apologetic look before wrapping me in a hug.

"Hey, pal..." She treads lightly, looking to my drink. "Everything okay?"

I shoot her a knowing look and a huff, rolling my eyes to tell her that everything has gone to shit since going out with her brother. Aspen sees the look on my face and grows a concerned look of her own.

"No wine tonight? Did someone feel your wrath?"

"Not yet, but they will."

The girls order their drinks, and we all sit at the table. Juliette orders a plate of chips for us to munch on, and by the end of my plate, I'm on my third drink. We start talking about our days and what's been going on in our lives for the last several weeks with work and such when my eyes land on a group walking in the door. I instantly narrow my eyes at them. It's Jimmy with two of his friends, who look just like him. All three of the men scream "alpha male" with their broad chests and bulky arms. The main difference between the men are *their hair colors. Where Jimmy has dark hair, the others are different shades of sandy blond.*

My gaze must be a dead giveaway who I'm staring at because the girls all turn their heads in the direction of the boys. Harper stays quiet and sinks in her seat.

"Who are they?" Aspen asks.

Harper's lips stick to the stirrer in her drink, and she takes a long gulp.

Juliette's eyes widen and she gasps, turning to me with a smirk she's trying to conceal. "Is that why you're pissed off today?"

My eyes can't seem to leave Jimmy. Looking at him makes my blood boil, especially seeing him look so carefree and smiling as he lifts the rim of his bottle to his lips.

I feel myself start to shake with anger in my seat as I watch him with his friends. I don't know why he is affecting me this much. There's never been a man who gets under my skin as much as Jimmy does, and it's irritating me that I can't figure out why. I'm not sure if anything would have come out of our arrangement. My night with Jimmy was nothing but pure sexual tension. From the moment my eyes landed on him and I realized who he was, all I wanted to do was climb on top of him, and I could tell the feeling was mutual. We didn't get anywhere deep, other than inside of me, so I'm confused as to why this ass is having such a major effect on me.

Yet I was willing to get to know him, to take a chance. It's not rejection that hurts; I've been through that before; we all have. It's the fact that he treated me like I didn't matter at all. Especially since he knew I was his little sister's best friend.

Harper looks to her brother and then back to me. It feels like a dirty secret between the four of us of who Jimmy is. Without revealing that aspect to the girls, I inform them on what went down last night.

"You see that man in the middle? The one with the dark hair?"

Juliette and Aspen nod their heads, their eyes staying on Jimmy and his friends. Maybe it's the stronger drink I've been sipping on

*mixed with my anger, but the blunt words that flow out of my mouth
don't take me by surprise.*

*"He fucked me last night and then dipped." I take a long swig of
my drink before adding in, "After we were set up by a friend."*

Aspen's mouth dropped. "Who is your friend that knows him?"

*I narrow my eyes at her while Harper sinks farther in her seat.
Juliette and Aspen are oblivious.*

"Are you serious?" Juliette asks.

*I nod my head. "Total ass. When I confronted him about it this
morning, it was all just a joke to him. He's a complete and total prick."*

"But... he's so gorgeous," Aspen breathes.

*She's really starting to get on my nerves, and I feel myself about to
lash out at her. Harper's hand reaches out to rest on my arm in a
comforting manner, but I'm already hopping down from my seat when
she does. The girls turn to me with confused glances.*

"What are you doing?" Harper asks.

*I fluff my blond hair and stand straighter. "If he wants to embar-
rass me the way that he did, then I'll embarrass him."*

"Blaire—"

*I don't respond to Harper's call as I start to walk toward Jimmy,
and I know she won't stop me at the risk of exposing that Jimmy is her
brother. Why she wants to keep that a secret beats me, but after
meeting him, I understand. I wouldn't want my friends to know I have
an ass of a brother. Jimmy's back stays facing me as he sits at the bar
with his friends. When I tap his shoulder, he spins on the stool. The
smile on his face quickly fades and is replaced with shock before
turning into a grin.*

"I know you. Brittany, was it?"

*Now his two friends turn to face me, their faces equally as hand-
some as Jimmy's, but I don't let that throw off my game. I size Jimmy
up by standing confidently and giving him a grin of my own.*

"Johnny, was it?" I bite back.

*Jimmy snickers, obviously amused at the situation. When he
regains himself, he looks at me with his boyish grin that makes my*

stomach bubble, warning me that this guy is more than just a bad decision. He's the type that'll ruin your life.

"It's nice to see you again, Blaire."

I know this is his way of trying to get me to keep my cool in front of his friends. It dawns on me that of course they don't know about their best friend's smash and dash tendencies, and if they do, they're proud of it because they're typical men. It's then I realize the power I possess in this situation to expose this man, which I feel is perfectly acceptable after the way he treated me last night and this morning.

Jimmy's friend to his left clears his throat and extends his arm out to me. "I'm Luka," he says with a smile as charming as Jimmy's.

"Alex," the other one says, lifting his beer in the air in greeting.

I smile at them both before planting my eyes back on Jimmy. "I'm Blaire. Jimmy's flavor last night."

Alex and Luka both give Jimmy the oh-shit-you're-in-trouble side glance, and I feel my confidence grow. Jimmy looks at me with a slight glare, his mouth pressed into a hard line, before glancing over my shoulder and finding his sister staring back at him from our table. His eyes travel back to me, and his shoulders lift as he takes a deep breath.

"Is there something you need?" he asks, even though his tone conveys that he wants me to leave as soon as possible.

"Actually, yes. There is."

I know I've had too much to drink tonight, but I'm feeling empowered from the alcohol. I clear my throat before embarrassing myself further in this situation and acting out in a way I know I'll regret in the morning. I clutch my drink tightly in my hands and start to yell at the top of my lungs.

"If anyone here is interested in hiring this man, Jameson Maxwell, owner of Four Forces Security for protection." I pause, making sure the entire bar's eyes are on me. "I highly advise you don't, unless you want to be fucked over... and I mean that literally, people. This man cannot be trusted!" I point directly at him as I watch anger mar his perfect face.

Murmurs and laughter at my intoxicated state start to surface in the bar. I giggle at the major scowl on Jimmy's face and feel hands pulling me toward the door. I mouth *fuck you* to him as I stumble from the chair I was standing on. The next thing I remember is the gentle breeze of the city's night air on my hot skin, nearly knocking the breath out of me from its sharp contrast to the heat of the alcohol.

"Blaire, what's the matter with you?" Harper seethes through her teeth when we're on the street. She's pulling me hard as Juliette and Aspen follow behind us with my purse and jacket, embarrassed looks on their faces.

I giggle as I stumble, trying to walk with Harper's tugs and my wobbly legs. "I was just giving that bastard what he deserved," I defend myself.

Harper scoffs. "Yeah, well, you embarrassed yourself in the process."

I can hear the anger and frustration in her voice, but I don't care. "Honestly, Harper, your brother is an asshole."

Juliette or Aspen—one of them—gasps behind us, and they stop walking at the revelation that Harper and Jimmy are related. Harper yanks me to a halt on the sidewalk and groans in frustration. "Nice going, Blaire," she says.

The scuff of feet jogging up to us surfaces, and through my now blurry vision, I can make out Jimmy's frame barging between Juliette and Aspen and over to me in a rage.

"Jimmy, don't—" Harper starts, but she's cut off immediately by Jimmy glaring at me.

"What the hell was that!" he yells in my face.

I roll my eyes. "You don't scare me, Jimmy."

"You can cost me my job over shit like that. Who the hell do you think you are!"

He's screaming inches away from my face, and I can smell the beer on his breath. Harper tries to pull him out of my proximity, and thankfully, his friends jog to us and pull him away.

"Take it easy, man." I think it's Alex that says that.

"No one got it on tape, I swear," Luka chimes in.

Jimmy still keeps his scowl locked on me as I back against a wall, scowling right back at him. It feels good to finally release the anger I've had bubbling inside me all day at the culprit despite the dignity I've lost because of it. I know that will be a different story in the morning.

Jimmy turns swiftly on his feet to Harper and points a finger in her face. "Do something with her. Now."

People on the sidewalk are starting to stop and watch the scene unfold, and I bury my face in my hands. The last thing our company needs is bad publicity. Jimmy storms off back in the direction of Murphy's, and his friends follow, leaving Harper and the girls with me. They all stare at me with unreadable expressions, and I huff, feeling incredibly tired.

"You really didn't need to act like that, Blaire. That was low, even for you."

I roll my eyes at Harper and try to steady myself on my legs since people are watching. I'm supposed to be one of the most put-together businesswomen in America right now, not trashed and yelling at low-life men in bars. I do my best to walk toward my apartment with the help of my friends. The longer we walk, the more the excitement of what just happened starts to wear off, and by the time we reach my building, the guilt rises inside me.

I twist the key in my doorknob to open my apartment and step in, turning to face my friends. They give me blank looks and I take a deep breath, feeling completely embarrassed for what I just did.

"I'm sorry, guys. Truly. I don't know what came over me."

Juliette and Aspen nod with tight smiles. I look to Harper, who has hard eyes and her lips pressed into a tight line. I know she's pissed at me, and she has every right to be. I don't expect her to say anything for a while.

"Get some rest and drink lots of coffee in the morning," she says flatly after a few moments of silence. "You're going to need it."

The girls leave my apartment, and I settle in for an early night in bed, but it takes me a while to go to sleep. I replay the events of tonight over in my head, and the more they resurface, the more I want to bury myself in the pillow and suffocate.

Screw Jimmy Maxwell for making me come undone.

———

PRESENT DAY...

Oddly, cooking with Jimmy is... fun. It's hard to find "fun" at a time like this when I shouldn't be smiling, but I appreciate all he's doing to get my mind off my father. There's no worse feeling than hearing your only surviving parent and family member has been kidnapped, and it's all I can think about.

When the news broke and our PR rep left me the urgent voice-mail, every single horrible thought filled my mind from my father getting hurt to him being held hostage or, worse, dying. I'm not sure what I'm supposed to do or how to feel, but I'm sure finding peace in cooking spaghetti with my bodyguard isn't the way to handle things.

Jimmy places the pot of water on the burner and turns the knob to high. As he waits for the pot to boil to put the noodles in, I mince the garlic and bell peppers to add to the jar sauce while the meat cooks in the pan. It's silent in the kitchen for several minutes as we maneuver around each other, but I can feel Jimmy's eyes linger on me every so often, like they are now. He's standing a few inches away on the other side of the stove as I pretend to not feel him stare at me as I chop the peppers. I don't want to be enjoying this—being stuck with Jimmy and him watching me—but I do. It feels wrong given the current situation. Now is not the time to enjoy playing house but I also am craving some sense of normalcy in this uncertain time.

I finish chopping the peppers and check to see if the meat is done. Seeing that it is, I ask, "Do you have a colander?"

Jimmy blinks. "A what?"

"A colander?" I repeat, looking at him with scrunched eyebrows. I read the blank look on his face. "You don't know what a colander is?"

He shakes his head. "No, but I know what a cylinder is."

I roll my eyes and sigh as I search his bare cabinets for a colander or anything that will suffice. So far, I've only seen the kitchen, and from the looks of it, you would think Jimmy doesn't live here. There's hardly enough equipment and furniture to call this place a home, and I haven't made it to the bedroom yet.

Bedroom... Will I be sleeping in Jimmy's bed *with* Jimmy? I force that question out of mind as I move from cabinet to cabinet with no luck of finding a colander. I open his drawers and find a spoon with a hole in the center. This will do.

Tearing off a few pieces of paper towels, I scoop spoonfuls of ground meat onto the paper towels before dripping the grease into a mug. Jimmy stands by and watches as I then pick up the cutting board and slide the peppers, garlic, and onions into the pan with the knife. I set the cutting board in the sink and turn to see Jimmy's eyes on me.

"What?" I ask.

"I'm still waiting to hear what a colander is."

"It's just this thing that looks like a bowl but has tiny circles around it for grease and water to drain out of. You use it for pasta mostly. Will you stir the veggies?"

Jimmy takes the spatula and mixes the chopped peppers and onions in the pan to soften. "You sure know your way around a kitchen," he says.

The simple compliment makes me smile. I pull two paper plates from his shelf and set them to the side. "Thanks. My mother taught me how to cook before she passed."

Jimmy looks up briefly. "What happened to your mom? If you don't mind me asking."

"Car accident. It happened when I was seven. She was on her way to pick me up from school, and someone ran a red light. Hit her head-on and killed her instantly."

Jimmy grimaces slightly, and he looks at me apologetically. "I'm really sorry."

I offer him a small smile. "Thanks. She was five months pregnant at the time too."

Jimmy's head snaps in my direction. "Really?"

"Mm-hmm. With another girl too. I remember when she and Daddy told me I was going to have a little sister. I was so excited. I had been begging them for months to get me a sister—because I thought that's how it worked at the time; you *buy* your siblings—and I asked for a little sister so we could play dress-up and Barbies."

He chuckles. "That's adorable."

I smile at the memory and shake my head. "Dad was never the same after that accident."

"How so?"

"Well," I say, leaning against the counter and folding my arms across my chest, "my dad met my mom in college. He was three years older than she was, but he always said the second he saw her walk into his personal finance class, he knew she was the one."

"Just at first glance?"

"Yes. Well, no. He said that he was smitten with her from the very first glance, but later that night, after he got back to his frat house, he said he spent the whole evening thinking about her and telling his fraternity brothers that the next time he sees her in class, he's going to ask her out. The next time they had class a few days later, she didn't show. Come to find out, she dropped the class and Dad thought he would never see her again. He told his best friend at the time—Mark —that if he runs into her again on campus, then it must be fate because he didn't get a chance to catch her name. So, fast forward to nearly a *month* later at one of his frat's socials, he came down the stairs of his house to see her standing there, leaning against the wall with a drink in her hand and *Mark's tongue* shoved down her throat."

Jimmy laughs. "Oh no. What happened?"

"What happened was my dad thought he didn't stand a chance, that she found Mark and liked him instead. So my dad walks by at the same time Mark and my mom break their kiss, and my mom sees my dad and instantly runs to him. She tells him that she recognized him from her personal finance class the other day and wanted to know his name. Dad tells her his name, and she tells him hers, and the whole time he's looking back and forth between my mom and Mark, trying to figure out what's going on. He comes to find out my mom was never interested in Mark. She saw my dad earlier at the party, but Mark grabbed her and kissed her just a moment later."

"So, how did Mark take it?"

"Once Mark found out that this was the girl from my dad's class, he backed off, and then they lived happily ever after... until the day she died."

The pot of water starts to boil. Jimmy opens the noodles to pour them in and gives them a stir with the same spoon I used to cook the meat. "Well, I'm glad your dad got to be with the girl he loved for a little bit."

I smile at his words. "Me too."

There's an awkward pause at the end of the statement as we stand in the kitchen. Something in the air between us feels different this time. It feels thick and laced with something I can't put my finger on. I try to appear busy as I unscrew the lid to the sauce and pour its contents into the pan with the softened onions and peppers. Jimmy checks the noodles by catching one on his fork and popping it into his mouth.

We stay like this for several more minutes, quietly stirring our dinner. When the noodles are ready a few minutes later, I turn off the burner and scoop the pasta into the saucepan and stir it all together. We each fill our plates even though I'm not hungry, and Jimmy walks to the small table against the wall.

I'm reminded that this is still the only room in his apartment I've seen. The day Harper told me to come over here, I stepped foot in his kitchen, and that was it. The kitchen offers a view into his living room, where a TV is sitting on a dark wood table, and there's a small gray couch against the opposite wall facing the TV.

Jimmy's apartment is a lot like him, simple and clean without a lot of clutter. Jimmy is a very upfront and blunt guy, so it doesn't surprise me to see he lives in a place that's barely decorated.

We twist spaghetti onto our forks and take the first few bites in silence. Jimmy hums in appreciation for the food across the table and nods his head as he chews. "This is delicious," he says.

I give him a small smile. "It's the jar sauce. Tastes like homemade if you add enough pizzazz to it."

I move my fork in my bowl as my loss of appetite settles while Jimmy clears his bowl in a matter of minutes. When he's finished, he looks at me with concern.

"Are you not going to finish it?"

"I'm just not hungry, Jimmy. I tried."

He nods his head slowly. "How can I help?"

It's not his simple words that make me smile; it's the sincerity in his tone. I can hear it in his voice that he wants to do everything he can to keep my mind off things. In all honesty, I just want to be alone right now.

"I think I want some time alone," I tell him, standing from the table. I'm unsure where to go, and the loss of comfort of not being in my own home stirs my nerves more.

Jimmy nods his head in the direction behind me. "The bedroom's that way."

"Where are you going to sleep?"

"In my bed."

"But... I'll be in there?" It's a statement that comes out as a question.

"I know and so will I."

I give Jimmy a look and his eyebrows arch.

"You don't think I'm sleeping on my couch while you hog my bed, do you?"

My cheeks flush in embarrassment as I frantically search my mind for words to say. "N-no, I just thought—"

"Blaire, we've *slept* together before. Twice, to be exact. I think we can manage actually sleeping in the same bed with our clothes on."

I gulp and nod my head, feeling small underneath his stare. Jimmy has this way of looking at a woman and making her feel stripped bare in the most vulnerable way. It's unnerving but I like it. I turn on my heel to walk toward the bedroom, and I can feel his eyes on me. As I walk to the room, I freeze with a sudden realization. What I'm about to do makes my shoulders sink in defeat, but it's what I want at the current moment. Over the last week, Jimmy has been inside of me, seen me in my most delirious state, and seen me cry. I think I can say he's cracked through my walls, whether I like it or not.

Jimmy looks at me with a questioning gaze. I don't hesitate to ask him what's on my mind.

"Will you... come lie with me?"

Jimmy's lips part slightly, but his eyes don't narrow at me. "What?" he asks softly.

"It's just... I don't... want to be *completely* alone right now."

My eyes lock with Jimmy's, and for once, he doesn't make me feel small. He doesn't have a smart remark or a look about him that embarrasses me. Instead, his eyes are soft. They look at me with tenderness and understanding, and he puts his fork in his bowl before standing from the table and walking over to me.

I feel breathless as I wait for him to come closer, and when he does, his height towers over me in the most comforting way. I feel safe next to him, and I want to cling to him tightly.

Jimmy's green eyes bore into mine and I feel captivated by him. We're silent as we stand like this for several heartbeats, and I wait for him to make a move. I wonder what he's thinking right now as he looks at me, and I want to know if he feels the same electricity that I do.

"Bedroom's this way," Jimmy says, breaking the silence.

I feel let down for some reason as he strides by me to open the closed door that reveals the inside of a room with a full-sized bed and one nightstand on the left side. It's big enough for the both of us but will be a stretch with Jimmy's big build. It also means that we will be squished together, a thought I don't particularly mind at the moment.

Jimmy pulls down the sheets of the bed as I stand at the edge looking at him. While he's right—we have been in bed together before —this time feels more intimate to me. Jimmy fluffs the pillows before standing up straight and looking in my direction.

"Everything okay?" he asks.

I nod my head and gulp.

Jimmy slides under the covers and lifts the other side for me to slip in. I walk over to the bed and slide under the sheets next to Jimmy, where I instantly feel warm and relaxed against his hard frame. Jimmy lifts his arm for me to nestle against his chest. It's the most comfortable and natural feeling. When my head meets Jimmy's chest, I realize how tired I am. I fight to keep my eyes open in the moment as my breathing becomes steady with his own. It's quiet in the room as Jimmy lies with me and smooths my hair with his hand, a gesture that makes me smile.

"Thank you," I whisper into his chest.

"For what?"

"Comforting me."

He lightly snickers. "If I didn't, you would have bitched all night."

"Do you always think of me as someone who raises hell?"

"Do you not remember that night in Murphy's when you screamed at the top of your lungs about me?"

I grimace. That was definitely not one of my finest moments. "Yeah. Sorry about that."

Jimmy chuckles. "It's fine now, but damn, you really almost fucked me with my job."

"Well, I'm getting payback for it now with you being my bodyguard."

Jimmy doesn't say anything, and I momentarily feel like I might have crossed a small line with that one. Jimmy continues to stroke my hair, and I revel in the soothing feel of it. My eyelids soon start to feel heavy. I feel myself going in and out of sleep, exhausted by the emotional toll of the day.

"Jimmy," I say.

"Hmm?"

"Are they going to find my dad?"

I feel him still next to me. "Yes," he says.

For some reason, I believe him. I have all the faith in the world that Jimmy knows what he's doing and that he has the capability to find my father. The question is, how long will it take? What do we do from here?

Sleep gets the best of me, and in a matter of seconds, my eyes close and I drift off into the night against Jimmy's chest, feeling completely safe and protected in his arms.

13

JIMMY

My eyes dart open sometime during the night, and the room is pitch-black. The crack at the bottom of the door reveals the lights in the kitchen I left on, and I try to gently move Blaire off me to go turn them off. Glancing down at Blaire, I don't want to move her. I can tell she's dead asleep, and she looks so peaceful and content that I don't want to disturb her. She had an emotional day and needs all the rest she can get. Thankfully, she groans and rolls over onto her side, leaving me with room to move off the bed.

I quietly step out of the room and close the door behind me so the lights in the kitchen don't wake her up. The entire apartment is quiet, and I tiptoe around the place as to not disturb Blaire. Noting the time on the oven clock, I see that it's three in the morning. Man, I was sleeping good. I turn the lights off in the kitchen and start to head back to the bedroom when my phone in my pocket begins to ring, causing me to jump at the suddenness of it. My hands quickly sink into my pocket to turn the ringer off, and I see that Harvey, one of my other Army brothers who works at the firm, is calling me.

"What the fuck, man? It's three in the damn morning," I whisper in annoyance into the receiver.

"Jesus, man, sorry to wake you, but it's urgent."

I huff because I don't have it in me to hear more urgent news. "What now?"

"The building of Hanson Holdings has a security camera that caught footage of the man we're after. He entered the building shortly after five when all of the employees were gone to kidnap Charles."

The hair on my skin stands straight up at the information. Typically, it's nothing this useful, but for once, I'm intrigued with what Harvey and the guys found. God, it kills me to be playing protector instead of doing what I do best, which is hunting down the bastards.

"Any leads on who it is?"

"It's hard to make out the face from the angle of the outside camera, but we're searching through the tapes of the cameras inside. All we can get from it is that it's a white male, probably around the age of fifty."

"Tall?"

"Average."

With how big the Hanson Holdings building is, they're sure to get another lead from a different camera in that place.

"Are you sure it's him?"

I know if I were with Harvey face-to-face, he'd be nodding at me. "Yeah. There's more footage from the camera in the back of him carrying Charles out."

"Anyone else with him?"

"Just another man helping him load Charles in a van."

This feels like something out of a horribly scripted crime movie I've seen before. It's one of the amateur kidnapping scenes I've heard of, and if we or the police don't catch this bastard, then we all need to resign from our jobs. What I really don't fucking understand is how Charles' own private security let this guy have direct access to Charles with no issue. Something isn't adding up.

"Has there been any updates on Charles' condition? Any monetary demands?"

"Not yet," Harvey says. "They will probably come soon, though."

I've stopped walking in my apartment, pausing in front of my windows that overlook the street I'm on. New York is such a massive fucking city that there's so much ground to cover in this mess. There's so many loopholes and twisted schemes that go on in this city with men like Charles that it's sometimes too complicated to crack. But knowing this situation, there will be something that pops up soon. Criminals are idiots and are always making mistakes.

"How's Blaire holding up?" Harvey asks.

Hearing her name causes me to turn around in the direction of my room as if she's standing behind me. Harvey's question gives me a feeling of power in the sense that I'm the one that's keeping her safe. *I'm* the one who's watching over her and making sure nothing bad happens to her like it has her father, and I'd say I've done a great job. Not only that, but I get to be with her and witness her every second. It makes me feel special in a weird way.

"As good as she can be in this mess," I tell him.

"We'll call you if we find anything else."

"I'll stop by the office tomorrow in case you boys need any help."

Harvey scoffs. "Yeah, because we've got so much fucking ground to cover."

There's stirring behind me, and I turn to see Blaire looking at me with sleepy eyes. She rubs her barely open eyelids and eyes me skeptically in a way that makes her look so cute in her just-woken state.

"I gotta go," I tell Harvey, keeping my eyes on Blaire. I hang up the phone and slide it back in my pocket, turning fully to face her. "What are you doing up?"

"I can ask you the same question." Her voice is laced with exhaustion.

"Let's go back to bed."

"Who were you on the phone with? Have they found my father?"

I sigh and shake my head. "No. I'm sorry."

"Any leads?"

The decision to tell Blaire about the security footage rattles in my mind. It's information I haven't verified myself and the last thing I want is to give Blaire any ounce of false hope. Deciding not to tell her about the footage of her father being shoved into the back of a van, I shake my head.

"Sorry."

Disappointment flashes on her face, and Blaire's shoulders sink. Her lips quiver, and I quickly stride over to her in an attempt to keep her from crying.

"Let's go back to bed. I was sleeping really well. I only came out to turn the lights off."

Blaire nods her head, and I follow behind her as we walk back to the bedroom. I close the door behind us and climb in on my side to resume our previous position, with Blaire nestled up to me. She doesn't hesitate to slide over to me, and I smile as I hold her. Something tells me that Blaire isn't going back to sleep immediately, and when I hear her voice pierce the silence a few seconds later, I know she's going to be awake for a little while.

"Have you ever had someone close to you die?"

Her question catches me off guard, and I still in the bed. I'm not thrown off by the question—I'm thrown off by what to say. Have I ever had someone close to me die? Yes. Eighteen months ago. Was it my fault, and do I live with the guilt of it every day? Yes. And it hurts like hell. It's why I can't look at Blaire as anything else other than a work mission or lay.

I take a deep breath and keep my response surface level. "Yes."

"Who was it?"

"I don't want to talk about it."

I'm hoping the assertiveness in my voice is enough to stop her, but Blaire lifts herself on my chest to look at me. I can see her searching my eyes for an answer.

"Who was it?" she asks again.

I look away. "Go to sleep, Blaire."

I feel Blaire's eyes linger on me before she slowly sinks back down onto the bed, this time off me. She rolls over onto her side facing the opposite direction, and I know I've upset her. A part of me feels guilty for doing so at the moment since she's facing the potential loss of her only surviving parent, so I offer some semi-encouraging words.

"Your father isn't going to die."

Blaire rolls back over. "What?"

"He's not going to die. More than likely, he was kidnapped for money. Whoever is pulling the strings and took your father, they just want his money in return. Keeping him alive is the only way to get it."

Blaire's eyes narrow at me. "What makes you think they won't just kill him?"

"Because what would they have left for leverage?"

"Me."

I scoff. "They aren't going to take you."

"Why not?"

I open my eyes and look at her. "Because if they wanted to, they would have by now, and if you think anyone is going to take you on my watch, then you must really underestimate me."

Blaire's mouth hangs open slightly. I can see that my words have calmed her just a little bit, and I close my eyes once again. "You have nothing to worry about, Blaire. We're going to find your father."

Blaire's head falls back on the pillow a few seconds later, and she's quiet for the rest of the night—well, morning. Even though it doesn't take her long to fall back asleep, I lie awake for another hour, thinking over her question, until my eyes close and I start to relive my real-life nightmare all over again.

EIGHTEEN MONTHS AGO...

On the rare occasion that I venture into town, I can always count on returning to the house and seeing Miranda on the swing I bought her, sipping a glass of tea. It's always a sight to see with her hair flowing in the wind and her eyes soaking in the views of the field near the house, and sometimes, she's even reading a book. Whatever she's doing, she looks absolutely breathtaking doing it, and every time I come home, she makes me want to go back out just to come back and see her all over again.

Miranda Shiplay was the woman of my dreams I didn't know I needed, and when I came home to see her not sitting on the swing, I knew immediately something was wrong.

I had known something was wrong the whole day, even the second my eyes opened in the morning. Miranda stirred next to me in bed. Her eyes slowly blinked open not too long after me, and she could see the worry on my face. The way Miranda and I were, we knew each other like the backs of our hands. I knew when something was bothering her when she did her best to hide it, just like she did with me. She proved it this morning.

"What's wrong, Jimmy?" she asks, her voice gentle with morning sleepiness.

I'm staring at the ceiling, trying to decipher the weird feeling that's settling in my stomach and telling me today is not going to be a good day.

"I don't know," I tell her. "I have this weird feeling in my stomach."

"You might be hungry. Let me go make you some breakfast."

I reach out to stop her from already trying to get out of bed. That was one of the many reasons why I fell in love with her—she's gentle and selfless, always wanting to take care of others before herself.

"No, it's not that," I say, gently pulling her next to me. For some reason, I need to feel her touch. I need to feel her beating heart against my chest and to feel her warm skin to know she's still alive.

"Jimmy, what is the matter?"

I can hear the worry and concern in her voice as I hold her naked body against mine. Our skin-to-skin contact leaves me feeling refreshed and charged for the day. The feel of her soft body always sends a wave of electricity through my veins like it's doing now.

"I don't know. I just... Something feels off, like today isn't going to be a good day."

Miranda chuckles, and I know she thinks I'm being ridiculous right now. "Are you psychic or something?"

I don't laugh at her attempt to be funny because the way I'm feeling right now really has me on edge. There's a pop from the kitchen I hear through our closed bedroom door that has me shooting out of the bed and swiftly reaching for the gun under my pillow. I hold it up to the door as if I were aiming at someone, and Miranda pulls the sheets to her body as she sits in bed.

"Jimmy! Calm down. That was the ice machine. It does that from time to time."

I dismiss her words as I creep to the door before yanking it open. I do a quick check of the one-story house to make myself feel better, and I feel relieved when I discover that it was, in fact, the ice machine that made that noise. With one last lingering glance from the window, I check the outside areas and walk back to the bedroom where Miranda is out of bed and sliding on her yoga pants.

"All clear," I say.

She huffs. "Told you. You need to take a Xanax."

I walk over to her and wrap her in my arms. "What I need is for you to be safe. I can't take any chances on missing something and you getting hurt."

Miranda smiles and wraps her arms around my back. "I'm fine, Jimmy. You're here protecting me. I'm not going anywhere."

"Good, because I can't lose you. I don't want to lose you."

It must be the urgency in my tone that causes her to search my face with worry. The way she watches me tells me she's wondering why I'm so on edge this morning.

"You're not going to lose me, Jimmy. I promise."

I lean into her to plant my lips on her in one of the most passionate kisses I can muster. Every kiss between us feels passionate and full of love, but this morning, I want her to feel it. I want to let her know how much I value her and love her with the way I kiss her and hold the back of her head, something she loves. When I pull away, I rest my forehead against hers and smile.

"I think I'll make some coffee," I say.

One of Miranda's and my favorite ways to spend the mornings is on the swing with our morning coffee. We usually start and end the days out there on that swing.

"Sounds wonderful. I'll make pancakes."

Miranda and I walk to the kitchen where I notice her recent book —the new Nicholas Sparks one—sits on the counter, her bookmark peeking out. I don't like to read, but I love seeing Miranda's excitement over the great book she's reading at the time, so I always make it a point to ask her about her books.

"How's the new Sparks book?" I ask, opening the cabinet to pull out the coffee filters.

"Oh my gosh, it's amazing! I love the characters in this book. It's unlike anything he's written before. This one is like a mystery thriller compared to all of his other sappy romances, and I—what's wrong?"

Miranda pauses when she sees me looking in the fridge with a disapproving glance. I search the holders and the drawers and move things in the fridge before checking the cabinets one more time. "We're out of coffee," I say. "I could have sworn I picked up another bag."

Miranda shrugs and pours a scoop of pancake powder in a bowl. "Run to the store really quick."

I shoot her a look. "You know I don't like to leave you here alone."

"Jimmy, I'll be fine. It's seven in the morning. The worst that could happen to me is dying from a lack of caffeine."

I shake my head. "Not happening."

"Jimmy, go. You're letting that weird feeling get to you."

"I told you I woke up feeling like today wasn't going to be a good day, and I'm not going to risk the chance."

"You are seriously overdramatic sometimes."

"That's okay. I'd rather be overdramatic than not cautious enough and have something happen to you."

"Nothing is going to happen to me! Jimmy, go to the store, pick up a bag of coffee, and come home. It's a simple task that will take you twenty minutes, max."

"That's twenty minutes where something could happen and I wouldn't be here. Just come with me."

Miranda stops stirring the pancake dough to give me a glance. "I'll keep my phone on me. Please, I really want some coffee."

Because she knows how to get to me, Miranda pushes her lips out to look as if she's pouting. It's a look she knows always works, and because I love her so damn much, I always cave. Even if I don't want to. I push aside the feeling inside of me screaming to stay home so I can go get the woman I love her coffee.

"Fine," I muster, swiping my truck keys off the counter. "You need to look outside every two minutes. The gun is in your drawer by your nightstand and the safe—"

"Safety is off in case I need it. I know." She smiles.

My eyes linger on her. Even in the morning with no makeup on, the woman looks like an angel. A smile spreads across my face.

"I love you so damn much," I tell her.

"And I love you so damn much too."

Miranda lifts onto her toes to kiss me, and I breathe in her scent before walking to the door, resisting the urge inside of me to not go. We can survive without coffee.

With my hand on the knob, I turn to look at her one more time. Miranda stands in the same spot in the kitchen with a smile and waves at me as I step outside of the door, not knowing that that would be the last time I see her alive.

14

BLAIRE

I'm jolted out of my sleep by loud screaming coming from Jimmy's side of the bed. At first, I don't recognize that I'm in his apartment with him. I had completely forgotten that we had come back to his apartment yesterday after leaving the airport to get away from the paparazzi, but as soon as I hear his voice next to me, it all comes rushing back.

"Miranda! Miranda!" he screams.

Jimmy is thrashing around in the bed with his eyes closed while he groans and wails, screaming the name Miranda. I act quickly and start to shake him.

"Jimmy! Jimmy! Wake up!"

"Miranda! Miranda!"

"Jimmy!"

I continue to shake him hard until I'm practically pushing his body from one side to the other. Jimmy groans once more until his eyes dart open and he pushes me off him, lunging out of the bed. Jimmy stands at the edge of the bed, gasping for air as he watches me with wild eyes. He's drenched in sweat, and the most horrified look is on his face. I don't know if I should be worried or glad that he's awake.

"Oh my God... Blaire... What was I—what happened?"

His hands lift to fist his thick dark hair, and I take a moment to make sure I've regained my own breathing.

"You had a nightmare," I say breathlessly.

Jimmy's eyes travel to the bed as if he's trying to piece together what happened. A million questions are now swarming in my mind, and I'm not sure when the right time is to ask them. I don't even know what time it is right now, so I reach for my phone on the floor by my side of the bed and see that it's almost seven in the morning. Makes sense. The sun is starting to rise enough to cast a pinkish glow over the city.

My eyes flash back to Jimmy, who's staring at the bed with an unreadable expression.

"Jimmy, are you okay?" I ask.

He doesn't say anything.

"Jimmy."

The second time I say his name with more force, and he looks in my direction. He lets out a deep breath and runs his hands over his face. "Yeah, I'm good."

After this morning's events, I'm no longer sleepy. I did get a decent amount of sleep, so I guess it's time to get up and try to start the day.

"Do you have any coffee?" I ask.

Jimmy shakes his head. "I don't even have a coffee maker. Usually, I get some on my way to work. There's a place down the block."

"Do they deliver?"

Jimmy gives me a look. I take that as a no and pull out my phone to DoorDash us some breakfast.

"What are you doing?"

"Ordering some breakfast," I say. I place the order and look at him from my side of the bed. "It'll be here in twenty minutes. Enough time for you to go take a shower because... you need it."

I walk out of the room to go find my bag with my own change of clothes and toiletries while Jimmy turns on the bathroom light and closes the door. Moments later, I hear the shower running, and for a split second, I picture Jimmy naked in there. It's not a horrible thought—Jimmy naked *is* a gorgeous sight—but it makes me wonder if he did the same thing when we were in Miami. Did he picture me naked when I was in the shower? I shake my head to get the question out of my mind as I start to sift through my belongings for what I want to wear today. I was supposed to be back at the office and operating on a normal schedule, but I know all of that will be altered now since my father isn't here. Someone is going to have to give an emergency press conference and update the company, and lo and behold, I know that falls onto my shoulders. I used to dream of the day where I would be the one leading the company and giving the speeches at the televised press conferences. I just never wanted it to be under these circumstances.

I am picking out my outfit for the day when my cell phone starts to ring. I check the caller ID and see that it's our PR rep, Jessica.

"Jess? Hi," I answer in a rush. Every phone call from the office right now is of the utmost concern to me. I can hear it in Jessica's voice, too, that things are just as important to her.

"Oh my God, Blaire! How are you? I wanted to call sooner but tried to wait as long as I could before bombarding you."

"You're fine. I'm... as good as I can be. Everything okay?"

"We need you to come in ASAP. Hanson Holdings' lawyer is here and has important matters to discuss with you."

I'm on my feet before she can finish that sentence. The feeling of urgency that is coursing through me right now is unmatched. Thank God for dry shampoo on days like this when I need to skip the shower. Speaking of showers, I hear the water turn off and the door to the bathroom open as I say, "On my way. Be there soon," and hang up the call. I don't have to look at Jimmy to know that he's staring me down right now.

"And where do you think you're going?" he asks.

When I turn, all trains of thought I had vanish at the sight of Jimmy's lower half wrapped in a towel. His wet chest glistens with trails of water droplets his towel didn't catch, and his hair is tousled from his hands running through it. I know I'm standing here like a gaping creep, but damn, he's sexy.

"Um... Uh... I have to get to the office like now."

I storm by him to go to the bathroom to get ready. There's a knock on the door, and I know it's the breakfast I ordered, so I rush back to my bag to grab a twenty and shove it in the delivery boy's face. I take our bags and tray of coffees and set them on the table before scurrying to get ready.

We make it to the office in thirty minutes and enter around back to avoid the press that has gathered like hawks in front of the building. I slide on a dark pair of sunglasses to further hide my face and keep my hair in a high bun until we're in the building. Jimmy walks briskly next to me and stays by my side the whole ride up to our floor and into the office where I meet Jessica and Stephen, our lawyer. The office is abuzz with more security detail than usual and several men and women in dark suits with notepads in their hands. I make a mental note to ask Jimmy who they are.

When Jessica sees me, she envelops me in a sympathetic hug. I know she's trying to be nice, but I can already tell that I'm not going to like the pity I'm going to be getting from everyone. I just want my father back.

"They're going to find him soon," she says with a sympathetic smile.

I smile back at her as I follow them to the boardroom, anxious to hear what they have to say. For now, I am going to be making the company's decisions.

We enter the massive room and take our seats at the big oak table in the center. Jessica sits at the end with Stephen across from me and Jimmy at my side. The whole time, my stomach rumbles with nerves.

Stephen's hands clasp together, and he looks at me with sad eyes as I wait to hear what he has to say.

"First off," he starts, holding my gaze, "I want to convey our condolences for your missing father—"

Whatever he says next, I tune out because I want to scream. If this whole meeting is going to be a pity party for me, then I'll just leave now. Jimmy must sense me tensing next to him because I feel his hand plant on my knee. His touch nearly makes me jump.

"Thanks," I say flatly. I shoot my eyes to Jessica.

Jessica clears her throat. "So, Blaire, we know that your father has left requests for you to be the person to take over the company in his... *absence*, and Stephen here has some regulations he needs to discuss with you."

I sit up straighter in my seat. My father has prepared me for this moment for years during the time I've worked for him, but I can't help but feel incredibly ill-prepared.

Stephen shifts in his seat and opens up a manila folder where I instantly recognize the company's logo plastered on the sheets and the words titled COMPANY NAME TRANSFER in all caps.

"Miss Hanson, as per your father's request that Mrs. Hennings here just discussed, you will be the individual responsible for Hanson Holdings once your name is transferred. However, there is a stipulation."

My stomach sinks. "What's the stipulation?"

I watch as Jessica and Stephen exchange glances, and it's in that moment that I feel as if I'm being ganged up on. Have these two already discussed this among themselves without me?

"In order to transfer the company over to you, you must be married."

I feel all the air in the room vanish as my mouth gapes open.

Did I just hear him right?

"I have to be *married*?"

Stephen nods his head.

"Why? How is that the stipulation in this predicament? My father wasn't married, and he owned the company."

I'm unaware that I stood up out of my chair until I feel Jimmy's hand on my elbow, tugging me to sit back down. What I said was a valid point, though. My father was unmarried after my mother died and still owned the company, so why should I be married to own it? I'm not sure this was a stipulation my father made so I ask to see the document. There it is; his signature is on it at the bottom of the page. There has got to be some kind of mistake.

"This can't be—it's so... weirdly archaic and sexist." I'm pissed; my father and I have never discussed this. Sure we've had our fights about my future, mostly him telling me that as an only child, I needed to produce children so they could run the family business someday. I never thought he was this serious about it.

"Blaire," Jess says sweetly, "in order for you to own the company and have the power of attorney, you need to be married. If you don't comply with the rules, then you'll have no say in the company's future endeavors and it defaults to the board."

I crumple back into my seat, defeated. Getting married is a big responsibility in itself, one that I wasn't even considering for myself at all in my life, so how am I supposed to get married in a hurry for the sake of the company? *Who* am I even going to marry?

There's stirring in the seat next to mine, and my head swivels to look at Jimmy. He's glancing down at his finger and picking at his cuticles in the most nonchalant manner. It makes me wonder if he's heard any of this conversation. I have an idea, one that I know won't go over well... one I'm not even sure about yet, but what the hell.

"Can you give me a minute, please?" I ask them.

Jessica and Stephen hesitate for just a brief moment before nodding and exiting the room. I wait for the door to close before turning to Jimmy. He keeps his head down, looking at his fingers in his lap.

"Whatever idea is running through your mind, the answer is no."

"Did you hear what they said?"

"Yes. I heard them loud and clear, and I knew you'd do this. The answer is *no*."

"But Jimmy, I need this. It's not like I want this to be a thing either. I don't want to marry you."

"Good. We're on the same page. No."

I feel my eyes starting to sting with tears. Apart from not being used to the word no, I'm not okay with the way he's so quick to dismiss my needs.

"Jimmy, please, don't dismiss this so quickly. I think this is the work of someone on the board."

This gets his attention.

Jimmy's head snaps to me. His eyes are serious as he studies me a moment. "Why?"

"Because they know of my father's assets and stake in this company. He's the majority shareholder so whoever has his power, controls the company. They're trying to find their way to his money, and they know since I'm not married and don't have children, if he's out of the way I don't have a leg to stand on and they win. You're already with me every day, and as soon as this mess is all over, we'll get our marriage annulled. Just, please, Jimmy. Please... marry me just for the sake of my father's company."

I never thought this situation would reach a point so low to where I'd be begging for Jimmy Maxwell to marry me. I sit beside him, feeling as if the fate of my life rests in his hands, and I study his face while he ponders my plea.

"I want a negotiator," he says. "If it's really someone on the board, let's try to talk them down."

I feel like sinking lower in my seat at Jimmy's words. He doesn't have to say anything else for me to know the thought of marrying is disgusting to him and a part of me hurts at the realization of that.

"Jimmy... come on. Do this for me. Please?"

This time it doesn't take him long to ponder it. Jimmy thinks to himself for a few seconds and scratches his chin with his fingers before nodding his head.

"Fine. Let's get married."

A wide smile spreads across my lips, and I feel as if a weight has just been lifted off my shoulders. I know that with Jimmy by side as my husband and business partner, we'll be able to crack down on this situation.

Jimmy shifts in his seat and offers me a boyish grin. "Only if we get to consummate the marriage later."

I scowl at his sly smile. "Then we can't annul it, so that's off the table." I wave Jessica and Stephen back in. They walk to the table with anxious smiles and sit down with both their eyes on me, awaiting my decision.

"Well," I say, holding up my left hand playfully, "I'm engaged to be married."

15

JIMMY

"You're *what?*"

Luka nearly spits his beer out after I tell him and the boys what went down in the Hanson Holdings office today, including the news of my upcoming wedding to Blaire. This is the first time I've been separated from Blaire, but I keep her tracker sitting on the table. Plus, she's in the building next to us. I made Blaire promise to stay in my apartment after we got back from our meeting while I went to the bar to meet up with my Army brothers. It's a big risk leaving Blaire alone, especially now that her father has been taken, but I'm confident in the two FBI guys standing outside my building. Plus, with these four guys with me, we could easily get to her before the fuckers leave the apartment.

Alex and Harvey exchange glances across from me at the high-top we're sitting at.

"You're kidding, right?" Harvey asks with a chuckle.

I knew it would be hard for the guys to comprehend at first what's going on. To them, it's ironic that I've agreed to marry the woman they saw rip my ass a new one when she was drunk out of her mind at Murphy's.

I take another sip of my beer and sigh. "Sadly not."

Luka chuckles beside me and runs his fingers through his blond hair. I knew he'd be the one that would find the most enjoyment out of all of this.

"You are in some deep shit, man," he says.

I scoff. "Yeah, but it's all for her father and the company."

It's what I keep telling myself since the meeting this morning. It's my way of justifying this situation. This isn't out of love or any mutual feelings between Blaire and me, obviously. It's for her own good, and the quicker everything is over, the better it'll be for me, and that all starts with finding Blaire's father and the fucker responsible for all of this.

But damn... the thought of marrying Blaire is comical.

"Oh, yeah, sure," Alex says in an annoying voice, wiggling his eyebrows at me. "Just for the company and Blaire's *father*."

I narrow my eyes at him. "What are you saying?" I ask, cocking an eyebrow.

Alex shrugs innocently.

"Come on, man," Harvey chimes in. "Don't act like there isn't anything going on between you and Blaire."

"There isn't." My response is quick and flat.

I can tell the guys aren't buying it.

"You mean to tell me that after all this time you two have spent together—literally spending every fucking second together—there isn't anything going on? Yeah, okay."

I glare at Harvey before turning my attention to Luka.

"I second that," he says.

I shake my head at them and try to tune them out. I know they're just giving me shit for what happened and the fact that we *are* spending every waking moment together, but that doesn't mean there has to be feelings involved. The only feelings that are involved are purely carnal and sexual, and they're going to stay that way.

"Think what you want." I shrug, swallowing the last long swig of my beer. I pull out my wallet and toss a few bills onto the counter.

I start to head to the door when Luka stops me.

"We're just playing with you, man. We know you can't stand the bitch."

I don't know why, but hearing Luka call Blaire a bitch makes something snap inside of me. I spin on my heel and narrow my eyes at him, causing him to narrow his at me in confusion. My pointer finger lifts in the air to point directly at him, and I feel my body growing tense.

"Don't call her that," I threaten in a hard voice.

"Jimmy, *you've* called her that," Alex points out.

All three of the guys are looking at me with raised eyebrows, and I sink back on my feet. What in the world has come over me?

"Whatever," I say, doing my best to shake off whatever this is. "I gotta go."

I quickly leave the small bar, ignoring their sly remarks, and walk across the street to my apartment building. What in the world has come over me, and why did I react so strongly to Luka calling Blaire a bitch? This day has been too fucking weird.

I nod at the agents, both giving me the all-clear signal before I step into my building. I make it up the elevator in my apartment building and to the door where I can hear some muffled music coming from inside.

What the—? Opening the door, I'm instantly hit with the most delicious fragrant aroma. Blaire is standing by the stove, stirring a pot of something, and I see the packages and spices she's used, including the empty jar of tomato sauce.

"Damn. If I would have known marrying you would get me home-cooked meals every night, I would've proposed a lot sooner."

Blaire shoots me a look from the stove, and I close the door behind me.

"Spaghetti again?" I ask. She shakes her head.

"Chicken parmesan."

"Well, it smells fantastic."

This gets her to smile.

"Just wait until you taste it," she says, opening the oven door and sliding in a tray of chicken to bake. "How were the guys?"

I freeze on my way to my room and turn around to face her. Blaire turns her head to me, and her eyebrows draw together once she registers the look on my face. "What?" she asks. I study her a moment.

Her question struck me funny. It sounded like the typical question a wife asks her husband when he returns home from work.

"Don't do that," I finally say.

"Don't do what? I just asked how it was seeing your friends?"

"Yeah, but that's... you know this marriage—whenever it's official —means nothing, and it's only temporary, right?"

I knew my words were harsh, but the hurt on Blaire's face she's quick to conceal proves it to be worse than I thought. She blinks rapidly and moves slowly as she turns her eyes back to the pot on the stove that's now boiling. I sort of feel bad for saying that now because I can tell I offended her more than I intended to. I sigh and rub my face before trying to offer her some sort of apology.

"Blaire, I'm sorry, I—"

"I heard you loud and clear, Jimmy," she snaps with her back to me.

Blaire opens the half-empty box of spaghetti noodles and breaks them in half before sliding them in the boiling pot. She keeps her back to me as she continues to stir the noodles and the sauce while pretending I'm not behind her.

My shoulders slump in defeat, and small bubbles of annoyance rise inside of me as I turn around and head to my room to shower and change before dinner.

The hot water of the shower soothes my skin. I stand under the downpour coming from my showerhead and extend my arms out to plant my palms on the walls to let the water roll down my body.

My eyes are closed, and I think of the stress I'm carrying that nobody knows about. Nobody knows how extremely hard it is to be in my situation right now, watching over this woman every second of every day to make sure she's safe, and now I have to marry her? We both know it's temporary, but what Blaire doesn't know is that I promised myself to never marry if it couldn't be with Miranda.

Miranda was supposed to be my one and only. Hell, she was the only woman to make me feel anything. The day I found her in the cabin wrecked me, and it was that very day that caused me to go through a type of pain I wasn't ready to battle.

A certain type of pain I'm still battling.

But what makes it all the more frustrating is that a small part of me enjoys being around Blaire every day. I take pride in being the one who watches over her and protects her. I like being the man she sleeps beside every night. I liked being the shield for her in the airport when the paparazzi wanted to bombard her after she received the news of her father's kidnapping and being the one she clung to. And now I like sharing a shower with her and seeing her shampoo and bath products next to mine in the shower rack.

I like Blaire Hanson, but I'm still in love with Miranda.

16

BLAIRE

You would think by the way I keep pacing the kitchen that I'm going insane. Maybe I am. So what? All I know is that if I stop pacing this floor right now, then I'm going to pick up one of these kitchen knives and walk in that bathroom where Jimmy is and do some damage to his manhood.

Never in my life have I met a man so cocky and arrogant and *rude*, and that's putting it lightly. I'm aware that this marriage isn't based on love, but it feels like every chance he gets, he has to rub it in my face that I'm nothing more than a hole for his dick.

A job.

An unwanted distraction.

I check the time on the oven for the chicken and jump at my text tone cutting through the air. It's Harper, responding to the text I sent her about her older brother being a gigantic ass.

Harper: *A nice, juicy gigantic ass? :)*

I roll my eyes at Harper and start to type my own response.

Me: *Okay, that's weird considering he's your brother. We need to talk later. There's something I have to tell you.*

The oven starts to go off at the same time I press send. Sliding my hands into oven mitts, I open the door to take out my beautifully crusted chicken and set the tray on one of the other pot holders Jimmy has in the apartment.

I heard the shower cut off a few minutes ago but haven't heard anything else from him. I don't wait for Jimmy as I start to prepare my own bowl of chicken parmesan and a glass of wine, which I had delivered with some more groceries. I tuck my phone underneath my arm and start to walk to the table to sit down to eat.

"Were you going to wait for me?"

I jump at Jimmy's voice. He waltzes into the kitchen with his wet hair and lounge clothes, which consists of gray sweatpants—*fuck me right*—and a white T-shirt. I have to practically force my eyes away from looking at his tan bulging biceps and the other delicious bulge a few inches south of his waist. I shovel a bite of food in my mouth to keep my mind on other thoughts and not this asshole I have to marry.

Jimmy makes his own bowl of food and joins me at the table.

"You don't have to sit here. I'm perfectly fine on my own," I tell him.

Jimmy flashes me a look that I match.

"I didn't mean what I said earlier," he starts before quickly adding, "I mean, I meant the part where I said it was temporary, but I didn't mean... I didn't mean what you thought it meant."

I can hear the sincerity in Jimmy's voice as he tries to find the right apology. It's cute watching him get flustered.

"It's fine," I say. "I mean, you were right. This marriage means absolutely nothing, and it's just temporary. Thank God."

My words are full of sass, and sure enough, he gives me a look.

"I'm trying to apologize here," he says.

I nod my head and purse my lips.

"And I'm trying to figure out what you have against me that makes you think being my fake husband is the worst thing in the world."

Jimmy falls silent and captures my eyes. I didn't mean for the question to fly out the way it did. The last thing I want is for Jimmy to get the impression that I'm happy about the marriage, even if it is fake, and tease me with it, but the comment he made earlier was uncalled for, whether he's happy about this or not.

We continue to lock eyes with each other for a couple more silent seconds. Jimmy blows out a deep breath and reaches an arm behind his head to scratch an itch.

"That's... not it, Blaire," he finally says, blowing out a deep breath.

I search his eyes. "Then what is it? I mean, I know we don't like each other, but you don't have to be an asshole to me all the time."

I'm not sure why Jimmy's comment bothers me so much. It's not the fact of what he said because even I can't think of anything worse than being married to him. It's the fact that he's so against me and said it in a hurtful way. I can't explain it.

Jimmy scoffs and twists some pasta onto his fork. "The same goes for you."

"Excuse me? What does that mean?"

"You know what it means, Blaire."

"No, I don't know what it means, so explain it."

Jimmy rolls his eyes, obviously annoyed at me, and sets his fork down.

"We argue. That's all we do. We don't get along; we can't stand each other. You're an asshole to me, and I'm an asshole to you. That's the dynamic of our relationship, and that's the way it'll always be."

If there is one thing I can say about Jimmy Maxwell, it's that he always stays consistent. I haven't known him for long, but he's proven to stay the same—frustrating and above all selfish. My appetite is no longer existent, thanks to the fumes that are scorching inside of me, and I narrow my eyes at him, standing up from the table.

"There you go, running off again like you do best," he mumbles loudly for me to hear.

I was on my way to the bedroom to get some work done on my computer when his comment stops me in my tracks. I spin slowly on my heel back in his direction, and his rigid back muscles flex underneath the thin fabric of his shirt.

"What did you just say?" I demand slowly.

"You heard me," he says through a mouthful of food.

"Well, I guess I learn from the best then, because you're really the expert at always running off, aren't you, Jimmy?"

I can tell my words have hit a nerve in him. The fork sitting between Jimmy's fingers falls into the bowl with a *clink*, and he slowly turns in the chair to face me with sinister eyes. There's something about seeing him so pissed off at something I said that I find satisfaction in.

"God, you are so..." He fails to find words.

"I'm so what? Finish that statement like a man, Jimmy. I'm so what?"

Jimmy flies out of his seat faster than I can blink. I can hear the legs of the chair slide against the hard floor before I register how fast he's moved to tower over me with his hard eyes piercing into me. His mint body wash wafts the air around us, and I find his intimidating presence striking me in a funny way.

"Maddening," he finishes in a low voice, inches away from me.

Our eyes are locked with each other's, and the tension between us is so thick, you could cut it with a knife. Being this close to Jimmy always results in the pull in my stomach I'm feeling right now, and my body reacts with a slight twitch to the thoughts I have of stretching up on my toes and kissing him.

"What are you going to do about it?" My voice is barely above a whisper.

Jimmy is towering over me and only inches away from my lips. I want him to kiss me. I want his tongue to mesh with mine and his arms to lead me into the bedroom where he can make me forget all about my troubles and worries. Because, for some reason, Jimmy Maxwell holds that power over me, and he's the only man that does.

My eyes study his, and I watch as they slowly skim down my face to stop on my lips. My heart rate begins to quicken, and I can see his light eyes turn dark with his thoughts, causing my breath to hitch. I'm ready for it, ready for however he wants to claim me in this moment, and my eyes start to close. I lean into him and press up on my toes to meet him when—

Everything in the room stops.

I quickly plant back on my heels, and my cheeks start to feel hot with embarrassment and the moment we were about to have.

We were saved by a ringtone.

It takes me a second to realize it's coming from my phone, which I left on the kitchen table. I storm to it quickly to get out from under Jimmy's intensity and pick up my phone to see Harper calling me. I scoff. If it's not Jimmy, it's his sister.

"Harper," I say in greeting, really for Jimmy to know who's called me. His eyes roll in annoyance when I say her name. "What's up?"

"Um, it sounds like *you're the one* who should be telling *me* what's up. Your text I just got? What is it that you have to tell me? You and my brother aren't expecting a love child now, are you?"

Now I roll my eyes at her.

"Oh, God, no. I just—" My eyes cut over to Jimmy who's watching me with a careful eye and plan my next words carefully. "Meet me at Murphy's in thirty minutes."

Jimmy gives me a glare.

"Murphy's?" Harper asks in disbelief. "Isn't that a good distance from Jimmy's apartment?"

"Yes, that's why I said thirty minutes," I say, walking past Jimmy to the bedroom to start getting ready. Harper blows out a deep gust of air.

"This better be good if I'm skipping Pilates for it."

"You'll be glad you came. Trust me."

"Yeah, you're right. I was probably going to skip Pilates anyway. My muscles have been sore lately. You know, I don't see how women do this every day, like I—"

I smile as Harper goes off on one of her many little rabbit trails. Sometimes, I still can't believe that she's related to Jimmy. There's such a stark contrast between the two of them. Harper is more flamboyant and talkative compared to Jimmy's quiet and standoffish nature.

I hang up with Harper after listening to her brief spill about Pilates, and Jimmy files into the room. I don't have to look at him to know the look he's giving me. I can feel it.

"Murphy's? Really?" he asks.

I continue to move around the room nonchalantly.

"It's important," I lie.

"Doubt it."

"Look." I slide in an earring. "Just go with me, drink a beer, relax, and let me have my girl time for a little bit before you have to start performing husband duties every night, like staying home with your wife."

I'm just teasing Jimmy, but I can't help but feel a small ounce of excitement at the upcoming fake marriage between us. I have to constantly remind myself of what Jimmy said, that it means absolutely nothing.

Jimmy's face doesn't give, and he leans against the doorframe with his arms folded across his chest, appearing to look tough. I reach into my suitcase for a going-out sweater and make a show out of pulling my shirt up my body and revealing the black bra I have on underneath. Jimmy tenses from across the room.

"And having sex every night," he adds.

I fight back my smile. "Not every married couple has sex every night. Have you read the studies? On average, married couples have sex one to two times a week, and that's pre-pregnancy."

I've never seen a man's eyes widen faster than Jimmy's did when I said the word "pregnancy." It makes me chuckle, and I slide my sweater over my head before pulling my hair out from under the collar.

"Don't say that word ever again," he says.

"Oh, come on, you don't want little Jimmys running around in the future?"

My voice is light, probably the lightest it's ever been, and it hits me that this is the first question I've asked Jimmy during this whole protection period where I've gotten to learn something about him, other than what makes him an ass. Jimmy's nose crinkles up as his eyebrows draw together, and he shakes his head.

"Absolutely not," he says with a voice full of disgust. "Never."

For some reason, this makes me sad. I try to picture Jimmy as a father with a little girl. I can see him being the kind of girl-dad who's tough as nails before children and then, when he meets his daughter for the first time, falls in love with her. The thought makes me smile, and I catch myself at the same time he does.

"Why are you smiling?" he asks.

"No reason." I shake my head.

"Don't get any bright ideas. The last thing I need is to pay child support once we divorce."

I chuckle and playfully swat at his chest. "Cute that you think you'd need to pay *me* child support."

"Do you want kids?" he asks.

I'm caught off guard at his question. I didn't expect to be asked that. Jimmy must notice because he adds, "You asked me, so I think it's fair that I ask you." There's the usual gleam in Jimmy's eyes as he looks at me.

"I used to like the thought of having children," I tell him, "but I think it's getting too late for me now."

Jimmy's eyes narrow slightly. "Explain."

I take a deep breath and sigh. "Well, I'm not getting any younger. I'm in my early thirties now, and you start becoming high risk for certain conditions I think once you reach the age of thirty-five."

"Then adopt."

I snicker at his response. "I don't think it works that easily. Plus, I kind of thought I'd be married by now, too, so that kind of puts a wrench in my plans. I don't want to be by myself taking care of a small human."

It's true. I think about these things constantly. Growing up, I used to dream of my wedding and having a family of my own, but some-where along the way, I lost sight of them. I let my job and success be the focal point of my life instead of family. It's why I hardly date as it is. That, and men are... *men*. Still, I can't believe I'm letting this spill so easily to Jimmy.

Speaking of Jimmy, he shifts on his feet and leans his body back against the wall.

"Well," he says, "I hear The Sims is still around."

I playfully roll my eyes at him and chuckle at his joke. Jimmy starts to chuckle, too, and there's something that shifts in the air between us, something different than the way things have been. It's almost enjoyable.

Jimmy and I both continue to chuckle until the realization of this moment hits us at the same time. Everything in the room starts to fall quiet, including us, and we're left standing inches apart and peering into each other's eyes. It's a sensual moment, completely different than the uncontrollable desire I've had before when I've wanted to shut him up and climb on top of him out of pure carnal desire for him. This moment is sweet, something that is way out of Jimmy's vocabulary when it comes to me, but I like it. Does Jimmy?

The small space between us grows smaller, and I find myself leaning into him, or is it him leaning into me? Whichever it is, the electricity of Jimmy is entirely palpable. My body tenses in the most glorious way when I think of him kissing me or touching me. The way his eyes focus on my lips makes my body burn with heat as the need to be satisfied by his gentle touch bubbles in my stomach. We're getting closer.

I close my eyes as I slowly lean into him until I reach him, completely aware that this one kiss is about to change everything between us. This kiss could force the words we can't bring ourselves to say out loud, the words we both know are there, the words that will reveal how we truly feel about this situation, and I'm completely ready for it.

Just a little bit more.

The final distance between my lips and Jimmy's starts to vanish the closer we get. I'm ready for this. I'm ready to tell him everything I'm thinking when I try to fall asleep at night beside him, that I'm falling for him. Because I am, and damn, it feels good to admit it.

It's funny, Jimmy and me. We go at each other's throats, hating being in the same room with each other, but I've never felt the way that I have these last few weeks with anyone else. There was something special about Jimmy that I noticed that night we went out months ago... before he was himself and showed his true colors. I couldn't place my finger on it, and for a little bit, I thought it was just his increasingly great looks and perfectly carved body. It took me until now to realize that there is something deeper there with him, and I'm on the cusp of figuring it out. I *want* to figure it out as bad as I want him. I can only hope he feels the same way.

I feel him getting closer. I can feel his steady breaths on my skin the closer I get to him when he whispers the words that completely shatter me.

"Maybe we should go."

What?

My eyes fly open, and I find him looking at me with gentle eyes. My feet plant back on the ground fast, and I can't help but feel completely embarrassed right now.

Did he not want to kiss me?

Did I completely misread him?

He and I are quiet, both of us trying to figure out what the hell just happened, especially me. I beeline past him to get out from underneath his eyes. The sting of rejection courses through me, and thank God my purse is on the kitchen counter where I left it after I tipped the grocery store delivery man earlier this afternoon. I grab it, then head to the door, slamming it on my way out.

I know Jimmy's behind me since he has to be, but right now, I need to be without him. I need my space as I try to navigate through my feelings and through the embarrassment of Jimmy Maxwell shooting me down right there in his apartment.

No matter what I think, things will never work out between Jimmy and me, and I don't know why I even entertained that possibility. He's proven himself time and time again to be just an ass that's not into me, so why do I even try?

It's a question I ask myself over and over as I make the small hike to Murphy's, where I find Harper smiling at me at a high-top when I walk through the door, a glass of red wine already waiting for me. She looks relaxed in her yoga leggings and one-shoulder top with her hair back in a loose ponytail. She embraces me in a hug when I approach the table, and I'm thankful to see it's just her and not Aspen and Juliette. Harper releases me, then looks for Jimmy.

"Where's my brother?" she asks when she doesn't see him.

I huff and take the seat across from her. "Give him a second. He'll be here."

"Uh-oh, are you guys *fighting*?"

I contemplate telling Harper the truth, that I'm falling for her brother who's obviously not falling for me, but I know Harper will take that information and run somewhere far with it.

"He's still being him," I say, taking a long swig of the wine.

Harper hums. "I know that can be infuriating."

You don't know the half of it.

The door to Murphy's opens, then Jimmy steps inside. Even in my mad and embarrassed state, I still feel my stomach churn at his attractiveness when I see him. I have to silently admire him from afar and act as if nothing's there while he quickly eyes me and then takes a seat at the bar. I feel Harper's eyes burning into me.

"Oh... my... *God*," she says. I grimace and turn around, avoiding her eyes.

"What?"

A knowing smile is spread on her lips. "You guys slept together again, didn't you?"

I nearly choke on my wine. She gasps.

"Oh my God, you *have*!"

"Stop," I tell her before she makes a scene. If there's one thing about Harper, it's that she can be very overdramatic. "There is nothing going on between Jimmy and me." I don't say that for her; I say that for me, and it's somewhat painful.

"Mm-hmm. Sure," she says with a smirk. "There's *nothing* going on between you two when you spend every waking moment together and sleep in the same bed every night... You do sleep in the same bed every night, right? Or does he sleep on the couch?"

Now is a bad time to tell her about the upcoming fake marriage between us. Harper is going to have a field day with that one, and now I regret telling her to meet me here in the first place. I've had enough of the Maxwells in a short span of time. Both of them.

"Harper," I start, trying to get her to see how serious I am. She's obviously enjoying this too much.

"I always knew he'd come around to you eventually." She shrugs, ignoring me. "I don't know what his deal was the first time you guys went out. Ever since he got back from his last mission, he's been different. I think it had to do with another woman who broke his heart." She snickers. "I didn't know he had a heart to begin with."

I feel uncomfortable listening to her saying this for several reasons, the first being there's nothing there being reciprocated on his end of the spectrum so all of my feelings for him are pointless. He's not *coming around to me* like she thinks. The second thing is that I don't really like picturing Jimmy and another woman. It's weird. I've never been the jealous type—I know my own worth and what I bring to the table—but I don't like thinking of Jimmy being with someone else who isn't me.

Wait a second...

My mind rewinds back to the other night when I woke up to Jimmy thrashing around in bed, screaming the name Miranda. I've never heard him speak of her, and I could tell getting him to talk about her in that moment was never going to happen. Does Harper know? My eyes shoot to her, and I see her looking around the bar without a clue what's running around in my mind. Come to think of it, I've never heard her mention Miranda's name either.

I glance behind me to find Jimmy at the bar. His back is to us and he's nursing a beer, way out of earshot. I take this opportunity to find out more about Harper's mysterious brother without making it seem to her that I'm interested in knowing.

"Has he been serious with another woman before?"

My question piques her interest. Her head snaps back around to me fast, and she studies me a second before thinking.

"I'm not sure. I'm sure you've noticed how closed off he is, and he's the same way with me. Always has been. Trying to get information out of Jimmy is like trying to pull blood from a turnip."

I nod my head in understanding. Jimmy Maxwell is a complete mystery, and I've just made it my new mission to solve it. It's a great distraction from the issue at hand with my father that is constantly running through my mind.

"So," Harper says, "enough of my idiot brother. What do you need to tell me so urgently?"

Harper loves some good gossip, and I can see how excited she is to hear what I have to say. Little does she know it has to do with Jimmy.

I take a deep breath and brace myself for what I'm about to share with her. She's going to lose focus on the reason why we're getting married and that it's not real, but the only reason I'm telling her is because she's my closest friend *and* Jimmy's sister. I don't think I'll ever be able to get over that.

"I have to tell you something, but you have to promise me you'll let me explain it before you freak out."

"Ooh. This is going to be juicy."

"I mean it, Harper."

She nods her head at my serious gaze and shifts in her seat. I lean in toward her over the table because my paranoia reminds me that even though Jimmy is far enough away, with his military ears he might still hear me. I'm not sure if he'd want me to tell Harper. I'm not even sure he's told anyone, not even the guys he works with.

"There's a lot going on with the company since my father was kidnapped. I can't really explain it all since it's confidential, but basically, I'm going to be the head of the company now—"

"Oh my God, Blaire!" she cuts in. "That's great!"

I snicker. "There's more. In order for me to take over the company... I have to be married."

Her eyebrows draw together. I don't say anything else for a little bit to see if she can put the pieces together on where this is going, but she doesn't.

"You have to be married? To run the company? Isn't there thousands of successful businesswomen in the world who are heads of companies who *aren't* married?"

"That's what I said, but that was the stipulation put forth in the contract by my father."

Harper blinks rapidly and shakes her head. "That is crazy. What are you going to do?"

"I'm going to get married."

Her mouth drops. "To *who*?"

I look at her without saying a word. She studies me for several moments before gasping, the realization hitting her. Her hands fly up to cup her mouth, and the shock on her face is quickly replaced with excitement.

"You're going to marry *Jimmy*? Shut up!"

Her excitement is starting to grow so I do my best to bring it back down. "Yes, but it's only temp—"

"You're going to be my *sister*! Oh my God! This is so great. I can't believe this. When is the wedding? Are you going to have a big one with a dress? Can I help you plan it? Are you guys going to go on a honeymoon? Can you even do that in your situation with your dad?"

This is exactly what I was afraid of happening—Harper's endless questions and pointless excitement.

My fingers start to rub gentle circles on my temples as questions continue to fire from Harper's mouth. It's best to just let her get it out, which is what I do for several more seconds before stopping her.

"Harper, listen to me. The wedding isn't real. It's just

temporary."

This puts a damper on her parade. Harper stops rejoicing and freezes in her seat to look at me funny.

"What?" she asks.

"It's just temporary," I repeat. "Jimmy is going to marry me so that I can be the head of the company, but once they find my father and things go back to normal, we're getting the marriage annulled. It's not a real marriage."

Her face completely falls.

"I don't mean this to be rude and to upset you, but what if... what if they *don't* find your father? What are you going to do then?"

I don't blame her for asking that question because it's one that I think of daily. It has been extremely hard knowing my father is out there somewhere, probably being tortured by whoever it is that took him, and the thought of not finding him alive kills me. I'm confident that my theory is valid—that this is the work of someone on the board and they're holding him just for money. It's the only way I'll be comforted until he is found.

I sigh deeply at Harper's question. "I'm still trying to figure that out."

I don't want this to turn into a solemn conversation even though I'm not sure it was going to be light to begin with, which is why I'm thankful for Harper's happy mood change.

"Well, I'm still going to enjoy the thought of you being my sister while it lasts." She smiles. "All I ask is that I can be there for the nuptials."

I force a smile at her because she wants one. We spend the rest of the evening talking about her life and random things until it's time to leave. The whole time I sit in front of her, I think of Jimmy. I try to keep my head in our conversation, but I'm too buried in my thoughts of him and the feelings I want to share with her, the feelings I have for her brother. It's hard to not turn around and look at him as he sits at the bar a few feet away.

It's also hard to not wonder who Miranda is.

17

JIMMY

I open my eyes and I'm sitting on the porch swing outside of the house I'm staying in with Miranda. It feels weird to see the sun shining so bright, overlooking the field that we used to picnic in. I had forgotten the vastness of this area and why I loved being here so much.

Seclusion.

Being secluded from others with Miranda was always the greatest part about protecting her. It was solely me doing the job. I treasured my time with Miranda, probably a lot more than she realized, and when the door to the house opens and she steps out, my heart leaps at the sight of her again. What is she doing here?

I'm about to ask her that question when she silences me by extending a glass of our usual iced tea. "This is my favorite part of the day," she says as she sits next to me on the swing.

Everything feels too familiar—the way the swing bounces when she sits down, the sound the ice makes as it rattles against the glass, the feeling of her head nestling softly in the crook of my neck, the hum she makes as she relaxes into me. God, I miss this. I miss her.

We sit on the swing for what feels like several minutes. I don't question the silence or overthink it because this is what we would do; we'd sit in silence and appreciate the time with each other.

"It's so beautiful out here, isn't it?" Miranda asks.

I smile at the question. She always says this every night we sit out here, and it's always then when I reach my arm around her and say, "Yeah, it is," but I can tell there's something else she wants to say tonight. I know her. I don't have to look at her to know something is bothering her or that she's lost in thought. I can feel it radiating off her, and I can hear the difference in her silence.

"Talk to me," I say.

Her head moves just a little to look up at me. She goes back to resting her head between my neck and shoulder.

"I'm not sure how," she replies.

"What do you mean? We've always been good at talking to each other."

Miranda tenses in my arm. "I know, Jimmy. But this is different."

"What do you mean?"

Miranda shifts out from me and sits facing me. My stomach instantly drops. It's been a while since I've seen her. Why do I get the feeling she's about to say something that will break me? I study the look in her eye and the smile that's barely there in the corners of her mouth. Miranda always had a way of being gentle in everything she did and everything she said. She could make the harshest insult in the world sound like a compliment, and I feel that's exactly what she's about to do to me.

"What is it?" I ask again, this time on edge.

She lightly snickers, and I feel her free hand gently hold mine.

"Why are you afraid of her?"

My eyes narrow. "Afraid of who?"

"Her," she repeats with a smile. "You know who I'm talking about."

I take a deep breath, and my eyes don't leave hers. I know exactly who she's talking about.

"How do you know?" I ask.

"Don't turn the question on me. Answer it. Why are you afraid of her, Jimmy?"

My eyes start to sting with tears. This is the first time I've talked to Miranda in months, and she wants to bring her up?

"Don't do this to me right now," I plead in a whisper. Miranda reaches out to gently cup my cheek.

"Jimmy, you need to learn to move on."

I shake my head in an attempt to get rid of the sting from her words.

"No. It hasn't been long enough."

"When will it be long enough? I'm never coming back."

"Stop this!"

I shoot up from the swing, sending it violently bouncing with Miranda still sitting in it and looking at me with soft eyes. This is the first time I've ever felt any kind of anger toward her in all the time I've known her. Why is she doing this to me?

"Jimmy, you need to face reality at some point."

"I face it every day, Miranda!" I shout, unaware of the tears that are falling down my cheeks. "I face it every day that you're not here."

"I'm never coming back," she repeats.

"I know, and it's all my fault. Stop reminding me."

"Stop saying that it's your fault." She stands to meet me with pleading eyes. "You did nothing wrong, Jimmy. You didn't know. I didn't know. Even if you were there, I'm not sure things would have turned out any different. You would probably be dead with me."

"That's better than being without you."

Miranda's head tilts, and she gives me a soft look. "Don't say that, Jimmy."

"It's the truth. A day hasn't gone by that I don't think how I'd be better off with you, or how stupid I was to leave you alone in that house."

"You mean this house?" She motions with her hands to the porch we're standing on.

"Why am I back here?" I whisper. I don't want to leave, but it's hard to *not imagine that day when my world completely shattered and she stopped breathing right on the other side of the very door I'm standing near now.*

"Because it's time we close this chapter. It's time you start healing and forgetting me, and it all starts with her."

I shake my head. "No, it doesn't. It absolutely doesn't."

"So you're going to live the rest of your life miserable? The rest of your life clinging to the past you can't change? There's nothing you can do to bring me back, Jimmy."

"I know this, Miranda. Stop saying it."

"Then move on. Why is it so hard to admit the feelings you have for her?"

I can't face Miranda when Blaire pops into my mind. I turn on my heel to walk away, to separate us as I mull over Miranda's words. I hear her feet behind me as she follows me down the steps.

"Don't push her out, Jimmy. Don't lose her over your pride."

My feet stop moving, and I spin around to face her. "Why are you so adamant about this? Why are you pushing me toward her?"

Miranda smiles softly. "Because I can see it in your eyes, the way you feel about her. What's stopping you? Why are you being so stubborn?"

"Because she's not you," I say, my voice cracking.

Miranda closes the gap between us and holds my gaze. It's then that I realize what the point of this whole conversation is. She's not getting me to admit my feelings for her. She's telling me goodbye.

I back away from her and Miranda grimaces.

"You're leaving," I point out. Her shoulders slump.

"I've already left."

I feel as if I'm reliving the past again. Images of the day I found her start to come back to me, and I fist my hair and close my eyes to find some way to block them out. My stomach twists in pain, and my heart hurts as I crumple to the ground.

"Please don't go," I beg her, crying. "Please don't go. I can't live without you."

Miranda bends down to me and places a hand on my back. I know no matter how much I beg her that she's still going to officially leave after today, after I open my eyes. I realize this is a dream, that I'm not really with Miranda, and I wish that I could stay here forever. Here is where nothing bad happens. Miranda is alive; I can feel her, and we could live as if nothing ever happened. Oh, how I wish I could just stay here.

The hand Miranda places on my back gently rubs me, and she hushes me sweetly. "It's time you let go," she whispers, "and start choosing her."

I can't be mad at Miranda because it's Miranda. My love and feelings for her will never vanish, no matter how hard I try, but I'll be damned if she thinks I'm going to wake up from this and be in love with another woman. Not if it isn't Miranda.

"Look at me, Jimmy," she whispers.

I'll do whatever she asks... except be in love with someone else, and I look at her through my blurry eyes full of tears and blink them away, so I can see her clearly for one last time.

"I love you," she says. "I've loved you since I first saw you, and I always will. I'm not asking you to completely forget about me. What we had was real and pure and intense. It's not something you can easily forget about overnight, but it will get easier in time. I promise. It was supposed to be us, Jimmy, and God, do I wish it was. It pains me more than you realize to know I'll never be the one with you in real life, the one that gets to love you in the way you should be loved. But I've seen the way you love, and I got to be a part of it for a short time. I'm okay with that. The last thing I want is for you to live a full life missing out on what is right in front of you because you can't let go of the things you can't change. It's time to start accepting the present to have a happy future. With her."

There's no winning this debate, especially when she's right. I know I need to start accepting that my future won't include Miranda in it, but that's a pill I'm not ready to swallow. It's only been eighteen months since she died. While this moment is hard, it's comforting to hear that she still loves me.

"What if I don't want her and I want to be alone?" I ask.

"You and I both know that is not true."

My stomach churns. Is she right? I haven't allowed myself to put much thought into my feelings for her. I try to dismiss them as much as I can.

"Let her help you heal, Jimmy."

I try to muster up the courage to agree. I'll do it because Miranda is asking, but deep down, I don't want to do that. Saying goodbye to Miranda feels like I'm ripping off thousands of Band-Aids at once. Death and loss are always painful, like millions and millions of Band-Aids that are being ripped from your body every second of every day. But it's time to rip the last one off, or the last bunch off, in my case. I have to do this because she's right. I do have to start moving on for myself. It's going to be painful, just like these last few months have been, but thankfully, I have the memories from when Miranda was alive to keep me afloat.

"Okay," I tell her, stealing a final glance at her.

Miranda smiles. It's not a warm smile, and it's not an excited one. It's a smile that doesn't reach her eyes.

She helps me stand from the ground, and feeling the skin of her palm electrifies me. I never thought I'd be able to see her or feel her ever again.

"Kiss me one last time," I beg her. I can see the timidity in her eyes.

"That's not a good idea," she says.

"One last kiss is all I'm asking. I can feel you. Let me have one more moment of what was robbed from me."

I don't have to convince her anymore. Miranda launches herself at me and gently kisses my lips, and it's more than I could have ever asked for. It's a sweet kiss goodbye, a tender one to help me move on, and while no one other than my Army brothers know about her, I love that I can say I was able to do this, to feel her kiss in my dreams as if it *were real, because I'm pretty sure I'm in an alternate world right now where I'm able to dream and still feel someone who is no longer living.*

I don't want this kiss to end, but I know it has to. I breathe her in one last time and let the scent of her comfort me as I relax, holding her. If this really is the last time I'll ever see her, it's a hell of a way to go.

Miranda pulls away from me slowly, and I feel my heart start to break all over again. Neither of us move, but gravity starts to pull us farther away from each other. I'm not ready. Tears start to sting my eyes again, and I take my final glimpses of her as the space between us starts to widen.

"I'll always love you, Jimmy. It's time for her to fill my place in your heart."

"I love you too," I tell her, not bothering to acknowledge the second part of what she said as she slowly starts to fade out of view and everything around me grows black.

I SHOOT UP IN BED, panting for air. My body is drenched in sweat, and it takes me a moment to realize that I'm in my room, the darkness of the night making the room difficult to see. My eyes adjust to my surroundings, and I look to the space next to me in bed where I see Blaire sleeping, her back to me.

What the fuck did I just dream?

It all felt too real with Miranda there and touching her, especially feeling her kiss me. It's like she never died. She's still alive but trapped in some other dimension.

I start to play the dream over in my mind from the way it all felt to everything that was said. It's painful when I think of Miranda, but it's a hell of a lot more vicious when I dream of talking to her and being with her. At least I don't have to go through that again, I hope. If that really was our goodbye, then it was a good one, one I'm satisfied with and can live with. But it'll never make the sting of losing her hurt any less.

My phone on the nightstand starts to ring. I lunge for it before the noise wakes Blaire, and I see that it's Luka calling me. I also see that it's four thirty in the morning. I guess I can go ahead and get up for the day. It's not like I'll do any sleeping after that dream.

I pull the charger out from my phone and hurry as quietly as I can out of the bedroom before taking Luka's call.

"This better be good for fucking four thirty in the morning," I tell him.

"Well, it sounds like you were already up," he says.

"Bad dream," I mumble, stumbling my way to the kitchen to brew some coffee.

"Listen," Luka says, "we have some news on Blaire's father."

This makes my ears perk up. I start to pray that whatever it is he has to tell me doesn't include the death of Charles Hanson. I'm not sure I can give Blaire the comfort she needs if she finds out her father has died.

"Go on," I tell him.

"He's still alive." Those three words have enough power to cause me to blow out the deep breath I didn't know I was holding in. Luka continues. "They're holding him for ransom. Said that if they don't get their money in forty-eight hours, it won't be pretty. My gut says they're more worried about gaining control of the company than the cash and it's just a distraction but I'm not willing to call their bluff."

"Have you found out who it is pulling the strings?"

"No, but we're closing in on 'em. Harvey thinks it's someone within the company."

"That's Blaire's theory too," I say, walking to stand near the front door. I'm sure Blaire is dead asleep, but I don't want to take a chance on her waking up and hearing anything that's being said right now.

"Keep an extra close eye on her today. Don't let her leave that apartment."

My stomach drops. "We were supposed to get married today."

It still feels funny saying that.

"Well, go another time," Luka says with a hint of frustration.

"Luka, we can't. We made this appointment last week."

"Find a way around it or make it snappy. We don't know what these fuckers have planned."

I groan in frustration, knowing he's right. It's been hard enough on Blaire to wait the two days before we can get in front of a judge, but this has to be legal. We can't just juke the system to make it look like we're married. It has to be done through the courts in order for the lawyers and board to release the company to Blaire. Of course, fate is playing things out for me like this.

The coffee finishes brewing, and I can smell its strong aroma. This woman has been in my house less than a week and she's already buying me appliances and nesting. My stomach starts to rumble, and I'm getting so damn frustrated between the dream I had last night of Miranda, Luka calling me and being pissy, and knowing that I'm getting married today that I feel like lashing out. Thankfully, Luka says he needs to go, and he quickly gets off the line.

I walk to the coffee pot and reach into the cabinet above it to pull out a mug. I pour some coffee in the cup and sit at the table to just think about everything. I've never been a man who lets stress control him. I've been in the midst of some of the most stressful situations during my time in the Army, but this is a new and different stress. This is stress that makes me feel as if I'm losing control of my life. I've never told anyone about Miranda and what I went through with her death. The boys don't know how deep things with her were, only that I met her on a mission. I purposely left out the part where I fell head over heels in love with her and was planning on proposing to her. Miranda is a touchy subject, and I've kept her to myself. I've learned that it's better that way.

Noise comes from the back hallway where my room is, and Blaire appears a few seconds later looking dead tired. Her eyes aren't even half open, and her blond hair is sitting on top of her head in a messy bun as she slowly trudges into the kitchen. She looks cute.

"Coffee is ready," I tell her, holding my mug up for her.

She groans and moves past me to the cabinet she knows the mugs are in to make her own cup.

I don't know what to say to Blaire. Granted, she's still in sleep mode, but all I can think about right now is the *her* Miranda kept bringing up. I know without a doubt that her is Blaire.

Blaire walks by, heading to the hallway with her mug in her hand, a little more alert now.

"Where are you going?" I ask her.

She keeps walking as she answers in a groggy voice, "Back to bed."

"You don't want to sit with your soon-to-be husband?" I tease.

Blaire stops moving. She doesn't turn around. I wonder how she's going to respond, and with every silent second that goes by, my stomach bubbles more.

She says nothing.

Blaire walks back to the bedroom like she wanted, and the door shuts behind her.

This is how it's been all week.

18

BLAIRE

I didn't talk to Jimmy the night after I tried to kiss him.

I was the one who decided the courthouse was the way to go with our marriage since it's not real in the first place and doesn't demand an actual wedding, so I called them one day on my lunch break to set the date for today after work. I did pick out a dress, nothing too fancy, and I set a reminder in my phone to bring my curling iron and makeup to work with me so I can touch up before we go.

It feels weird to know that when I go to sleep tonight, I'll legally be a wife. I won't be one in the literal sense, but I'll still be married to Jimmy Maxwell. God, this is odd.

There's still been no news about my father, and I'm starting to grow worried that I'll never see him again. It's hard to walk the office of the company he built with my mother and know that he's somewhere out there waiting for someone to find him. It's kept me up at night lately, except for last night when I was able to get some shut-eye.

I felt Jimmy thrash around in bed again and get up sometime in the night, which is why I woke up so early. I found him sitting at the kitchen table with a coffee mug in his hand and lost in deep thought before he saw me. I know whatever he dreamed about has affected him. I wonder if it was Miranda again. Since that night he woke up screaming her name, he hasn't spoken of her again. I feel bad for being nosy and wanting to know who she is, but if it affects him that much in his sleep, maybe she's worth talking about.

I bring a cup of coffee back to the bedroom where I am now scrolling through Pinterest on my laptop before it's time to get ready for work. I'm thankful for the extra time I have this morning to lounge around before going into the office, but the gentle knock on the bedroom door tells me that all of that is about to change.

Jimmy slowly opens the door and peeks his head in as if he's going to open the door on something wild.

"Can I come in?" he asks timidly.

I eye him suspiciously. "Sure. It's your room."

Jimmy walks in and leaves the door open. He sits down at the end of his side of the bed and puts one knee on the mattress before looking at me. I study his eyes for any indication of whatever it is he's about to say to me. My heart begins to race.

"You can't go to work today," he says. It's not at all what I was expecting.

"What?"

"It's not safe."

I study him to see if this is some kind of joke, and when I fail to see anything, my stomach drops.

"What is going on?" I ask. I feel as if I'm standing on the edge of a building, waiting for his news to push me off.

Jimmy sighs. "I got a call this morning about your father—"

"Is he alive?" I rush out, holding my breath until he answers.

"Yes, he is."

I instantly feel like crying.

"You can't repeat this to anyone. I mean it, Blaire. This stays between us," Jimmy says with a hard, serious tone. I shake my head and let him continue. "Your father is being held for ransom, and whoever it is behind this wants your father's money by tonight, or things are going to get ugly."

"I have access to all his money." I jump out of bed, unable to control myself or think straight right now. My body feels jittery, like I've consumed enough caffeine to jump start an elephant. "It's—it's in the house in the safe. And he has more in the bank. All of it. I can get to all of it. Just tell me how much they want."

"Whoa, whoa. Hold on, calm down," he says gently, getting off the bed to meet me where I'm standing. Jimmy reaches his hands out to steady my jittery body. "We're not giving them any money."

"*What?*" I jerk out of his touch. "They'll kill him!"

"No, they won't. Look, I do this for a living. I've seen this before. They don't want your father dead. They want what he has, and the only way to get it is by holding him."

"Then what are you going to do?" I ask, still not feeling comforted by any of this.

"We're working on it. Right now, you just need to call the office and tell them you're sick. Don't say anything else. Do you understand me?"

I nod my head at his instructions and fight back the tears wanting to break free. "Understood."

"Good. It's all going to be okay. I'm not going to let anything happen to you or your father."

I believe him. I feel completely protected with Jimmy, and I hate that my father can't say the same. I also hate that there's nothing I can do in this situation but wait. That's been the hardest part in all of this, waiting for things to calm down. My life has completely flipped in the last few weeks, and I'd give anything to get out of this mess right now. But I can't ignore the fact that I'm absolutely grateful that it's Jimmy here protecting me. I'm not sure I would have made it this far if it wasn't for him.

"What about the wedding?" I ask. "Can we still go to the courthouse?"

Jimmy blows out an unsteady breath and scratches the back of his head. "Yes. We'll just have to be quick."

"Why? Is it unsafe there too?"

"We'll be in a government building, so no, not entirely. But I want you home as much as possible until we figure out who these people are."

"Am I in danger?" It's a question I'm not sure I want the answer to but need to ask.

House arrest is coming. I can feel it.

"Not with me you aren't."

Jimmy's response nearly makes me melt. I completely trust that he'd do whatever it takes to keep me safe, and the way he looks at me as he says this further confirms that feeling. We never talked about the moment we had the other night, and I wonder if we ever will. I also wonder what he's thinking right now as he looks at me like this, like he's trying to tell me something with his eyes.

I nod back at him. "I should go call work."

I turn on my heel to reach for my phone, which is charging on the floor, and dial the office to speak with my assistant and let her know I'm not coming in today. I tell her that I'm sick with an intense migraine and need to take the day off, and once I hang up, I see that Jimmy has left the room.

━━━

I DO GET some work done today on my computer in Jimmy's apartment before it's time to go to the courthouse while Jimmy spends the day doing whatever it is he does in the living room, essentially giving each other space.

I shower later in the afternoon, closer to twelve, and start getting ready slowly. I dry, then curl my blond hair into loose waves before pinning one side back and slipping on the dress that I pulled from my closet before Miami. It's a simple white maxi dress with a sophisticated deep V-neckline that stops just below my breasts. There's a slit in the left side that stops slightly above mid-thigh that's perfect for showing off my tan legs. It's a casual dress that's still "formal enough" for a courthouse wedding, and I wonder if Jimmy will have any kind of reaction to seeing it, although I'm not counting on much. I put on my makeup and finish with my Chanel perfume before slipping on my heels and walking out of the room.

"I'm ready," I say as I enter the kitchen. I freeze once I see Jimmy.

My breath hitches, and all the air inside of me vanishes. When did he change? Jimmy leans against the counter, peering down at his phone, but the moment his eyes land on me, he freezes with the same reaction as me.

We stand a few feet apart, taking in how the other looks. I take a mental screenshot of the way he looks so casual yet so handsome in his white collared shirt tucked into his navy dress pants. And when did he trim his beard? I've never seen Jimmy look so cleaned up and rugged at the same time. I don't know how to act. I've always appreciated the way Jimmy looks and know that he's sexy enough to make me go wild, but this? This is too sensual, even for me.

I'm not blind to the way he's looking at me with the same wonder either.

Jimmy's eyes slowly rake my body from head to toe, then all the way back up again, and I feel my body heat under his appreciative gaze. Jimmy's jaw clenches when his eyes find mine again, and my cheeks start to redden as I blush, feeling empowered at the words he's conveying through his eyes alone.

"Do you like?" I ask quietly.

Jimmy nods his head. I expected a sly remark.

"I do," he responds.

I lightly snicker. "You're not supposed to say that yet."

Jimmy doesn't smile at my joke, but his features don't harden. It's almost as if he can't peel his eyes away from me, and his body softens. There's even a very light trace of a smile at the corner of his mouth. Never have I felt so truly seen by Jimmy.

"If you aren't going to tease me about this later," I start, "I like what I see too."

This gets him to crack a more appreciative smile, and he shrugs.

"What can I say? I clean up nice."

There's the typical Jimmy response.

Jimmy moves from the counter to walk toward me and extends his bent arm in my direction. "Ready to get married?" he asks.

"Depends. Where are you taking me for the honeymoon?"

"To a nice blissful place I like to call Poundtown."

My mouth drops open at his crude remark, and it sets Jimmy laughing.

"I'm sorry. That probably wasn't the right time for that joke," he says, trying to regain himself.

I playfully roll my eyes. "I thought you'd have a little bit of decency on our wedding day."

"You never know. I might have a surprise for you later this evening."

My head snaps in his direction as we walk down the hall to the elevator. Jimmy has a surprise for me? This news is shocking, and I can see he reads that on my face.

"What? You didn't think I'd take our fake wedding into consideration?" he asks as we step into the car.

"No, it's just... it's what you just said, a fake wedding."

"Yeah, but it's still a wedding. Still needs to be celebrated, even if it will be short-lived."

Something about him saying our wedding will be short-lived makes me sad, but I quickly dismiss it. We ride the elevator down to the bottom floor where I expect us to meet an Uber outside, but instead, I see a black BMW waiting by the curb. Jimmy motions to it, and I eye it skeptically.

"What is this?" I ask, knowing there's no way this is his car.

"Our ride. What do you think?"

"Yeah, right. Where's the Uber?"

"You really think low of me, don't you?"

I eye him. "Um, kind of. You don't own a BMW."

"For the night I do." He pulls out a pair of car keys from his pocket and jingles it in my face. My eyebrows draw together as I look at him. "One of my three surprises," he says as he opens the car door for me. I can't help but smile as I slide in.

"Three surprises?" I ask as he rounds the car and slips into the driver's seat.

Jimmy starts the car and checks the busy streets of New York before he pulls off to head toward the courthouse.

"Yeah. Three surprises."

"What are they?" I don't think I'll be able to stop smiling.

Jimmy flashes me a quick look. "I can't tell you. They're surprises."

"I hate surprises."

"Well, suck it up for a few more hours."

I sit back in the leather seat and enjoy the ride to the courthouse as Jimmy drives. He even pairs his phone to the car and plays us a wedding playlist that elicits a small giggle from me. I get to see Jimmy in a new light as we ride through New York, and I like this carefree and fun side of him—two words I never thought would fit his personality.

We get to the courthouse and park along the street before walking in. I'm sure everyone will be able to guess what's going on, and I duck my head so no one recognizes me on the street. Jimmy does his best to shield me as we successfully walk in the building to the floor where marriage licenses are handled. As we round the corner, I gasp when I see Harper standing there with a big smile on her face and a small bouquet of white roses in her hands.

"You look *gorgeous!*" she says and steps back to observe me from all angles. "I mean, you look more fantastic than I will at my real wedding."

I smile at her words. "Thank you. What are you doing here?"

Harper eyes her brother with a suspicious smile and a wiggle of her eyebrows. I feel Jimmy's hands on my shoulders as he leans into my ear and says, "Second surprise."

"I'm your witness," she says with a squeal and a little jump. "Here are your flowers. Because every bride deserves flowers on her wedding day."

I take the flowers from her and turn to Jimmy with a smile. He nudges for me to go through the double doors. "Let's make this thing official so we can get out of here."

"Do you guys have rings?" Harper asks as she grabs the door to yank it open.

"Harper, this is a fake wedding," I tell her, and she rolls her eyes at me.

The three of us file through the doors to the office where Jimmy and I will get married. The whole thing goes by in a flash. The judge rattles through the proceedings like a routine, and since this isn't my real wedding, I don't take offense to it. She has us hold hands and look into each other's eyes as we repeat the statements and vows, and the longer I stare into Jimmy's eyes, the more I feel as if I'm doing something real. I wonder what Jimmy is thinking.

Today will be the first time I've kissed Jimmy in what feels like a while. While the lady continues reading her script, I think back to last week when I tried to kiss him and he rejected me. Now he has to kiss me to make me officially his wife. I still can't believe I'm standing in a courthouse and marrying Jimmy Maxwell. Who would have known three months ago fate would decide to be funny?

"Alright, you two," the disinterested judge says. "You may kiss."

It's the moment I've been waiting for. I hadn't been nervous about anything until this part of the "wedding," and now my nerves start to act up as Jimmy leans in closer to me. I close my eyes as I wait for the soft impact of his lips that will seal the deal for however long time will allow.

Jimmy's lips softly collide with mine at the same time his hands cup my cheeks in the most gentle way. I softly moan into him, completely forgetting Harper and other people are in the room as I start to melt into my new fake husband. Jimmy's lips move to deepen the kiss in such a tender way, and damn if this isn't the sexiest, most sensual kiss I've ever experienced. I can feel it between my legs. I don't want this moment to stop as I enjoy the feeling coursing through me. Jimmy slowly breaks the kiss to look at me with soft eyes.

I feel like I can't breathe.

Something just passed through us, and I know he felt it too.

"Congratulations. Have a happy marriage. Exit the same way you came," the judge says.

Jimmy's hand reaches for mine as the three of us leave the room. I'm smiling from ear to ear as we walk down the stairs of the building, laughing. I feel as if I'm riding a high I don't want to come down from. I'm a married woman now. It's weird to wrap my head around but not near as weird as the fact that I'm *Jimmy's* wife. Even he doesn't look so bothered by it with the gigantic smile he's wearing.

"We should all celebrate," Harper says as we file down the stairs. "You guys up for drinks at Murphy's?"

She's looking at me, but my eyes shift to Jimmy. As odd as it sounds, I don't want to go to Murphy's with Harper. I want to spend time with Jimmy alone.

"Probably not, Harp. I need to get Blaire home. Safety purposes."

Jimmy's arm slides around my waist, and he gives me a slight squeeze that makes me stifle a smile. His words are true, but I can read the real truth behind him. Harper makes a disgusted face.

"Ew. Oh, God, I know what that means."

"You had no problem with it in the past," Jimmy teases her.

"Yeah, but now you're like... *married*. It's all too much."

Jimmy and I chuckle at Harper. We approach the doors to go outside. Jimmy halts us in the lobby.

"Thanks for coming today," he says to Harper. She gives us both smiles.

"I wanted to. I'm so excited to have you as my sister-in-law... even if it is temporary."

I force a smile, not wanting to remember the temporary nature of our arrangement. I want to keep this happy feeling going for a little bit, even if it is just for tonight. I remind myself it's all for my dad. I have to do everything I can to get him back.

Harper gives me a hug and heads for one of the side doors while the BMW comes into my view as we exit the front door. We hastily get into the vehicle and pull away to head back to Jimmy's apartment. The air between us feels different. Now I'm nervous.

"So, how does it feel to be married?" I ask him after a few seconds of silence.

He smiles. "Like I'm about to have the same candy bar for the rest of my life."

I playfully roll my eyes as he chuckles. "Can you just be sweet for one day?" I ask.

The second his eyes turn to me—even though it's brief—I feel my breath hitch. The sight of his emerald eyes glimmering in the sunlight mixed with the emotion of knowing that he's my husband is too much for me to bear, especially with the softness in his eyes.

"Don't underestimate me," he says.

Something inside of me tells me to believe him. I sit back in my seat and let the rest of the ride back to Jimmy's apartment take its course. In the silence, my mind drifts to my father and his situation. He's still out there somewhere, probably terrified, while I'm here trying to carry on life at the company without him. It feels strange and wrong for me to feel happy in this moment. It feels strange and wrong to feel happy at all.

Jimmy parks the BMW in front of his apartment and turns to me. I can feel his eyes watching me while my head is turned, facing out the window. Tears have swelled in my eyes from thinking of my father, and I blink rapidly to get rid of them so he doesn't see me cry.

"What's bothering you?" I hear him ask softly.

I take a deep breath, keeping my head facing out the window. "Nothing. Just... thinking of my father." I pause and turn to look at him. "How did you know something was bothering me?"

The left side of his lips curve upward in a soft smile. "I *am* your husband. Husbands are supposed to know their wives." He winks.

I smile softly but have no words to speak. If I open my mouth now, the dam will break. Thankfully, Jimmy opens his car door to get out, and I straighten in my seat. He comes around to my side to open the door, and I step out of the car to follow him inside. As we walk, Jimmy holds my hand with a tight grip, the feeling finding its way into my stomach, as if he's clenching me there too. Feeling Jimmy's strength does something to me I can't explain. When I'm with him, I feel as safe I can ever be. I wish he could have been protecting my father. Maybe if Jimmy were his bodyguard instead of mine, this would have never happened, and I would have never had to marry—

My train of thought freezes when the door opens to the apartment.

"Jimmy..." is all I can whisper.

I'm frozen in the doorway as my eyes scan the scene before me. The whole apartment is dimly lit by the candles scattered across the kitchen counter and table. There's the soft smell of vanilla and roses. I then spot the rose petals trailing from the kitchen to the back bedroom. It looks like a scene from a movie.

"What is this?" I ask, stepping farther into the apartment.

Jimmy closes the door behind him, and he stops walking a little bit behind me. I can feel his presence just behind my back.

"I told you I had a few surprises for you this evening."

I turn on my heel to face him. "When did you have the time to set this up?"

"I didn't." He softly smiles. "But don't worry about it. Just enjoy it."

Jimmy closes the small gap between us. His hands reach up to cup my cheeks as gently as he did in the courtroom, and his lips gracefully cover mine in a tender kiss. I inhale the scent of him—the scent of Jimmy and his cedar cologne—and relax in his arms, melting into him. Whatever it is that passed between us in the courtroom has led to this moment, and it's euphoric and sensual. All I want is more of him. Jimmy opens his mouth to deepen the kiss and slowly slides his tongue in to touch mine, earning an appreciative hum from me.

I pull away from him and whisper his name, resting my head against his as I bask in the safety of his arms wrapped around me. We stand like this for several seconds in the silence of each other and the flicker of the candlelight. I pull my head back just enough to stay in his embrace while twisting my head to follow the path of rose petals to the bedroom.

"Where does this path take us?" I ask softly.

Jimmy's eyes lock with mine with captivating force when I turn my head back around. "Let's find out."

His lips claim mine once again with a slight urgency, and he bends down to wrap his arms around the bottom of my ass as he lifts me into the air. My legs wrap around his waist as he carries us through the living room and to the bedroom where the smell of vanilla and roses intensifies once he opens the door. He sets me down on my feet, and I turn to walk away from him. I don't want to be separated from him, but I feel as if I need to be. I'm enjoying this too much, being with him. I can't think straight. When I hear the door softly close and feel his eyes on my back once more, I start to breathe raggedly.

Turning on my heel, I find him looking at me, his face glowing in the candlelight. My breath leaves my body. The air in this room feels tense as we can both practically read each other's minds. I want him, plain and simple, and I can see it in Jimmy's eyes that he wants me too.

He watches me as I face him. I slowly bring my hands up to the straps of my dress to slide them down my shoulders, but Jimmy interjects. "I want to take your dress off."

His voice is soft and low, barely above a whisper, and he strides over to me in two short steps. I feel like I've been consumed with fire under his gaze, and when he touches me to turn my body around... I feel like I'm going to explode.

My back is to him as his fingers pull the zipper down on the dress. I stare blankly at the wall, breathing deeply when I feel his fingers lightly slide underneath the straps on my shoulders. God, my skin feels as if it's burning from his touch.

Jimmy slowly slides my straps all the way down my arms until his fingers hook with mine. My bare chest pebbles with goosebumps as my skin is exposed to the cool air of the room. Jimmy's hands slowly trace their way up my stomach to cup my breasts and hardened nipples. I revel in the way his fingers gently pinch them and my eyes close as my head falls back to meet his chest. I push my chest out to have him touch more of me as I shimmy out of my dress, exposing the lace thong I have on underneath. I hear Jimmy's sharp intake of breath. His hands roam back down my stomach to plant on my hips. Jimmy spins me around to face him, and I watch as his eyes rake my body from head to toe.

"You are so beautiful," he whispers.

I'm already an empowered woman—I don't need a man to tell me how beautiful they think I am—but hearing the appreciation in Jimmy's voice and seeing it in his eyes is a whole other level of empowerment, especially since he's now my husband.

"I want to see you," I whisper to him, holding his gaze. I start to unbutton his shirt. I release all the buttons and slide the fabric down his impressive arms to reveal his sculpted chest. Now it's my turn to marvel at the beauty of him. My fingers trace the contours of his chest, and I study him in a way I haven't before. I run my fingers all over him, noting how soft and hard his skin feels and appreciating the dedication he's put into making his body as strong as it is. My eyes travel back up to him, and I find Jimmy peering down at me with an intense gaze. I reach up on my toes to reclaim his mouth, and Jimmy pushes me until my back falls onto the mattress.

We've done this before. I've seen Jimmy, felt Jimmy, sucked Jimmy, but this feels much different. Watching him slowly stride to me from my position on the bed leaves me lying in a newfound anxiousness. I want him in a way I've never wanted him before. Now it's a *need*. I *need* to feel Jimmy's mouth, hands, fingers, and anything else on or in me or I might explode. I wriggle on the bed, wanting to feel his fingers pull my thong down my thighs, but I know what he has planned for me will be far greater than anything I expect.

Jimmy stands in front of me at the end of the bed. His fingers wrap around the ankle of my left leg, and he lifts my leg in the air, planting a trail of kisses all the way up my leg and thigh until he stops on my bare stomach. His arms hook under both legs, and he pulls my body closer to him on the edge of the bed. I feel the wetness between my legs growing by the second, and the ache intensifies with every second that passes without his mouth on me. His lips cover my wet mound through the small fabric of my thong, and a moan escapes my lips as he softly kisses my wetness. My hands fist his hair, wanting to feel him there without anything between us. I know he's going to torture me and go slow. This is our "wedding night" after all, and he's trying to make this special just for me.

I melt into the bed as he continues to lap me up through the fabric. I wriggle underneath him and lift my head to watch his head between my legs.

"Jimmy," I say, causing him to look up at me. "Please take these off. I need to feel you."

A smirk spreads across his lips. He doesn't refute me or deny my wish but slides my thong down my legs slowly before bending my legs and pushing them far apart with his hands. I'm fully exposed to him, my pussy clear in his view, and his eyes plant themselves there, absorbing me. I like being this exposed to him and watching him look at me. What I like—no, *love*—even more is the feeling of his tongue on my sensitive bud as his head dips to lick my wetness.

My head lulls back against the bed, and my back arches off the mattress. I start to see stars and feel tingles as a powerful sensation washes over me. The feeling of Jimmy's tongue on me is almost too much, and I start to moan loudly, completely losing myself in him.

"Jimmy." The word comes out in a strangled groan, my head thrashing around as I dig my fingers deeper into his hair.

His tongue continues to lap me in its vicious way that leaves me gasping for air. I feel my body tensing as an orgasm starts to quickly build. "Jimmy," I moan again. "I... I want you..."

Jimmy pulls away. "Get up," he orders.

I look at him, momentarily confused, before quickly obeying him and sitting up on the bed.

"*Off* the bed," he instructs gruffly.

I fall to his command and stand up at the side of the bed. Jimmy pops open the button of his chinos and slides them down, along with his boxers. My eyes widen at the impressive length of his full erection. I lick my lips, waiting for my turn to taste him and feel him in my mouth.

"Get on your knees," he says, looking at me while he slowly strokes himself.

This feels erotic, and I love it. I sink to the floor on my knees and waste no time gripping his hard shaft and guiding his cock into my mouth. Jimmy's head falls back, and he hums as his hands wrap my hair around his fist behind me while his hips start to gently rock into me.

"That's right, baby. Take all of me."

I hum as I suck him, pumping him into my mouth. Jimmy's pace quickens as he starts to rock into my mouth faster, lightly huffing. I feel his muscles start to tense, and I think he's on the verge of coming when he stills himself and grips the back of my hair tighter. His hand pulls my mouth off his erection, and he jerks me off the ground by my hair. I wince at the delicious pain.

"Lie on your back," he orders me.

I do as he says and fall onto my back. The bed dips with Jimmy's weight as he crawls to hover over me, pressing my knees apart with his own. He stills at my slick entrance, his eyes holding mine intensely as I wait to feel him stretch me, filling me with him.

The head of his cock starts to press through my slick folds, and my hands reach for Jimmy's back. All at once, I scream when Jimmy slams into me, forcing me to take all of him without warning. My eyes shut tightly as he slowly pulls out before pushing into me with a painful force. A cry escapes my lips as we fall into a pattern, with Jimmy pulling all the way out before rocking into me hard. His pace is slow and steady, almost as if he wants to enjoy this for himself, and I don't mind at all.

Not one bit.

"Jimmy," I moan.

"*Fuck*," he groans. "You're so tight."

I can't help but let out a small cry every time he thrusts into me. He dips his head and captures my mouth with his own, his tongue exploring mine as he whispers how crazy I drive him. His words are filthy as he describes the thoughts that go through his head when he looks at me. He grips my wrists in one hand, pinning them on the pillow above me as his eyes bore into me. Our bodies move as one; he reaches his hand between us and circles my clit. I can feel tension building in my body as our eyes stay locked on one another.

It feels like bliss. It feels like heaven. It...

Tears start to swell in my eyes. Why the hell am I starting to cry? I close my eyes tightly and do my best to not look as if I'm getting emotional. Jimmy is starting to tense, which I know means he's close, and I let him continue to make love to me because it registers that this is exactly what this is—love.

I'm falling in love with him.

Jimmy thrusts inside of me a few more times before emptying himself and crashing onto the space on the bed beside me. I can hear him pant for air after exerting all that energy. His head turns in my direction.

"Did you come?" he asks.

I shake my head.

"Oh, I'm so sorry. I really tried to get you there."

"It's okay," I say as best I can without sounding upset.

"Did you enjoy it?" he asks with genuine concern in his voice.

I nod my head, and we lie like this for a few minutes until I hear his breathing become steady, and I know he's asleep. I turn my head to look at him, and sure enough, his eyes are closed. I study Jimmy's face and all his features as my mind tries to process the emotions that are running through me. It's true; I'm falling in love with Jimmy. As much as I didn't want to admit it, I've been falling in love with him during this whole process. Being with him and being protected by him has done this to me, and I'm not sorry about it. There's just one harsh reality.

He's not in love with me.

19

JIMMY

I wake up a few hours later alone in the bed. At first, I'm confused by all the candles that are lit in the room and why I'm waking up here alone, but then I remember what transpired a few hours earlier. Blaire and I got married, then we came back and consummated it. It's weird knowing that I am a married man now, even though it's not a real marriage, but legally, I *am* a husband. But... where is Blaire?

I get out of the bed and rub my face. I catch sight of my lit phone screen and note that it's after midnight. How long was I out? I grab my boxers from the floor and slide them on before leaving the room to go find Blaire, wherever she is in the apartment. When I round the corner from the hallway, I find Blaire sitting at the kitchen table with her face in her hands. It's an odd sight, and I freeze before slowly making my way to her.

"Blaire?"

Her head snaps up to me, and I see her eyes are slightly red. Has she been crying? I study her face some more before growing concerned for the sadness I see in them. "What's wrong?"

She sniffles and sits back in the seat. "Nothing," she mumbles. Her eyes avoid mine.

"I'm pretty sure that's a lie," I say, taking the seat across from her.

She's quiet as she continues to look down at her hands folded together on the table. Something is definitely bothering her. I can see it plain as day. When she finally looks up at me, my stomach sinks.

"Who's Miranda?" she asks weakly.

All the breath within me vanishes from my body. I'm not sure how to react or feel at this moment, or how she even knows who Miranda is, and more importantly, why her eyes seem to be red as she asks this.

"How do you know about Miranda?" I ask. While this is a topic I'd never planned on discussing with anyone, I want to know how she knows.

"You woke up screaming her name a few nights ago when you thrashed around in bed."

Shit. There's no avoiding this now. I know married couples tend to tell each other everything and are not supposed to have secrets, but does that still count when you know your marriage isn't real? I don't want to talk about Miranda for the simple fact that it's too hard to, especially when I feel myself forgetting more about her every day when everything happened not that long ago.

"Who is she?" Blaire presses at my quietness.

I stand up from my seat and start to pace around the room. "No one," I tell her, praying that she'll drop it.

"I think that's a lie," she mimics my words, and I can hear the screech of the chair as she slides it out to stand up herself.

"Blaire, go back to bed."

"No. Tell me, Jimmy. Who is she?"

"She's none of your damn business!" I shout at her, shocking her and myself.

Blaire's face whitens, and her mouth parts open in shock. I'm breathing rapidly. I take a few deep breaths to calm myself back down, rubbing my face with my hands.

"Sorry," I start. "I didn't mean to yell."

Blaire watches me intently from the table and sniffles, wiping underneath her eyes. "I just want to know," she says in a pleading voice. "Is she your girlfriend? Is she why you didn't want to marry me?"

My heart aches thinking of Miranda and how yesterday was supposed to be something I dreamed of doing with her. I close my eyes to push away the growing thoughts of Miranda. Visualizing her will only make this more difficult for me.

"No." I shake my head. "She's not my girlfriend."

"Then why did you scream her name a few nights ago?"

"You're not going to leave it alone if I tell you I don't want to talk about it, are you?"

Her eyes hold mine momentarily. "Only if you ask nicely."

I start to slowly walk back toward the kitchen table and reclaim my seat. Blaire follows me and slowly sits down in her own chair, maintaining eye contact with me even though I can't bear to look at her right now. Why? Because it's too much. It's too much to think of Miranda while looking at Blaire because, maybe, somewhere inside of me, I know the truth. The truth I'll be damned to ever admit because it's better to not acknowledge.

"Miranda was a client of mine a long time ago," I say, trying to carefully choose my words, not because I'm afraid of hurting Blaire, but because I'm afraid of bringing up the past. I lived through that dreadful day and just swore to Miranda a few nights ago in my sleep that I'd start to move on... but maybe moving on starts with talking about it.

Maybe moving on starts with Blaire.

"What happened to her?" Blaire asks.

My jaw tenses. "She died."

Blaire's face stiffens.

"Under my watch," I add. "Or lack thereof."

Flashbacks of the day I came back home and found Miranda lying on the floor with the bullet wound bleeding from her head resurfaces in my mind, and I shudder. I feel the gentle touch of Blaire's hands on my shoulders, and I look up at her to see her gentle eyes. If she could communicate with them, I know they'd be telling me that it's okay, that I don't need to go into detail with this if I don't want to, but I *do* want to. I want to talk about Miranda for the first time in eighteen months, and I want to talk about her with Blaire. I take a deep breath. "It's a long story, but I'll just shorten it."

EIGHTEEN MONTHS AGO...

Something told me to make the trip to the store a quick one. I didn't want to leave in the first place, but I was willing to do anything to make Miranda happy, and if that meant getting her coffee, then I was going to get her coffee. I walk into the grocery store briskly, and since I'm familiar with the joint, I book it to the coffee aisle. I zoom down until I find the familiar orange and blue bag of Miranda's favorite coffee—Dunkin' Donuts French Vanilla. I grab the bag and book it toward the cash register. I'm just about to pull my wallet out of my back pocket when my phone rings.

Miranda.

I pull my phone out of my pocket as quickly as I can, but I read Harvey's name on the screen. Clicking the side button to ignore the call, I slide it back in my pocket and pull out a five-dollar bill to cover the coffee and sprint out of the store to my car. There's an odd feeling settling in the pit of my stomach, but I try to push it out of my mind. It's just nerves from leaving Miranda alone. My phone starts to ring again, and I pull it out just to make sure I'm not missing Miranda, and I scoff when I see that now Alex is calling me.

"Son of a bitch," I mumble, annoyed, tossing my phone to the seat next to me. Why the hell do they keep calling me?

As I drive down the road, Miranda is all I can think about. Today is the day. Today is the day I'm going to ask her to marry me. It's crazy, I know, planning to propose to my client, but I love her. I love her with all my being... and I've never been a man to say cheesy shit like that. I didn't plan on asking her to be my girlfriend, and I surely didn't plan on falling in love with her. All I know is that I don't want to spend any more of the days I have left on this Earth without her. I shudder thinking of parting from her when this mission is over. The solution is simple; I need to make her my wife.

The closer I get to the house, the more my excitement grows. I'm going to propose to her tonight. I've had it planned for weeks and have been trying to find the right time to do it. There's a pack of steaks in the fridge I bought the other day and a bottle of wine that's been chilling for weeks. After dinner, I'm going to propose to her when we have our nightly sit on the porch swing. Then, after she—hopefully—says yes, I'm going to take her to the bedroom, bury myself in her, and make love to her the whole night. It sounds so perfect.

I turn down the gravel road our safe house is on past the forest. Once the tires crunch the gravel, an overwhelming feeling comes over me. A bad one.

Miranda.

I straighten in the seat and stiffen. My hands grip the wheel so tightly, my knuckles turn white, and when I see the flashing blue and red lights of the police cars sitting in front of the house, vomit starts to make its way up my throat.

MIRANDA!

I bring the car to an immediate stop and bolt out of the seat. I'm pretty sure I even forgot to turn the car off. I sprint to the front of the house and try to make my way up the stairs when I feel a pair of hands grab my arm.

"Get the fuck off me!" I scream at the man. Sprinting up the steps, I ignore the shouts and demands of officers telling me I can't be here and I make my way into the house, searching around. "Miranda!" I yell, looking around for her. "Miranda!"

I turn my head to the kitchen where I see a small circle of police officers and investigators all standing near the island. All of them looking at me.

"Hey, pal. You can't be in h—"

I push through the circle and freeze, all the bile in my stomach making its way up my throat. My shoulders sink with the big burst of breath that leaves my body, and my eyes start to sting and become blurry with tears. "Miranda," my voice croaks. She's lying crumpled on the floor at my feet.

Dead.

A single bullet hole in the middle of her head.

Her beautiful eyes are open but are blank; her soul is no longer here on this earth. Whatever it is she's seeing, it's not me.

I fall to my knees and hover over her body. My face plants into her stomach as I fist her shirt. A cry escapes my mouth. I don't care that a bunch of men are watching me break down right now. Miranda is gone. The love of my life is dead.

And it's all my fault.

I cry a little bit more until I feel gentle hands on my back. "Get the fuck off me!" I shout again, sprinting to my feet in a rage to look at whoever it is that just touched me. I find the faces of Luka, Harvey, and Alex all looking back at me with confusion and shock.

"Who did this?" I shout at them through tears. "Who killed Miranda!"

I know they're confused right now, wondering why I'm losing my shit. None of them knew about Miranda or the love that we share.

"Jimmy, I... I tried calling..." Harvey says in a small voice.

"Who did this to her!" I shout again. I need to know who this monster is that just took my forever away from me. I need to find this scumbag and wrap my hands around their neck and watch their life vanish at the hands of me.

"Jimmy, why don't you come over here and sit down—"

"No, Alex! I don't want to fucking sit down! I want to know who killed MIRANDA!"

The rage inside of me is no match for anyone trying to stop me. In a flash, I turn back to the counter and sling all the contents off it, including that damn Nicholas Sparks book Miranda was so desperately glued to all the time. I feel like punching the wall. I feel like yanking my gun out of my pocket and shooting it at someone, prefer- ably the prick who shot Miranda.

"Jimmy!" Luka shouts. "There's something you need to see!"

His voice stills me. I don't feel like I can walk, but I follow behind him despite how badly I don't want to leave Miranda behind. Luka leads me into the bedroom, to the left side of the bed where a man in all black lies on the floor with a bullet wound in the side of his head and a gun on the floor right at his fingertips.

"What the... Who is this?" I ask, stifling the tears I feel like shed- ding. I can't do that in front of the guys no matter how much I feel like bursting at the seams.

"Perry Stroup, Miranda's ex-boyfriend."

Ex-boyfriend?

"He's been stalking her, Jimmy. He was watching her the whole time she was here."

I don't know what makes me more upset, the fact that Miranda is dead or the fact that she died from my own lack of supervision. I've failed her.

"He snuck in here when you left this morning. Killed her before turning the gun on himself."

Dammit! I kick the body out of rage. Bastard did my job himself. Alex steps forward behind me and places his hand on my shoulder. "Sorry, man," he says with a gentle voice.

I fall to my knees on the floor and place my face in my hands. There are voices behind me speaking, asking me questions, but there's only one thing I can hear clearly—my own thoughts. I fucked this up. I blew our cover. I should have never left the house this morning.

How in the world did I not keep her safe?

20

BLAIRE

I wipe at the tears that are running down my face and pull my knees closer to my chest, listening as Jimmy finishes telling me the story of Miranda. I'm surprised at how much he's telling me since he said he was going to shorten it, but it's as if once he got started, he couldn't stop.

"I thought my world was ending," he says, dipping his head between his shoulders. "It sure felt like it was."

I sure hope this Miranda woman died knowing how much Jimmy loved her. He reminds me an awful lot of how my father loved my mother, and I'm jealous to hear that Jimmy's experienced this feeling before. It makes me wonder if I'll ever experience it with someone.

"She sounds like she was incredible," I tell him. He hasn't offered a lot of details about Miranda, but from the little I've gathered, he thought the world of her. A faint smile spreads on his lips while he looks off into the kitchen as if he's remembering her in his mind.

"She was," he replies, full-force smiling now. "And beautiful too."

I'm not going to lie. It pains my heart to hear Jimmy speak like this of someone else. I'm ashamed to admit I'm actually jealous.

"I hate that you had to walk in and see her like that," I tell him.

Jimmy nods his head briefly. "Me too. I'll never get that image out of my head."

I look at him and study his face. I can now actually see the pain that he's carrying and has been carrying. It explains why he was the way he was a few months ago.

"Is she the reason you didn't stay with me that night at my apartment when we first met? Because it was so recent?"

Jimmy's eyes trail back to mine. "Yes. Harper doesn't know about her. No one knows the extent of it, that I was going to propose to her. Not even the guys."

I fight the urge to smile at this small piece of information because I find it monumental that I'm the only one he's shared this with. I also feel guilty for wanting to smile at this devastating news in the first place. Jimmy takes a deep breath, and I stay silent as I wait to see if there's anything else he wants to share on the subject of his dead should-have-been fiancée.

"Why were you crying when I walked in here?"

My cheeks flush, and heat rushes through my skin. It's not what I expected to come out of his mouth next. I could take the easy way out and tell him it's because of my father and all that I have going on at the moment. But I also feel like telling him the truth, the truth that I'm in love with him and I know he's not in love with me. I know that with even more certainty now after hearing him speak of Miranda.

"It's really nothing. Just everything going on." I'm not sure my heart could handle Jimmy's truth right now.

"I still don't think you're telling me the truth," he says.

"There's no truth to tell you that you don't already know."

He gives me an odd look and then looks down at his hands.

"Do you still love her?" I blurt. I need to know for my own sake.

Grief and loss are both bastards.

You can never get over them as quickly as you'd like, and I know that. It took me forever to get over the loss of my mother. But with Jimmy, someone who's already a stranger to love... Who knows how long it will take him to move on from the tragic death of the only woman he's ever loved, especially when he feels as if her death was his fault.

The look in Jimmy's eyes tells me everything I need to know about the answer to my question.

"Are you asking me to confess my feelings for another woman on our wedding night?" he offers as a small joke.

I know he's trying to infuse humor for his own good, but it doesn't draw a smile to my lips. Jimmy notices this and takes a deep breath. "I do," he answers. The same two words he said to me earlier in the courtroom when he pledged to be mine now carry a whole new weight to them. "But I know she will never come back to me."

There's sadness in his voice that rattles my core. I'm jealous of a dead woman, and I feel guilty for being jealous of a dead woman. Miranda sounds lovely. How on earth could I expect to live up to her in his eyes? How could I expect him to ever love me after loving her?

"I figured as much," I tell him.

Jimmy looks at me. "Blaire—"

I hold up a hand to stop him. "You don't have to say anything else," I say. I try to smile so he believes me, so that I'm not transparent to him.

"It feels good to talk about her," he says. "It feels... liberating."

I shrug. "Well, that's what friends are for."

A silent moment passes between us. Jimmy is looking into my eyes with a soft gaze that pains me. Standing up from the table, I fake a yawn. "I should go back to bed," I tell him in a much happier tone. "You coming?"

Jimmy shakes his head. "Not this second. I think I'll watch some TV."

"Okay. See you in the morning." I'm relieved by his answer. It would be too hard for me to fall asleep with him lying next to me after this weighty conversation. I start to walk by him when the sound of his voice stops me.

"Blaire."

My name has never sounded sweeter coming from another set of lips.

I turn around to face him and find Jimmy looking at me intently. It makes my breath hitch. He's still sitting at the table with his elbow propped up on the flat surface and his muscular fingers resting on his upper lip.

"Yes?" I ask.

"Thank you."

I'm not sure what he's thanking me for, but I'm also not sure I want to know. I give him a small smile before turning back around and walking to the bedroom. I can feel Jimmy's eyes on me the whole time.

THE NEXT MORNING I march into my father's office with our attorney. I called an emergency board meeting to discuss the next steps now that I'm officially head of the company. The FBI and NYPD are also involved. We need to keep everyone abreast of how this situation is being handled. First order of business per Jimmy's command, communicate with the kidnappers and demand proof of life before agreeing to their monetary demands.

I wasn't prepared for the brief fifteen-second call with my father. I could hear the fear in his voice as he instructed us to comply with their demands. I try to remain stoic, to choke back the panic that grips my chest like a vise. They want a wire transfer which we agree to but only for half the amount; the other half will be a physical drop at a destination the kidnapper chooses. Jimmy explains that this will be law enforcement's chance to set up surveillance and catch the kidnapper in action at the drop.

Two days pass by, and we fall into a familiar routine. As much of a routine as we can have while waiting for the drop with the kidnappers. I'm a nervous wreck but Jimmy assures me dozens of times that there's no way in hell the kidnappers will let this fall through, not with fifty million in ransom money on the line, especially since they know he's good for it.

I work from home every day now while Jimmy stays in the living room, and we eat dinner together. Some nights we order takeout, and some nights we cook. I can't remember the last time I've gone out of the apartment to Murphy's or seen the girls, so tonight is girls' night at the apartment. I tried to get out of it because mentally I'm a mess, but at their insistence, as well as Jimmy's, that it would be good for me, I agreed. Stressing myself into chronic heartburn and insomnia isn't doing me any good.

Speaking of apartments, I miss mine. Since I'm being closely watched by Jimmy, I can't go back to my apartment without him being there. I made a quick stop the other night to pick up a few items I needed, and walking into my home felt unfamiliar. I've grown used to living with Jimmy. I've grown used to having him by my side.

We agreed to switch rooms for tonight while the girls are over. Harper, Aspen, Juliette, and I will be in the living room while Jimmy takes the bedroom. I offered for him to invite the guys over, but he quickly shot it down, reminding me that they're working.

Jimmy hovers over me in the kitchen while I empty a bag of popcorn into a serving bowl I bought for Jimmy's apartment. I decided that if I have to live here, we needed to upgrade his kitchen. Jimmy plucks a piece of the popcorn from the bowl and hums as he chews on it.

"This popcorn is good. What kind is it?"

"White cheddar," I reply, walking the bowl over to the table in the kitchen.

"So, I have a question," Jimmy says from the kitchen.

"Shoot."

"What *really* happens at girls' night?"

My eyebrows arch at his question.

"I'm just curious," he adds quickly.

I snort and grab some wineglasses from the cabinet. "You're really asking me that?"

"Yeah?" he says, drawing his eyebrows together. "Why?"

"Jimmy, what do you *think* happens at girls' night?" I pull the fridge open to grab the chilled bottle of wine and set it on the counter before grabbing the corkscrew.

"I don't know." He shrugs. "I always figured pillow fights... gossiping... painting each other's nails—"

"Oh my God!" I half laugh, finally pulling the stubborn cork loose. "You're one of those guys that thinks we pillow fight in our underwear?"

Jimmy wiggles his eyebrows. "Or less."

I roll my eyes at him. Of course he would think this way. "Those things are completely made up by Hollywood for their movies. You really want to know what happens?"

My voice turns seductive as I seize the opportunity that's right at my fingertips. I stick my hip out as I rest my weight on my left leg, arching my eyebrows at him. Jimmy studies me. I can see how intrigued he is.

"I'm dying to know," he says in a deep voice.

I take a small step closer to him and look down at his chest, running my index finger down his rock-hard abdomen. "We talk about men," I say, my voice dark. Jimmy's breath hitches as my slow touch continues to roam farther south.

"What about men?" he asks.

This is going to be fun.

"Nothing too *detailed.*" I shrug. "Just their eyes, their fingers, their lips..." My finger slowly traces down his chest and to the tip of his belt. "How satisfied they make us in bed..." I start to trace his jeans and lift up on my toes to be closer to his ear where I whisper, "But not nearly as satisfied as we are from a woman's touch."

I hear the sharp intake of breath from Jimmy and feel how his growing erection pulses underneath my finger. I slowly sink back on my heels and meet Jimmy's wild eyes. He's looking at me darkly, with pure desire lacing his pupils and tiny chills pebbling his skin.

"Really?" he asks, fully invested in what I had to say.

I take my bottom lip in between my teeth and give Jimmy my best seductive gaze. "Oh yes," I tell him. "Women know how to please other women." I pause. "Especially with their tongue."

His lips part in bewilderment. Jimmy's eyes widen, and I can't contain it any longer. I bellow a laugh. I bend over and clench my stomach as tears start to form in my eyes from how hard I'm laughing, and I can see out of my peripheral vision the scowl Jimmy is giving me. Man, that was too good.

"You fucking suck," he says, throwing a discarded piece of popcorn at me.

I continue to laugh and try to regain myself as I wipe away the tears that have started sliding down my cheeks.

"I thought I was about to watch a fantasy in my living room later," he adds, starting to chuckle himself.

"You are such a guy," I tell him when I've finally regained my calm. "Girl on girl is such a teenager's fantasy."

"Well, call me a teenage boy, then."

"Well, here's a bucket of ice water for that fantasy; your sister comes to girls' night."

There's a knock on the door, and our heads both turn in the direction of the knock. I look back to Jimmy and shoo him out with the flick of my wrists, and he rolls his eyes, picking up another piece of popcorn from the counter and popping it in his mouth.

"This is *my* apartment," he teases.

I hold up my bare left hand. "What's yours is mine, *honey.*"

I open the door and meet the excited faces and squeals of my best girls as they each give me hugs before walking into the apartment. They're all a squealing mess.

"How does it feel to be *married?*"

"There's the new Mrs. Maxwell! When are the kids coming?"

"How in the hell did *you* get married before *me?*" They ask one question after another.

Once they're all in and I close the door, I register the silence that has fallen upon the room as the girls all stare at Jimmy, who's still in the room. I can tell by the looks on their faces that they had the first same thought as me the first time I saw him in all his glory—*that* is Harper's sibling?

"Aspen, Jules... this is Jimmy. My... husband." It's weird saying that word, and it's really awkward right now in this kitchen with all of the silence and stares.

Jimmy stretches out his hand for the two girls and says, "Jimmy. Blaire's *fake* husband slash bodyguard and Harper's brother."

A pit of sadness and embarrassment forms in my stomach as he adds in the word "fake." Luckily, Aspen and Juliette are too busy staring at how beautiful he is to notice his ad lib.

"N-nice to meet you," Aspen says.

"Yeah," Juliette nervously snickers. "Likewise."

"Okay, I'm going to get sick," Harper adds. "Get out of here, Jimmy."

Jimmy turns to head to the bedroom, then turns back on his heel, looking directly at me. "If you need me, I'll be in the bedroom."

I don't know what it is about Jimmy when he talks to me in front of people that turns me on so much. Maybe it's the way he looks at me as if I'm the only one in the room. I nod my head at him.

"Got it," I say. With one last slight head nod, he turns and finally walks to the bedroom. The second we hear the bedroom door shut, I feel all of their heads turn to me.

"Okay, you need to spill *now!*" Aspen says.

"Does he have any single friends?" Juliette asks.

"Harper, how could you keep *him* from us?" Aspen adds again.

Harper and I look back and forth between each other.

Maybe girls' night wasn't such a good idea.

21

JIMMY

I hear the many wine giggles coming from the living room as I try to watch TV in peace in the bedroom. It's been hard to focus. I don't like not physically seeing Blaire. It makes my hair on my skin stand straight up. It's hard enough to give her space when she works during the day, and now I have to do it some more for girls' night. The only reason I agreed to this was because I needed my space from her to clear my head. Ever since I told her about Miranda a few weeks ago, something has been different. At least, on my end. I keep remembering what Miranda told me in the dream I had, that I need to let her go and start moving on with *her*.

Blaire.

Moving on is not easy. I've seen friends try to move on from death and heartbreak, and I saw how fucking painful it was, which is why I swore to never have to deal with it myself. When everything with Miranda happened, I was reminded why I swore off this shit in the first place. I don't need Blaire distracting me again. But fuck, she is too distracting. She's just so damn beautiful and sexy. If I didn't know better, I'd say it's starting to kill me.

There're more loud giggles from the living room, and I light up my phone screen to check the time. It's after one in the damn morning. Don't these girls need to be going? I open the Uber app to order these girls a cab and walk out into the living to inform them of their impending departure. When I round the corner to the living room, I freeze.

Blaire is on top of the coffee table, holding an almost empty glass of wine.

Oh yeah, I'll be cleaning some puke up later this morning.

I stand against the wall and watch the scene before me. The other girls—including Harper—are so drunk, they don't even notice me. The blond one—Juliette, I think—presses a button on her phone, and music starts to play in the room through her phone speakers. It's sensual music, and I watch as Blaire starts to dance to it. And when I say dance, I mean dance in a way it looks like she's trying to turn herself on.

She slowly bends her knees until she's low to the table, and she runs her free hand over her body. She starts at her chest and draws her bony fingers over the curve of her breast and down her side and hip until she skims the skin that's showing from out of her shorts. The girls drunkenly laugh and cheer her on as the music continues to play and Blaire continues to rub herself and sexily dance to the music. Fuck, if I'm not growing hard at this.

Blaire's knees connect to the surface of the table, and now she's sitting straight up. For someone who's drunk, she sets the wineglass next to her with grace and plants her palms on the table and arches her back, spreading her knees further and pushing her ass in the air. My dick fully hardens then as I look at the position she's in and the way she's wildly swinging her hair. *Damn, I'd fuck her like that.*

Blaire turns to sit on her ass, which then positions her to face me, and when she catches me watching her from the entryway, she gasps. The other girls finally find me in the hallway, and they start to laugh uncontrollably. So does Blaire.

"Jimmy!" Blaire slurs. "Were you watching me?"

I don't say anything. This girl is definitely wasted right now, and so are her friends. The girls and Blaire continue to laugh, and I can't help but keep my eyes on my fake wife.

"The Uber for your friends will be here soon," I finally say.

Blaire sticks out her bottom lip as if she was pouting. "But, baby... they wanna stay."

Baby? What the fuck?

"Well, they can't. Start sobering up." They're way past that possibility.

Blaire moans. "You're such a killjoy, always ordering me around and shit."

"That's what husbands d—"

"You think you can control everything and that everyone is at your mercy. Fuck you, Jimmy. Fuck you."

My lips press together in a tight, hard line. Now she's getting bold. Her friends continue to laugh with her, and I stand there, ready to spank Blaire. No more girls' nights for her.

"Oooh. Is someone getting mad?" Blaire notices my expression and moves on the coffee table. Her elbows plant on the table, and she lowers onto her knees to push her ass in the air, bending in a way I've never seen a woman bend.

"I bet you liked it when I was doing this," she says with a wiggle of her eyebrows. She earns more laughter from her friends and a *ping* sound comes from my phone.

"Uber's here. Time for you girls to go." I walk over to the couch and lead the girls to the front door and escort them out. I feel Blaire behind me. She pushes herself against my chest and peeks her head out the door.

"Text me later!" she shouts down the hallway, and I push her back inside.

"Do you not know how to use your inside voice?" I scold her. "There are other people that live on this floor."

Blaire rolls her eyes. "There you go again being a Debbie Downer."

I make up my mind that I don't like drunk Blaire. I don't like drunk Blaire at all. I ignore her as she continues to slur pointless words while I lock the door and turn back around. Blaire is trying to walk to the bedroom and is stumbling around. It's quite comical. She tries to make it out of the kitchen but trips on her feet and starts to fall. Thankfully, I'm right there to catch her. I can see how drunk she is from her eyes, and when they slightly open as she lies in my arms, she chuckles.

"Always saving the day, aren't you, Jimmy?"

Her drunk words strike me in an odd way. I pick her up in my other arm to cradle her lifeless body against my chest as I carry her to the bedroom we now share. Her fist bunches my shirt as I lay her down, and I have to pry her strong fingers free. I pull the covers up her writhing body and slide the trash can in my room to her side of the bed before trying to leave.

"Where are you going?" she groggily asks.

I pause by the door. "I was going to let you sleep this off."

"Alone?"

The tone of her voice captivates me. The neediness in it pulls at me.

"You don't want to be alone?" I ask.

Blaire violently shakes her head. "I want to be alone with you."

Maybe drunk Blaire is cute... once she's not trying to stir the pot with me. I stand still, pausing by the door as I look at Blaire through the dark. She's fighting the sleep that's starting to take over her body. Her heavy eyelids fight to stay open as she stares at me from her spot in the bed. I don't know why I'm debating on crawling in that bed, as if I haven't slept with her before. I've slept with Blaire plenty of times. Why does this time feel different, as if it will solidify something?

"Please, Jimmy?" she asks.

That's all she has to do. Those two simple words have me acting before I even realize it, and I toss my shirt and pants to the floor. I walk over to the bed and lift the covers to crawl in next to her, and Blaire instantly slides over to rest her body on my chest. I settle into the warmth of her and rest my hand on her hand as I start to gently massage her hair. She hums in appreciation against me, and I can hear the steadiness of her breathing.

"Go to sleep," I whisper, pressing a gentle kiss to her hair. I can feel the curve of her lips against my skin.

"Jimmy," she whispers. I think she's falling asleep, but I freeze at what she whispers next. "I love you."

My whole body stills. It feels as if it's been captivated by flames. I'm pretty sure my heart has stopped beating, too, as I look at the top of her head in the dark. Did she just say what I think I heard? I don't say anything or move for a couple of seconds because I'm unsure of what to say or do at this moment. Someone once told me that drunk words are sober thoughts, and while that might be a made-up saying, it does hold some truth to it. If that's the case, then Blaire just admitted that she loves me, and I'm unsure how I feel about it.

I lie awake in the darkness and feel the steady rise and fall of Blaire's chest as she falls into a deep sleep. I can't sleep. Any sense of tiredness I felt from earlier is gone. Those three words she just whispered to me a few minutes ago keep repeating over and over in my mind. Miranda is the only woman I've said those words to, and I swore to never say them to anyone else. What will happen if I say those words back to Blaire? Will Miranda fade out of my memory? I'm not sure I even love Blaire. I know I have... feelings for her. But love?

I'm pretty sure an hour or two have drifted by, and I've finally dozed off to sleep when I'm awakened by Blaire shooting up in the bed. She starts to gag, and I instantly know what's about to happen. I move fast and reach for the trash can I placed at her side and hold it out for her to take while I gather her hair in my hands. Blaire gags some more before finally heaving into the trash can. If this isn't love, then I don't know what is.

"That's it. Get it all out," I tell her as I rub her back. Blaire heaves a few more times before handing me the trash can and falling back onto the bed. I set the trash can back on the floor at her side in case she needs it again, and I press the back of my hand to her head. She's breaking out in a cold sweat.

I hop out of bed and run into the bathroom to heat up a wash rag before bringing it back to her. She tries to take it from me with a groan, but I gently shove her weak hands out of the way and place it on her head myself. She looks at me through her squinting eyes.

"Thank you," she groans.

I smile. "You're welcome. Do you feel better?"

"Better is not the word I would use right now."

"I meant, do you feel like you got it all out?"

"I think so." She sighs, closing her eyes once again. I continue to dab the rag on her head. "You don't have to do this."

"I want to," I tell her.

Her eyes pop back open minimally.

"Close your eyes and go back to sleep. You can deal with feeling like shit tomorrow," I say. Blaire smiles and her eyes finally close. It takes her just a second before her breathing falls into a steady rhythm, and she's back to sleep. Damn, what a crazy twenty-four hours this has been.

I dab the rag on Blaire's head until it starts to cool completely. I sit awake to see if she's going to get sick again, and after twenty minutes of watching her sleep, I start to get sleepy. After setting the rag on the floor, I crawl back into bed and feel Blaire's body curl up next to mine. It's like a natural instinct for her and for me, as much as it feels natural for me to lift my arm to cradle her. It doesn't take long for me to become overwhelmed by sleep, and when I wake up a few hours later, I find that we're still in this position.

———

ONCE I SLIP out of bed, careful to not wake Blaire, I saunter into the kitchen to make breakfast. I can't remember the last time I actually made something to eat in the mornings other than a microwaved Pop-Tart, but since Blaire has stocked the place, I figured I could wake her up with food she'd like to eat. She's going to feel like crap and will need the coffee and pancakes to soak everything up.

I pull the box of pancake batter out of the cabinet and start the coffee pot. It's only a little after nine in the morning, but who knows when Blaire will wake up. She was out like a light.

I start to rummage around in the kitchen as best I can, which ends up turning into a complete mess. Pancake powder is all over the floor and countertops—even my hands—but thankfully, there's one perfectly golden pancake sitting on a plate. The smell of fresh coffee fills the apartment, and I hear the shuffle of feet coming in behind me. Turning around, I see the pale, hungover face of Blaire Hanson. Her brown hair is knotted in a messy nest on top of her head, with strands hanging down on all sides, and her eyes aren't even fully opened. The sight makes me chuckle.

"*Vogue* called. They want you to come in just like that for the front cover shoot."

Blaire glares at me and slides into a chair at the table. "Very original," she says in a raspy voice.

I whistle. "Damn, girl. How much did you drink last night?"

"More than what came up," she says, putting her face in her hands. "Thank you for holding my hair during that embarrassing episode last night."

"In sickness and in health," I tease, flipping the second pancake over. "I'm surprised you even remember that."

"Me too," she says.

I freeze with my back to her, remembering her whispered words before she woke up to puke. "What else do you remember?" I ask, wondering what she'll say and if she remembers telling me she loves me.

"I remember you putting the rag on my head. I remember feeling like shit—which I do now, too, by the way—and, um... I remember..."

Blaire starts to comb back through her memory as I slide another pancake on top of the other. I walk the plate and a steaming hot cup of coffee over to her. Blaire is still in deep thought as I set her food down in front of her, my heart racing.

"Not much else," she finishes.

I search her barely open eyes. "That's it? You don't remember anything from before then?"

"No. Why?" Blaire's face grows concerned. "What did I do?"

Oh, it's more like what you said.

"Nothing." I shrug. "I was just curious."

Blaire's eyebrows scrunch together as she studies me. I start to think she's going to press me for more information when her eyes finally look down to the plate of food I made for her.

"Looks good," she says, looking back up to the mess at the stove. "First time?"

I snicker at her joke and raise my own coffee mug up to my lips. Blaire starts to eat her food when my phone in my pocket rings. I fish it out and see Luka's name on the screen. My eyes flash back to Blaire.

"Hello," I answer timidly, keeping my eyes on Blaire.

"We got him," Luka says.

22

BLAIRE

My whole world stopped the moment Jimmy says those words. "They found my father?" I ask breathlessly to confirm it. Every next second feels like an eternity.

"Yes. We need to go now."

He's frantic as he stands from the table and pushes his phone back in his pocket. I'm still frozen in place, my appetite now gone, and suddenly, so is the evil hangover I woke up with this morning. My father has been found! I feel as if I can't move. I don't know what to do next.

"I can't go looking like this," I say when I finally snap back to reality. I stand and pace back and forth. This is everything I've been waiting for, for my father to return home! I stop moving and look back to Jimmy. "Is he... is he alive?"

"Blaire," he breathes frustratedly. "I don't know, but we need to go *now*!"

"Okay, okay. Just... let me g-get ready."

I move without thinking. The world feels like it's actually stopped. I try to think of my father's face, of the last time I saw him.

God, I hope he's alive. If he is, I can't wait to hug him and feel him again. I feel like crying both sad and fearful tears.

I move quickly in the room to run a brush through my extremely matted hair, and I pull it into a bun on my head. I dress in some dark jeans and a flowy shirt before sliding on my jacket and brushing my teeth. My makeup from last night will have to do for this morning. I walk back into the kitchen where Jimmy is waiting for me, and we leave in a rush out the door. He's moving fast down the hall as if every second counts that we aren't there.

"Why are we moving so fast?" I ask as we step into the elevator.

"Because we need to get down to the police station."

I don't ask any more questions as I follow Jimmy out the door and into the black Cadillac belonging to Jimmy's company. It's the first time I've seen this vehicle, but I slide in the back seat, and Jimmy slides in after me as the driver—who is some man in his late fifties— takes us to the police station.

"Who told you?" I ask, turning to Jimmy. He's staring down at his phone again and doesn't look back up as his fingers type on the phone.

"Who told m—oh, Luka."

"What did Luka say?"

Jimmy stops texting and looks up at me. His intense eyes somewhat soften my nerves, but my heart still feels as if it's going to beat out of my chest. I need all the answers I can get before we get there. I need to be as prepared as possible.

"Blaire," he says calmly. He places a steady hand over mine resting on my knee. "Breathe."

It's not exactly the word I was looking for, but I try not to read into it and do as he says. Just breathe. The rest of the ride to the police station feels a lot longer than it really is, and I almost jump out before the Cadillac comes to a complete stop. I hear Jimmy calling after me as I run past the flashing cameras belonging to the paparazzi and into the building of the local New York Police Station. The coolness of the building knocks the wind out of me as I run in. I freeze at the desk. The scuffle of Jimmy's feet behind me comes into earshot.

"Blaire," he says at the same time someone says, "Jimmy." It's a clean-shaven man about Jimmy's age with dark-brown hair and piercing gray eyes. One of the men I saw that night at Murphy's when I went off on him. He has a similar build as Jimmy, and I can't help but wonder if every man who goes through the military comes out this stout.

"Luka," Jimmy says, giving this Luka guy some kind of bro hug. I interject myself into their moment.

"I'm Blaire Hanson, Charles Hanson's daughter. Where is he?" I can't wait much longer.

"He's right this way," Luka says, placing his hand on the small of my back. Luka starts to lead me away from Jimmy, and I pause to look back at him.

"Aren't you coming?" I ask.

Jimmy looks at me. "You go ahead."

I give him one last glance before Luka leads me down a hall through two metal doors. Lights in police stations are weird. They glow differently and darker. It's an odd feeling being in a police station as I wait to see my father who's been missing for nearly a week. It feels like Luka and I have been walking for miles in a maze as he weaves through the varying halls.

"Is he—is he alive?" I ask as we continue to walk. I hear Luka lightly snicker, and he finally freezes in front of a door.

"See for yourself," he says as he twists the knob.

23

JIMMY

Alan Stephenson, Hanson Holdings' former chief financial officer, was arrested last night for the abduction of Charles Hanson. Thankfully, Charles was kept alive as Alan tried to have Charles wire over money from the company before stooping to lower threats such as kidnapping or killing Blaire. It turns out, this was all just payback for Alan after he was fired last year for being caught embezzling from the company.

I wait in the front of the police station as I give Blaire her time with her father once Luka brought her back to him. I want to be there for her, but I also don't want to see the lucky man standing there. That would mean this will all be over. Blaire finally makes her way back to me thirty minutes later with a soft smile on her face. I rise out of the chair when I see her approaching.

"He's alive and well," she says in a gentle voice.

"That's good to hear."

There is a pause between us as Blaire holds my eyes for a moment, and I know exactly what's coming next.

"Jimmy—" she starts, but I hold a hand up to stop her. I just smile at her and take a deep breath. I don't need her to say what it was she wants to.

"I'm going to stay with him tonight," she says. It sounds almost as if she's asking for permission. I nod my head and slide my hands in my pockets.

"I figured you would." And it's true. I knew Blaire would want to spend the night with her father and bask in his safe return. It's completely understandable.

Blaire wears a timid face and fiddles with her hands. It's clear that neither one of us knows what to say next. I decide to be the first to break the awkwardness. I step toward her and pull her to me before planting a soft kiss to her hair. The smell of her vanilla body spray and honey shampoo fill my nose as I take in one last inhale of her since our time together was drawing to a final close now.

"Goodbye, Blaire," I whisper before pulling away.

⸻

IT'S BEEN a week since I've seen Blaire after her father's return, and this man wasted no time getting back to work. I was wondering when I would get the call from him to come in and end our contract. I guess today's the day. I walk through the sophisticated and clean halls of Hanson Holdings, passing by several offices. I've never seen Blaire's office, and I wonder which one of these is hers. I also wonder if she's in today.

My eyes scan the plaques on the doors. When I finally find the office that belongs to Blaire, I freeze and my heart rate quickens. The door to the office is open, but Blaire isn't inside. My eyes find the bright-pink purse of hers on the floor, which means she's here, just not in her office. The sight of her purse gives me a small sense of hope, and I walk to Charles' office to make this quick. I have to see Blaire. Oddly, I've missed her this last week.

I make my way toward Charles' office. I tap my knuckles on his office door and hear him gruffly say, "Come in." As I open the door and saunter in, Charles looks up at me from his computer screen.

"Jameson! Hello!"

"Nice to see you, Mr. Hanson. Glad you're okay." I shake his hand and sit down in the same chair I sat in when I was told I'd be watching over his daughter. I think back to that conversation and how at first I didn't want to be near that spoiled brat who's now my wife. Well, my wife for a few more days.

"Thank you, son. I'm doing well and so is my daughter. Thank you for keeping her safe."

"Just doing my job," I tell him.

Charles picks up a pen and a checkbook. "I called you in today because I wanted to give you this." It's quiet as he writes on the check and then rips it out to hand it to me. My eyes scan the several zeros I see, and I keep my posture calm and collected as I look back to him.

"I added in some extra for your hard work," he says. "I know what you had to do for Blaire to be promoted in my absence."

I look back at the check Charles has just written me. It's a symbol for the end of our relationship we never had. When I walk out of this office today, legal action will have to be taken for it to end. Permanent action. Who knows the next time I'll see Blaire Hanson.

"This isn't what we agreed to," I say, handing the check back to him. "I don't need anything extra."

Charles' eyebrows scrunch together. "But Jameson—"

"It's Jimmy, sir, and your daughter's life isn't measured in zeros to me." I set the check down on his desk and stand up, giving him one last final glance. "Send over a check with the remaining amount we discussed to my office when you're ready. It was a pleasure doing business with you."

I don't shake his hand as I walk out of his office for the last time. I feel his eyes on me as I exit his expansive room and head back down the hallway that brought me here. I start to come up on Blaire's office, and I peek my head in to see if she's back in, but the office is still empty. I know what I have to do. It feels weird being in Blaire's office alone as I step in farther. I walk over to her desk area and scan around the contents of her desk until I find a small notepad and one of her flair pens. I write my note and place it on her keyboard when my eyes catch sight of one of her photographs sitting to the side.

It's of her and Harper.

I pick up the white photo frame in my hand and study the picture. Looking at Blaire makes my heart pang with sadness. The picture looks to be a recent one of her and Harper at Murphy's, both of them laughing and holding up their pink cosmos. I take in Blaire's carefree appearance and the way she looks so light and happy. It brings a small smile to my face. Who would have thought I would have actually fallen for this girl during the time we've been together? But none of this is real. Blaire is going to go back to living her life as it was before me, and I'm going to do the same.

24

BLAIRE

I quickly scan the papers in my hands and freeze as I step back into my office.

Someone has been here.

My eyes narrow as I scan my office for any sign of things being stolen. There's a feeling that's come over me as I step farther into my office, knowing I haven't been the only person in this room. I quickly check the space in front of my desk where I have a small sitting area and coffee table but see nothing as I walk toward my desk. I set the papers in my hand down when I catch sight of the bright-pink paper with scribbled words on it. A pit forms in my stomach as I start to scan the words before I pick up the paper and hold it closer to my face. A single tear escapes down my cheek.

Before I know it, I'm storming out of my office in a rage.

———

I POUND my fist on the door profusely. In my hands, I'm clenching several papers that were delivered to my apartment in a manila folder earlier today when I returned home from work and the note that was left on my desk. The door doesn't open so I continue to pound on its hard surface, and a door down the hall opens, an older woman stepping out. She gives me a concerned look, and I ignore her as I continue to beat on the door. I'm about to resort to screaming when it's yanked open, and I'm thrown off-balance for a split second. My eyes meet Jimmy's, and I can tell by his deer in the headlights look that the last thing he expected was to see me standing here.

"*Divorce papers?*" I shout at him, stepping into the apartment and shoving the papers hard into his chest. "The *audacity!*"

Jimmy looks back and forth between me and the papers he's holding against his chest. "Blaire, I—"

"*I'm* speaking," I stop him. My rage has fully taken over my body. "What the hell, Jimmy? We haven't spoken in a week and you sneak into my office to leave me a note saying I need to sign these and return them immediately? What the hell is wrong with you!"

"What are you so mad about? Wasn't this the plan in the first place? The two of us getting married until your father comes home and then we go our separate ways?"

I don't know why I'm so upset about this. My face falls, and I bring my fingers up to rub my temples. "I can't believe you," I say.

"Admit it," he says.

I open my eyes to look at him. "Admit what?"

"Why you're so upset. Admit the real reason."

I scoff. "What the actual fuck are you talking about? Are you really this arrogant to insinuate something?"

There's a shift in Jimmy's eyes. He folds his arms across his chest, and his massive biceps bulge out of the sleeves of his black T-shirt. He eyes me suspiciously with a hint of amusement.

"Maybe I am," he says, "but I know you, Blaire. You're not mad about me leaving you a note and mailing you divorce papers. You're mad about something else. Something your stubborn self never wants to admit."

My skin starts to prickle as I stand under Jimmy's direct gaze.

The proud smirk he's wearing makes my stomach flip-flop. "That's not true," I tell him. Jimmy takes a step closer to me.

"Yes, it is." He takes another step. "There's something you want to say."

I back up every time he takes a step toward me. "I don't know what it is I could possibly say."

"Say it." He takes another step.

"Jimmy..." I continue to retreat until my back meets the door. I have nowhere else to run. Jimmy is inches away and towering over me with his intimidating height. His eyes pierce into me.

"Say it, Blaire. You've said it before."

"I've said what before?"

"That you love me."

A small gasp escapes my throat. "I've said no such thing." Is he serious?

Jimmy nods his head. "Oh, yes, you have. You said it the other night when you were drunk."

"Well, there you go. I was drunk. And I'm sure that is not what I said."

"Have you ever heard the saying 'drunk words are sober thoughts'?"

I gave him a look. "What kind of made-up proverb is that?"

"It's not a proverb, Blaire. It's true, and I know what I heard because you said it clear as day." He plants both of his hands on either side of my head, and my knees start to wobble. He's captured me, and I'm all his. My eyes fall to his lips, and my heart begins to beat as if it could burst out of my chest. I want to reach out and claim his lips. I'm dying to feel them on me, but I can't let him know that. I can't let him see right through me.

"You're mistaken," I whisper. He lowers his head closer to me and I feel my breath catch.

"Am I, though?"

I feel as if I can't breathe. My eyes can only focus on his lips and the feeling of his touch. Why is he making this so painful? If this really is our last goodbye, why does it have to be like this?

"You admit it," I say, turning it back on him. This gets Jimmy to saunter back a few steps, and I feel relieved to not be under his intense scrutiny. "Admit why you're such a coward you won't say goodbye to me in person."

Jimmy's jaw tenses. His eyes hold mine intently, and I start to feel breathless as he watches me. Then everything happens in a flash. Before I can blink, Jimmy takes one long stride over to me and jerks me by the waist into him. His lips crash onto mine with a force that causes me to moan at the suddenness of his kiss, and he starts to walk us to the back room. He's kissing me all the way there, and our hands are frantic, both searching for each other's bodies. I remove Jimmy's shirt and toss it somewhere behind me in the living room, and he pushes me against the frame of the entryway to the back hall to grab the silk of my blouse and pull it free from my pants. His fingers work to pop open the buttons while he kisses my lips and deepens the kiss by inserting his tongue in with mine. I feel the bite of the cool air against my bare flesh as he pushes open my shirt further and wastes no time pulling it down my arms and discarding it onto the floor. We shouldn't be doing this right now; sex isn't the answer. I know what he's doing. He's avoiding the question, but damn, I'll let him.

"Jimmy," I whisper when he pulls his head away. I'm not sure why I said his name. I have nothing to say. His eyes search mine briefly before pushing me down the hall and through the open door of our—*his*—bedroom until the backs of my legs meet the mattress. I fall onto the soft sheets as Jimmy hovers over me to kiss me while his fingers work to pop open the button of my work pants. Our movements are fast and rushed. It feels as if this is the last time we'll be together in this way and we can't get enough of one another. Our lips can't leave each other's.

I help him out by lifting up enough to reach around my back and unclasp my own bra. I sling it somewhere in the room and go back to putting my sole attention on Jimmy. The last thing that needs to be removed are my panties. Jimmy's lips leave mine to start a trail of kisses down my neck and to my hardened nipple, which he takes gently in between his teeth and gives it several flicks with his tongue. I writhe underneath him and fist the sheets at the wonderful sensation that is coursing through me with every touch, flick, and kiss this man gives me. He starts to kiss a line down my chest and to my stomach, but all I can think about right now is how much I want him.

"Jimmy... please..." I beg breathlessly. I'm not sure I can handle feeling him give me pleasure in every way possible for one last time. I don't want to be reminded of the feel of his tongue on me anymore or the way he sucks my breast.

His fingers hook under the fabric of my panties, and he pulls them down my legs. I lie in anticipation, spreading myself for him as he slips down his boxers and places himself against my slick opening. My hands reach for Jimmy but then fall to grab the sheets as he rocks into me. It's a delicious pain as he fills me with his thick and wide length, stretching me in the most glorious way. My eyes close tightly as he pulls out to rock back into me harder this time and he grunts.

"Say it," he says, rocking his hips into me. Beads of sweat are starting to outline his head. "Say it."

"Jimmy," I beg, my eyes wildly searching his before closing to savor the feeling of him.

"Say it. Say you're mine."

He pulls out and slams into me. I scream loudly and grab the bedsheets harder.

"I'm..."

"Say it, Blaire," he gruffs.

Jimmy's thrusts become harder and deeper, knocking a groan and moan out of me with each one. God, I hope no one in this apartment can hear how loud I'm screaming. Tears start to sting my eyes as so many emotions begin to roll through my body, from love to pain to anger. I love Jimmy Maxwell. I love him so much, and the thought of never seeing him again—that this is really the last time we'll be together—saddens me. I don't want to confess my feelings just to leave here once we're through.

I feel a tear starting to slowly slide down my face when Jimmy's gruff voice fills the room once more.

"Dammit it, Blaire, *say it!*"

"I'm yours," I cry. "I'm yours."

"Tell me you love me." He pushes into me hard.

"I love you! I love you, I love you, I love—"

Pure ecstasy fills me, and my voice fails as it leaves my body and I'm left arching my back on the bed as the greatest, most tingly orgasm takes over me. I'm gasping for air yet screaming at the same time. Jimmy grunts as he pounds into me several more times before stilling and emptying himself in me and then collapsing onto me in a sweaty mess.

He doesn't pull out as he catches his weight on his elbows while hovering over me. We're a panting pile of limbs. Neither of us say anything as we lie here, still connected, both trying to steady our breathing. Jimmy slowly pulls out of me after a few more seconds, and he falls into the space next to me. It's quiet in the room, and the tears in my eyes haven't receded. Instead, they intensify, and I'm on the brink of full tears when I feel Jimmy's hand reach for mine in the room.

"Blaire?" he asks.

I take a moment to make sure I don't sound stuffy with tears. "Yes?"

There's a pause in the room as I wait to hear what Jimmy has to say. He shifts on the bed to look at me, and his eyebrows draw together with concern.

"What's wrong?" he asks, noticing my teary eyes.

My lips start to quiver, and I shake my head, trying to keep the dam from opening, but it's hard. My emotions win, and a small cry escapes my lips. Jimmy starts to pull me into his chest, but I push away.

"No," I say, sitting up in the bed and covering myself with my hands. "I need to leave."

I stand up from the bed to search for my bra and panties on the floor when Jimmy stands up behind me.

"Blaire," he says. "What's wrong?"

"All of this! All of this is wrong, Jimmy!" I turn back to face him, tears falling down my cheeks. "What we just did was wrong. You *used* me. You took me and forced me to say things I didn't want to say."

"You didn't mean it?"

"Of course I meant it, Jimmy! I meant all of it. I love you, I do." I pause. "But you don't feel the same about me."

Jimmy lightly scoffs and looks away as his fingers scratch at his chin. He's quiet a few seconds before looking back at me with unreadable eyes.

"You want to know why I left that note for you today?" he asks.

I shake my head.

"Because I couldn't bear to say goodbye to you in person."

My mouth parts slightly. Jimmy stands from the bed and keeps his eyes on me as he slowly takes the few steps over to me.

"I don't want to say goodbye to you, Blaire." I search his eyes and see nothing but the truth. Jimmy raises a hand to gently cup my cheek and the corner of his mouth slightly curves in a smile. "Because I love you, too."

A gush of breath leaves my body as I sink in relief. I relax in his touch and feel a single tear escape down my cheek. Jimmy wipes it away with his thumb. I can't tear my eyes away from his as we stand in the room, both looking at each other. Jimmy loves me. *He* loves *me*. The world feels like it's spinning just from the things he's said.

"You do?" I ask.

"Yes." He smiles. "Wholeheartedly."

I don't know how much more relief can wash out of my body at his words, but another wave of relief does.

"What do we do now?" I ask.

"Well, did you sign the divorce papers?"

I snicker. "Not yet, but there's still time."

Jimmy smiles, and he looks down at my hands as he picks them up in his hands. "I want you, Blaire. I've had someone taken from me without saying goodbye, and I'm not ready to face that again when I have the opportunity to control it this time."

Jimmy lets go of my hands and walks over to the dresser in his room and pulls it open. He digs around until he finds what he's looking for and pulls out a small box in his hands. As Jimmy walks back over, I register the red velvet covering it. Jimmy stops in front of me, and I gasp when he opens the box in my view to reveal a beautiful ring.

"Since we didn't have them the day we got married, I figured we could start wearing them now," he says. Jimmy plucks the ring out of the holder and slips it onto my finger. My eyes produce a fresh wave of tears, and they fall down my cheeks as my shaky hands extend my fingers so I can get a better look at the circular diamond that's sitting on my ring finger.

"I want to still be your husband, Blaire," he says. "And I want you to still be my wife. Will you stay married to me?"

I gasp and look up at him as he takes my hands in his. Jimmy is smiling softly at me and looking at me with pleading eyes. I smile back at him.

"Sure... if you move into *my* apartment."

A bark of laughter escapes Jimmy's throat. "That pretentious place? No way, sweetheart. Not a chance."

"Oh, darling, what's mine is yours. Remember?"

Jimmy's eyes narrow playfully. "And what's *mine* is yours. We're staying here."

"Absolutely not. My place."

"I'll move in with you under one condition," he says, placing kisses on my lips between each word.

"What's your condition?"

"We always fight naked."

I wrap my arms around his neck. "Deal," I say before kissing him with every ounce of my being, knowing that Jimmy Maxwell, the man I thought I hated more than anyone else, turned out to be the love of my life.

If you LOVED *The Protector*, make sure you check out Harper and Luka's story in The Savior.

LOVE A SEXY ALPHA?

I'm not Mr. Settle-Down-and-Start-a-Family.
Tried it. Failed at it.
Don't want it again.

I like my solitary life in the mountains. I mind my business and I keep to myself.
I learned the hard way that life ain't easy or fair.
One minute you think you've got it all figured out and the next, you find your wife in your bed with your own best friend.

Then Quinn Prescott shows up to rent the lower level of my cabin.
Sweet, innocent Quinn with her persistent attempts to get to know me and her constant questions.
Those big doe eyes have a story behind them.
She wants more than just a casual hookup and she deserves more.
But I'm not the man who can give it to her, and the quicker she understands that, the better.

I tell myself just one small touch.

One lingering glance into her piercing blue eyes.
One taste of her sweet, pouty lips.
But it's not just once, it's an all-consuming desire to claim her, to make her mine.
I can feel myself losing grip on the situation but I don't care.

Then my ex shows up with a baby, claiming it's mine and reminding me why I live by the rules that I do.
Only it's too late, I've let Quinn in and now she's carrying a secret of her own.

No matter how many times I try to lie to myself, this thing between us isn't just lust—it's something so much more and it's something I'm about to lose forever.

Read Claiming Her Forever, FREE in Kindle Unlimited!

PROLOGUE
QUINN-TWO MONTHS EARLIER . . .

"Quinn, sweetie, we need to leave."

I don't know how long I've been staring at the casket that's been lowered into the ground. My toes have gone numb from standing in my uncomfortable black heels that I bought for the funeral. My mother's funeral. The words bounce around my head as if I can't actually believe them. I reach over and grab my cousin Genevieve's hand, which is resting on my shoulder, and squeeze it gently.

"Okay, I'm ready." I look toward the sky, holding back my tears even though I know there's no more left to cry. I run my hand down the smooth, cool wood of the casket, saying goodbye one last time.

"Are you going to be okay in that house tonight? You know you can stay with Livy and me."

I link my arm through Gen's as we make our way toward her car.

"I know, and I appreciate it. I promise I'll be okay. If I'm honest, I think I just need to process everything. It still doesn't feel . . . real."

She pats my arm before we separate and climb into her car. "Well, Livy is always excited to see her Aunt Quinn, so please let me know if you need anything or just want to chill out, drink wine, and look at old pictures."

I know I'm not technically Livy's aunt, but Gen and I have always considered ourselves sisters, and I've always been Aunt Quinn to her daughter.

I give her the same pathetic smile I've had plastered on my face all day. Gen and I have been close for as long as I can remember. We're the two youngest cousins and spent most summers and weekends together. She even lived with us for a few months when her parents were dealing with some pretty serious marriage issues when we were in grade school. They ended up separating for a few years, but they eventually worked things out and have been together ever since.

"Your mom is . . . *was* . . ." I see her glance over at me quickly before turning her eyes back toward the road, "the most amazing person, Quinn. I know you know this, but she was always there for me when I was a kid, ya know?"

"Yeah," is the only word I can muster as I feel my eyes glaze over.

I know everyone means well telling me these things, but I'm exhausted emotionally and mentally, and not just from the activities of today. The last two years of my mom's life were a horrible fucking emotional roller coaster. I've always heard that the only thing stronger than fear is hope, but I never realized the truth in that saying until my mom went through cancer. You can't help but cling to any sort of hope as you go from oncologist to specialist desperate for second opinions and answers. You start putting faith in statistics that are *so* not in your favor, but you're desperate.

"When my parents were going through their shit, and when I got pregnant at 16, she was the first one to show me love and support instead of judgment."

Gen is two years younger than me, so when she got pregnant at such a young age, her parents didn't take the news very well. They felt they were losing control. Now they worship the ground that Olivia "Livy" walks on and there are no hard feelings between them.

I don't respond, and instead just watch out the window as she drives me back to my childhood home. I'm not looking forward to all the things that need my attention now that my mom has passed away. I know I have to go through all of her things and put the house on the market. I briefly considered keeping the house since it's paid for and it's all I've ever known as *home*, but I need a fresh start.

A few nights ago, I reached out to the owner of an Airbnb in Colorado. I've had this fantasy since I was young, where I'd find this gorgeous mountain retreat and spend a few months writing my novel. It sounded silly once Mom was diagnosed with cancer and our entire world was turned upside down, but now it's all I have to cling to.

My mom and I were best friends, always. We did everything together and despite the fact that the last few years of her life were hell for her, she never stopped encouraging me to pursue my dreams. For the longest time, I lost sight of those dreams. I felt guilty for even imagining what my life could look like had I not been taking care of her 24/7.

Gen pulls into the driveway and puts the car in park before turning to face me. I don't feel like another heartfelt *you're going to be okay* talk. I pull her in for a hug before she can say anything.

"Gen," I pause, not wanting to cry again, "thank you." She gives me a tight-lipped smile, clearly picking up on my exhaustion, and I exit the car.

I don't look around as I walk into the house. I'm not ready to take that trip down memory lane without my mom's hospital bed in the front room. Instead, I head straight to the bathroom to strip out of my funeral clothes and wash the day off of me.

I let my head lull forward as the water runs over my tense shoulders. Every time I close my eyes, I see my mom's smiling face. Something that always brought me comfort is now a reminder of loss. I can feel tears start to bubble up again, so I shut off the water and grab my towel.

The music streaming from my iPhone on the counter is interrupted by the ping of a text message. I slide the screen open and I'm immediately greeted by a message with a smiling selfie of Liv and Gen, their faces smooshed together.

Gen: *Hey, just checking in . . . we looooove you.*

I laugh—a genuine laugh—something I haven't done in weeks. I type out a response and snap a selfie making a kissy-face toward the camera and hit SEND.

Me: *I love you guys so much.*

After lathering my face and body in lotion—because mom always taught me to never skip it no matter what—I grab a bottle of red wine and make my way to my couch. I pick up my laptop and plop down to check out the Airbnb in Colorado again.

I sent a message to the owner this morning, asking him if three months would suffice for his request of *long-term tenants only* after he'd previously replied with a very curt *NOPE*—yes, in all caps—to my request to stay for a month. I open the app and see a red dot indicating I have a message. I open it and read:

MISS PRESCOTT,
  Yes, three months will suffice.
  —Sawyer

MY HEART JUMPS a little at the message and I smile. I haven't told Gen yet, but I've decided to move away from Idaho just to focus on myself and try to figure out life for a little bit. The cabin I found in the Rocky Mountains looks like the perfect retreat to finally write my novel—a dream I thought had passed me by. I don't overthink it, and instead just reply back to him:

MR. ARCHER,
  Great! I'll take it!!
  —Quinn

. . .

I HIT SEND BEFORE I can second-guess the number of exclamation points I included. I select the dates on the calendar, enter my information, and hit BOOK. I scroll through the photos of the cabin again and squeal a little to myself that this gorgeous place will be mine for three whole months.

The listing states that the upper floor of the cabin is the owner's private residence, though it doesn't give any information about him. When I look at his profile picture, it's just the back of a guy's head looking out over a ravine. His dirty blond hair is long enough that it brushes the bottom of his thick neck.

The rooms look spacious but quaint. As I scroll through again, I notice that the bathroom mirror caught a reflection of the person taking the photo. I can see a man from mid-chest down standing off to the side. He's dressed in black jeans and a flannel shirt that has the sleeves rolled up—showing one muscular forearm. *I wish I could see more of him,* I think to myself as I pinch the image to zoom in.

Gen's words from the last year of my life echo in my head: *"You need to stop neglecting the lady downstairs and get laid!"* I always brushed off the idea, reminding her that I didn't have time or energy for anyone else in my life.

In truth, getting laid, or any sort of romantic feelings or inclinations, have been so far removed from my brain for the last six years that I'll be surprised if I ever learn to ride that bike again. Not that I ever really, fully rode that bike.

I'd messed around with my college boyfriends but have yet to go all the way. No one knows that little fact. It's not like I've run around shouting from the rooftops that I'm a 27-year-old virgin. Once in a while, I'd let myself fantasize about finding *the one* and having a few kids of my own, but then guilt would creep in and I'd shove those thoughts aside.

It was like I'd convinced myself I was betraying my mother by wishing for a different life. In truth, that's one of the things my mom always talked about since her diagnosis: hoping I'd find someone to love me and give me my own family.

I close the laptop, pour myself a hefty glass of wine, and settle back into the couch. I mentally count down the days till I can pack up what life I have left and get the hell out of here. Tomorrow I'll start selling off most of my possessions and working with a realtor to list the house.

Read Claiming Her Forever

WANT A FREE BOOK FROM ME?

SIGN UP FOR MY NEWSLETTER AND GET *MY BEST FRIEND'S BROTHER* FREE!

It's no secret I've always had a crush on Damon Strickland.
My best friend's older brother and the center of every single one of my fantasies.

He's a walking, talking temptation.

That cocky grin and those broad, athletic shoulders.
You know what they say about a man with big hands right?

Growing up, we always tormented one another.
I was the nagging, annoying little girl he hated
And he was the man-whoring, douchebag I couldn't seem to get over.

Now as adults he actually came through and helped me land a job at my dream company.

*How the hell am I supposed to focus when all I can think about is
tearing that tight suit from his tempting body!*

**What's even worse?
He forgot to mention, he's my boss.**

**SIGN UP HERE AND GET A SECOND FREEBIE SENT
RIGHT TO YOUR INBOX!**

ALSO BY ALEXIS WINTER

Men of Rocky Mountain Series

Claiming Her Forever

A Second Chance at Forever

Always Be My Forever

Only for Forever

Waiting for Forever

Love You Forever Series

The Wrong Brother

Marrying My Best Friend's BFF

Rocking His Fake World

Breaking Up with My Boss

My Accidental Forever

The F It List

The Baby Fling

South Side Boys Series

Bad Boy Protector-Book 1

Fake Boyfriend-Book 2

Brother-in-law's Baby-Book 3

Bad Boy's Baby-Book 4

Make Her Mine Series

My Best Friend's Brother

Billionaire With Benefits

My Boss's Sister

My Best Friend's Ex

Best Friend's Baby

Mountain Ridge Series

Just Friends: Mountain Ridge Book 1

Protect Me: Mountain Ridge Book 2

Baby Shock: Mountain Ridge Book 3

Castille Hotel Series

Hate That I Love You

Business & Pleasure

Baby Mistake

Fake It

ALL BOOKS CAN BE READ AS STAND-ALONE READS WITHIN THESE SERIES

ABOUT THE AUTHOR

Alexis Winter is a contemporary romance author who loves to share her steamy stories with the world. She specializes in billionaires, alpha males and the women they love.

If you love to curl up with a good romance book you will certainly enjoy her work. Whether it's a story about an innocent young woman learning about the world or a sassy and fierce heroine who knows what she wants you're sure to enjoy the happily ever afters she provides.

When Alexis isn't writing away furiously, you can find her exploring the Rocky Mountains, traveling, enjoying a glass of wine or petting a cat.

You can find her books on Amazon or at https://www.alexiswinterauthor.com/

Follow Alexis Winter below for access to advanced copies of upcoming releases, fun giveaways and exclusive deals!

Printed in Great Britain
by Amazon

79984940R00132